She had to watch  **man. This wasn't** **her family.**

She dropped down on the couch and stared out the sliding glass doors at the beautiful snow-covered trees illuminated by the moon.

Reed sat beside her and clinked his glass with hers. "To going through a lot and coming out the other side," he said. "A bit beat-up, but standing."

She smiled. "I will definitely toast to that."

He smiled back and she suddenly couldn't take her eyes off his handsome face. *I'm falling in love with you*, she realized, butterflies letting loose in her stomach. Danger, danger.

Dear Reader,

Small-town Wyoming police detective Reed Dawson finds a newborn baby on his desk with an anonymous note: *Detective Dawson, I'll be back for her, I promise. Just a few days.* Reed has no idea who left the infant. All he knows is that he feels honor-bound to protect the little girl...

And when Social Services arrives in the form of single foster mother Aimee Gallagher to take the baby, Reed can't just hand her over. Aimee's home is set up with a nursery, so they go there to hash things out while the newborn naps. But an October storm snows them in...with a baby who has Reed and Aimee questioning everything they ever thought they knew about love, what they both want, and commitment.

I hope you enjoy Reed and Aimee's story. I love to hear from readers, so feel free to email me with your thoughts about *Snowbound with a Baby*. You can find more information about me and my books at my website: melissasenate.com.

Warmest regards,

Melissa Senate

Snowbound
with a Baby

——

MELISSA SENATE

HARLEQUIN
SPECIAL
EDITION

Recycling programs
for this product may
not exist in your area.

ISBN-13: 978-1-335-59428-0

Snowbound with a Baby

Copyright © 2023 by Melissa Senate

For questions and comments about the quality of this book, please contact us at CustomerService@Harlequin.com.

Harlequin Enterprises ULC
22 Adelaide St. West, 41st Floor
Toronto, Ontario M5H 4E3, Canada
www.Harlequin.com

Printed in U.S.A.

Melissa Senate has written many novels for Harlequin and other publishers, including her debut, *See Jane Date*, which was made into a TV movie. She also wrote seven books for Harlequin Special Edition under the pen name Meg Maxwell. Her novels have been published in over twenty-five countries. Melissa lives on the coast of Maine with her teenage son; their rescue shepherd mix, Flash; and a lap cat named Cleo. For more information, please visit her website, melissasenate.com.

Visit the Author Profile page at Harlequin.com for more titles.

For Max

Chapter One

Det. Reed Dawson pulled open the door to the Bear Ridge Police Department with three things on his mind: (1) ordering in a chicken Milanese sandwich with a side of fries and a fizzy lemonade from Pimoni's Italian Café, (2) writing up two reports for the chief on a lead he'd followed this afternoon on one case and the potential suspect he'd questioned for another, and (3) getting home before the impending snowstorm—a blizzard unwelcome anytime in Wyoming but particularly in mid-October—made getting anywhere impossible.

He would have been back a half hour ago, but he'd gotten a call from the temp at the front desk that Whiskers, an orange tabby cat, had gotten out of her house and was missing. The McAllister family had searched for hours, six-year-old Brady inconsolable at the idea that poor Whiskers wouldn't get home before the storm hit. Reed to the rescue. For the past thirty minutes he'd driven the family around in his SUV, checking places he figured a cat would go to get warm on an unusually cold day. Nearby drainage pipes. A car with a window accidentally left open. He'd actually come across one and alerted the owner to close it before the car filled with wind-whipped, heavy wet snow—but no cat. Neighboring garages and barns had also been a bust. Ten minutes ago, he'd been lucky to find Whiskers sleeping in the bed of a pickup truck at a ranch a quarter mile away from the McAllister's house. The utter relief on the boy's face made it all worth it. And knowing Whiskers wouldn't become a catsicle tonight.

Reed gave a hello-nod to the front-desk temp covering for their regular attendant. Diana, in her early twenties, was on the station landline phone and looked stressed. No doubt she wanted to get home too. The phones had been ringing off the hook all day with residents worried about the storm, if the power would go out, if their plow service didn't show. All six lines on the phone were lit up. Reed sighed and glanced at his watch—5:15 p.m. He'd get his reports done fast, then help out the temp by sending her home and taking over the phones until the two night-duty officers arrived at 6:00 p.m. That was when the snow was supposed to start in earnest, the worst of the storm getting going by 7:00 p.m.

As Reed pushed past the wooden gate to the bullpen, he could see something big and pink on his desk in the back. What the heck was that? It looked like an infant car seat.

He took one more step and stopped in his tracks.

It *was* an infant car seat. As he rounded his desk, he could see there was a *baby* nestled inside. Fast asleep.

Um, what?

Reed looked left, right, in front of him, behind him. For a parent. A guardian. Someone, anyone.

And no one was here except for the clerk and him. The six desks in the bullpen were empty; Reed's cousins Rex and Ford, both officers, were out on patrol, and the rookie was shadowing the other detective on a cattle-rustling case. The chief was likely in his office, but if he'd seen someone put a *baby* on Reed's desk, he would have called.

Reed stared at the infant. What was she doing here? And who'd left her? He looked over at the two restrooms across the station. Both doors were ajar, so no one had set the carrier on his desk to use the facilities for a few minutes. The break-room door was open, the lights off, so no one was in there, making a cup of coffee.

At the sound of a car peeling out of the parking lot, Reed ran to the window, just in time to see red taillights speeding down the side road. The person who'd left the baby? Had they waited until they were sure he'd gone inside? It was dark already, and he could barely make out that the car was compact and charcoal-colored. He tucked away that tidbit.

Reed took off his leather jacket and draped it around the back of his chair, his eyes on the sleeping infant. He instinctively went into detective mode, noting details. Newborn, no more than two or three days old, he'd say. A girl, given all the pink, from the carrier to the fleece pj's to the cotton cap to the blanket tucked up to her chest. Breathing: check. The baby looked healthy, coloring good. He grabbed his phone from his back pocket and quickly snapped photos from the left and right, just in case he'd need them for evidence and a time/date stamp.

"Diana," he called out to the clerk. "Who left this here?" He pointed at the car seat.

She looked over at him, then at the carrier. From her position, he doubted she could see that there was a baby inside. "Oh—a woman did, about ten minutes ago. I was on the phone, of course. She said she had something important to drop off for you, but I didn't even pay attention to what it was, sorry." Diana turned her attention back to the phones.

"Diana," he called again. She put the caller on hold. "What did the woman look like?"

She thought for a moment. "Long wavy red hair. Oh— and she had on big black sunglasses and a long black puffy coat."

Reed wracked his brain. Long red hair? Did he know anyone with long red hair—and a compact dark gray car? Wearing sunglasses indoors on an overcast day in October at 5:00 p.m.

Sounded like someone had disguised herself to drop off the baby.

Who? And why?

He studied the infant for any signs of familiarity in the sweet little face—there were none at all—then very gently moved the pink cotton cap to check the hair color and type: brown wisps. The eyes were closed but he figured they were newborn slate blue. Reed shifted the blanket and gently felt along the sides; he found two tiny diapers, a baby bottle, a sample jar of baby formula and a burp cloth.

And a folded piece of paper. A clue? He snatched it up, hopeful it would reveal the baby's and parents' names.

It was a brief letter, typed on plain white paper.

Detective Dawson, I'll be back for her, I promise. Just a few days. Take good care of her as I know you will. She doesn't have a name yet but I'm thinking Summer.

Whoa.

No signature. Nothing to indicate who'd written it.

But the baby belonged to someone who knew Reed. In what capacity? The "Detective Dawson" suggested it was a professional basis—and he used that word loosely. Could be anyone he'd come into contact with as an officer of the law. And likely someone from Bear Ridge versus from his old life in Cheyenne. The city was three hours away—a long trip for someone who'd just been released from the hospital yesterday or today.

He carefully picked up the car seat from the bottom, so as not to disturb potential fingerprints on the handle, and brought it over to the chief's closed office door. He slipped out a hand to knock.

"Come on in," called Chief Alex Taylor.

Reed got the door open and went in, his boss looking up and then at the car seat. The chief raised a graying eyebrow.

Reed explained the situation, and Alex let out a hard sigh.

"I suppose Wyoming safe-haven laws apply," the chief said, "given that the infant was left in a police station and she did sort of alert the front desk clerk. What do you make of the note?"

"The parent or guardian is clearly someone who trusts me," Reed said. "If I take the note at face value. Something about the wording feels genuine, but who knows? I'll work on figuring out who might have left her for me. At the moment, though, I'll take her over to the clinic to get her checked out. She looks healthy enough."

The chief nodded. "They'll alert Family Services. Definitely get this squared away before the snow starts. Weather app says the first flakes are coming at 6:00 p.m. Keep me updated."

Family Services. Reed's brain hadn't even gone there yet. The anonymous note was specific—addressed to him, asking him personally, if Reed's interpretation was correct, to keep the baby until she or he could come back—in a few days.

His brain hadn't latched on that bit either. A few days. How could he possibly babysit a newborn for an hour, let alone a few days? He certainly didn't *want* to.

"Will do," Reed said, and went back to his desk. He set down the carrier, eyeing the baby, who was still sleeping. *Let's go get you checked out*, he silently said, shrugging his jacket back on. So much for his chicken Milanese sandwich, the reports or giving the temp a break; the chief would likely send her home at 6:00 p.m., anyway. He grabbed the carrier, grateful that the Bear Ridge Health Clinic was just half a mile down Main Street.

And that's when he heard the first cry.

His gaze darted to the baby. Her tiny eyes were lifting

a bit, into slits. They fluttered shut, then opened wide. Her face scrunched some, and she let out a wail.

Amazing that such a loud sound could come from such a tiny human.

The temp popped up and looked his way, phone to her ear, eyes wide.

Reed put the carrier back down on his desk and unbuckled the harness, very carefully lifting the infant out. The crying stopped.

The temp went back to her call.

As Reed cradled the newborn gently in his arms, swaying just slightly, he had the sudden thought that maybe he was over his past. That this didn't hurt a bit. Holding a baby. Rocking a baby.

Like he'd once done.

But then the raw ache hit him, hard and deep in his chest. He blinked, trying to force away any memories that might dare come. But come they did. The face, the voice, the laughter of a baby, a three-year-old now, who he'd thought of as his own—but who he hadn't seen or heard a thing about in a year. His ex-wife had been pregnant with another man's child when Reed had married her, and she'd been quick to remind him during the separation and divorce mediation that Kayla wasn't his biologically. That he had no claim to her.

His heart had said otherwise.

Reed looked at the little one in his arms. Every time he encountered a baby or a toddler, he'd feel a little pinch, just for a second, but *holding* one was rubbing that old ache in his chest raw all over again.

Was he really going to take care of this infant for

days? Possibly longer? Till the mystery parent returned? *If* they returned?

How? He had a busy job. And a past that insisted he keep whatever distance he could from the tiniest of civilians, no easy feat for a cop or a man with a big family and *a lot* of young relatives.

But duty came first—far ahead of his own feelings. For now, he'd get the newborn to the clinic. Before the snow started. Before keeping her in his arms twisted the knife in his chest any deeper.

Aimee Gallagher had just gotten the call she'd been waiting for since she'd started the process of becoming certified as a foster mother a year ago. A child—a *newborn*—needed a rush placement. Was she available? Oh yes, she was.

She pulled her SUV into a spot in the parking lot of the Bear Ridge Health Clinic, where she was to meet Det. Reed Dawson. In the cargo area of her vehicle, she had an infant's rear-facing car seat, a child's seat and a booster seat. She had diapers in every size. A bag of clothing and pj's in every size. An emergency stash of child-friendly snacks. A bag of stuffed animals and toys. Aimee had long prepared for this moment—and for any-age child that might come into her life.

A social worker with the Wyoming Department of Family Services in Ketchum County, Aimee hadn't been very surprised to hear about the baby that had been left on a police officer's desk. Five years in, Aimee was sure she'd heard and seen it all. She didn't judge, she didn't speculate; she simply acted—did what was necessary based on state law and the needs of both the particular case and the individuals involved. All she knew at this point was that Reed Dawson had taken the newborn to the clinic to be checked out. Her last text from her boss indicated that the baby had a clean bill of health and Aimee should pick her up. The moment she took guardianship of the infant she'd be on leave with Family Services and begin her fulltime service as a foster parent.

She got out of her car, her heart racing—nerves, excitement, sadness all in there. A baby was off to an unusual start at just two or three days old. *I'll take good care of you, I promise*, she silently sent to her tiny charge. As Aimee locked her car, she glanced up at the overcast sky. There was not so much as a flake falling as of yet. Good. She wanted to get the baby home well before the storm hit.

The cold, humid, misty air definitely hinted at the snow to come. But maybe it would be a bust—just a couple of inches and not the forecasted blizzard that folks in the area had prepared for. Flashlights, nonperishables in case the power went out, shovels, and bags of sand and rock salt were impossible to find in the shops. Thankfully, Aimee had a walk-in closet full of all that stuff already.

As she approached the automatic double doors, she immediately spotted the detective. He stood facing away from the doors in a small waiting area, and he was holding the infant, swaying very gently. She could just make out the baby's head, the wispy brown curls, every time he moved slightly to the left.

"Detective Dawson?" she called. He sure was tall. At least six-two, lean and muscular. He wasn't in uniform, which she supposed he wouldn't be, since he was a detective and they wore "plain clothes."

He turned, cradling the infant so tenderly in his arms that she was rendered speechless for a second. Intense blue eyes—the man's, not the baby's—took her in. "I'd extend a hand, but tiny as she is, I'm afraid to hold her one armed. The pediatrician said she's likely three days old."

"Aimee Gallagher," she said, stepping closer, her gaze on the newborn. "Wyoming Department of Family Services. What a beautiful baby." She stared at the infant girl in wonder for a moment, unable to drag her eyes off the sweet face. Three days old. A marvel. She wore pink-and-white fleece pajamas. Her eyes, that newborn slate blue, were just barely open.

My first placement. Her heart practically soared out of her chest. She wanted this baby in her arms, to shower her with love and affection, to care for her.

"She was crying a few minutes ago, which is why I took her out of the carrier," the detective said, gesturing at the chair where the car seat sat, a pink cotton cap beside the handle. "She's emotionally stable now," he added, his deep voice as gentle as the rocking motion he continued to make.

Emotionally stable. She smiled to herself at that. The man was all business, which was good.

And he clearly *cared*, which was also good.

"Well, I'd like to get her home before the snow starts coming down," she said. "But if you could just briefly relay everything that happened, from finding the baby on your desk. My boss at Family Services filled me in, of course, but I'd like to hear it all firsthand."

He was staring at her, eyes slightly narrowed. "Get her home?" he repeated.

"Well, yes. I'm not only a social worker with Family Services, I'm certified as a foster parent. I'm taking custody of the baby until the person who left her is found and/or next steps are determined."

Except he wasn't nodding or putting the baby back in the carrier. In fact, he was stepping back a bit, his eyes narrowing even more. "The note I found in the carrier was addressed to me personally. 'Detective Dawson, I'll be back for her, I promise. I'll only be gone a few days. Take good care of her as I know you will.'"

"Right," she prompted. *You will be taking good care of her by turning her over to me, the foster mother.*

"So I'm not sure about just handing her over. The mother or father or whoever left her asked me to take care of her for a few days."

She tilted her head, unsure of the protocol in this situation. When he'd brought the baby to the clinic, a nurse had called Family Services upon hearing that the baby had been left on his desk. If Detective Dawson had mentioned his intention to care for the baby, per the note's vague request, Aimee's boss hadn't mentioned it. And since her boss *had* mentioned that Aimee's leave of absence would start immediately, as they'd planned if her first placement was under preschool age, the detective *hadn't* told anyone he wasn't turning the child over to Family Services.

Had he just decided? What was going on here?

"I've spoken to my chief about the situation," he said. "Safe-haven laws apply since the baby was left in a police station and the front desk clerk alerted that something was being left for me."

"Something?" she asked, her own eyes narrowing now. The baby wasn't a *thing*.

"Well, the woman who left her, who seems to have been in disguise, didn't specify that it was a baby. But as it stands, it's not a criminal matter."

Aimee bit her lip, her gaze dropping from the detective's face to the baby in his arms and then rising back to the detective. "What are you saying exactly?"

He took in a breath. "To be honest, I don't know what I'm saying. I just know I don't feel right about turning her over to the state when she was specifically left in my care. Until I know who left her and why, I intend to…babysit, I guess."

How was it that her heart deflated *and* inflated at the same time? Her first placement was quickly going south. But here was a man, a law enforcement officer, who had a serious sense of responsibility. She liked that. She *respected* that.

This was all very unexpected. Aimee wasn't easily rattled, which her job demanded, but she was definitely thrown here. She came to the clinic expecting to bring a baby home. She glanced toward the door, the impending snow worrying her. "Well, Detective, why don't we continue this conversation at my house? I'm all set up with a nursery. We can get this little girl fed and changed and put down for a nap if need be, and we can…further discuss. I'll need to call my boss too."

He eyed her. "You have kids?" His gaze slid to her left hand, which was bare and had been for over a decade.

For a split second, she wanted to say: *Yes, four, actually.* And then recount a cute story about the kids she didn't have but wished she did. Just as she'd once imagined—heading toward thirty-five with her four children, two boys, two girls, maybe even two sets of twins, which ran in her family. But the life she'd expected, the one she'd thought she'd been on her way to having? Gone, *poof.* "No. No kids. I'm set up so I can be ready at a moment's notice for any-age child I might be paired with."

"Which was the case today, I assume—the moment's notice."

She nodded. "I'm newly certified, so this was to be my first placement."

He seemed to be taking that in. "I agree we should tend to the baby's needs and get her squared away. I'll follow you to your house. And the name is Reed."

"Reed," she said, watching him settle the baby in the carrier. He gently put her cap back on, then tucked the blanket securely around her. He'd clearly done this before, given how comfortable he was. Her gaze went to *his* left hand. No ring. Not married? No kids? Cops were trained in baby care, so perhaps he'd just been paying very good attention during those lessons, given the way he'd handled the infant so far.

"And call me Aimee."

He gave her something of a smile in acknowledgment. She expected him to hand her the carrier, but he didn't. He held on to it and she led the way outside, where the snow was now coming down. The snowfall was still light at the moment, but the ground was already getting a fine coating.

"There's my car," she said, pointing to a small silver SUV. "I live here in Bear Ridge, about fifteen miles from the center of town. Old white cabin." She gave him her address, just in case the blizzard came early and he lost sight of her car.

"With the red door?" he asked. "I know the place. Not many white cabins in town. Or anywhere."

She smiled. "I grew up in that cabin. My mom was an artist."

"Ah," he said, then turned to his Bear Ridge police vehicle.

"Oh," she called. "Detective. Reed," she amended. "What's her name?"

He turned around, the white snow a contrast to his thick dark hair. "The note said she didn't have a name but that 'I'm thinking Summer.'"

"Summer," she repeated. "That's pretty."

He didn't respond since he was busy attaching the car seat into the back seat of his SUV. He got the job done fast. Another sign he'd done *that* before.

Was she about to lose her first foster child before she'd even welcomed the baby into her life? Maybe. Both her boss and the director of the foster parent program had spoken at length about the dangers of becoming overly attached to a child in your care. She hadn't even *held* this baby. But she already felt attached. To the little one herself. To her story, the mystery of why she'd been left, who her parents were. To who she was and what she meant to the detective. There was a reason the parent or guardian had left the baby on his desk with that anonymous but personal note.

Yes, she was attached already. So this whole thing was

already off to a very unusual start. And *that*, Aimee Gallagher, with thirty-four years under her belt and five with the Department of Family Services, was well used to.

Chapter Two

The entire way to Aimee's cabin, Reed kept looking in his rearview mirror at the baby—not that he could see her in the rear-facing car seat. Maybe that was for the best. "Out of sight, out of mind" had never worked on Reed, but not being able to see her face had helped restore his equilibrium.

Holding the infant girl in the clinic, giving her a bottle, burping her, the relief he'd felt when the pediatrician pronounced her in good health and handed him a newborn starter kit with all the necessary supplies and information sheets had brought memories rushing back. Taking Kayla to her first well-baby checkup at a week old. The instant love, the surge of an overwhelming instinct to protect and care for her, had informed everything he'd done in those days. The nighttime feedings and crying jags hadn't bothered him a bit. He'd *loved* that little girl.

Despite his strong sense of responsibility to *this* baby, "Maybe Summer," as he thought of her, he didn't feel the same immediate bond. Which was fine with him. Welcome, really. He was glad to have developed a natural defense mechanism to never put himself in the position he had with Kayla. Summer felt like the stranger she was, baby or not. If he had to put how he felt into words, only one came to mind: *numb*.

What *was* overwhelming was that sense of responsibility to her, though. She'd been left in his care—not the state's. And he wasn't handing her over. No matter how hard it was to be responsible for her. To hold her.

And no matter how kind the foster mother seemed. There'd been something steely in Aimee Gallagher's eyes that probably came from a job that could tear your heart in pieces if you weren't careful. He knew all about that. But he'd seen depths of compassion in her expression, warmth, and he knew she'd take good care of the baby.

No matter. He wasn't handing over his charge.

Reed had spent the fifteen-minute trip to Aimee's house trying to figure out who could have left Summer and why. He'd already made calls via Bluetooth to all hospitals and clinics within two hours of town, to get names of those who'd given birth to a baby girl in the past five days. The doctor had confirmed Summer was three days old, but Reed was covering his bases. Two names of new mothers were familiar, and the chief was looking into their backgrounds; perhaps he'd arrested the mother at some point. It didn't seem like the best reason to trust a man with your newborn, but if she associated him with law and order, and she was in a bad spot right now, maybe she'd thought of him when she'd needed a sure, safe place for Summer for a few days.

The silver SUV he was following made a right up a long, gravel drive. The white cabin with the red door, two shovels on the porch, came into view. Aimee had driven slowly, which he'd appreciated because he'd been keeping under the speed limit, aware of the snow and the baby. He parked beside her and hopped out, nodding at Aimee as she did the same.

She waited while he unlatched the carrier, then led the way up the three porch steps, also painted white, and through the red door.

The cabin seemed bigger inside than he'd expected. The entryway was cozy, displaying a short, padded bench with a boot tray beside it, a shoe rack, coatrack and hooks for coats, of which she had many. As she took off the long red wool one she wore, his gaze ran over her cream-colored sweater, knee-length plaid skirt and tall brown leather boots. Her long blond hair was captured in a low ponytail with a plaid scrunchie. He told himself it was just instinctual, taking in details of a person—the hallmark of his job. But the fact that Aimee Gallagher was very attractive didn't escape him, even in this crazy situation.

"I'll take your coat," she said.

He set down the carrier and took off his down jacket, handing it to her. She hung it beside hers. They both removed their boots, setting them on the tray. "I fed her when we were in with the pediatrician at the clinic. Even got a burp from her. I guess she's due for a change and a proper nap by now."

"I'd be happy to change her," Aimee said, her face

brightening for the first time since he'd said he wasn't handing over the baby. "Like I said, the nursery is all set up. The cabin is small but it does have three bedrooms."

He nodded and picked up the carrier, following her up the stairs and down the hall, the wall lined with what looked like family photos.

"You've clearly taken care of a newborn before," she said.

He was glad she was walking ahead of him and couldn't see his expression, the frown pulling at his mouth more from the comment itself than the answer. He certainly didn't want to talk about his experience with newborns.

"Yes" was all he said.

She glanced back at him, seemingly waiting a beat for him to elaborate, then gave him something of an awkward smile when she realized the *yes* was it.

"Here's the nursery," she said, opening a door and stepping in.

The small room was painted a pale yellow, stenciled along the moldings with white crescent moons and stars. The floor was covered with a pastel, round ABC-123 rug. A white crib stood along one wall, a changing table/dresser combination along another, next to a bookcase with board books and childcare nonfiction. A padded rocker was by a window.

"Wow, you really are all set up for a baby," he said, following her inside.

Was it his imagination or had she winced, just for a split second? Perhaps she was disappointed she wouldn't be fostering the baby, since he planned to care for the infant himself? She had said this would be her first placement, so she'd likely been looking forward to that.

He glanced at her, suddenly aware that he didn't know a thing about Aimee Gallagher, other than her profession, that she had no kids and that she was certified as a foster mother.

"May I?" she asked, reaching for the carrier.

"Sure," he said.

Again, her pretty face brightened. Her gaze didn't leave the baby as she removed Summer from the car seat, carefully cradled her against her cream-colored sweater and walked over to the changing pad atop the dresser. She laid the baby down, putting up a protective hand as she opened the top drawer to get a newborn-sized diaper, ointment and cornstarch.

"A whole drawer just for diapers," he observed.

"Well, I was told to be prepared for any age and I took that to heart," she said with a smile, taking off the diaper and using the ointment and cornstarch before putting on a fresh one. "There," she said. "All changed." She picked up the baby again, holding her for a moment and rocking a bit before turning to face him. "I'll put her in the crib. I wonder if she'll put up a fuss? The teacher of my parenting class said newborns sometimes do. Heck, that any age might."

"Yeah. They like human contact and warm arms," he said, the frown returning. Kayla had been a big crier as a baby and always calmed down when she was held. Whenever he'd attempt to sneak her into the crib after she'd fallen asleep, her eyes would pop open.

So it was happening. He was thinking about her, remembering, comparing. He had to watch that. "How was the class?" he asked to get out of his head. "Helpful?"

"Very. The teacher went over every age, from newborn to seventeen, since a placement can be any age under eighteen. I took copious notes."

He went to the window by the rocking chair and instinctively pulled the closed curtains more tightly together so that the only illumination in the room came from the gentle glow of the pale yellow lamp with its tiny painted farm animals on the base.

She seemed reluctant to put the baby in the crib. She rocked Summer a bit more, her eyes closed now, giving her a gentle caress on her head. She seemed to be lost in thought.

Yeah, she wanted this placement. That was very clear. *What's your story?* he wondered, watching her, her gaze so soft on the baby. Social worker. Foster mother. A single woman living alone way out here in the middle of nowhere instead of near the small but vibrant downtown.

"In you go," she whispered. He could tell by the care she took that she was concentrating on not waking Summer up. The baby lay down without a peep, her tiny arm shooting up along her head, her bow lips giving a quirk, the tiniest sigh escaping her.

"Oh my heart," Aimee said, hand going to her chest. The emotion on her face had him frozen in place. Yes, there was a story here.

And he'd stepped right in the middle of it. The beginning of it, he supposed.

"Yeah, babies are like that," he said—without intending to.

She turned toward him then, head tilted, her green eyes full of...what? *Wistfulness* came to mind. "You clearly have experience, Reed. Kids of your own?"

He felt a tight polite smile forming. He'd asked her the same question, so he should have expected it back. "Nope. It's just me. I'm divorced." He glanced away but felt her gaze shoot to him.

"Me too. It's been ten years."

"One for me," he said.

Her green eyed widened. "Ooh. That's that first milestone where you're probably close to over it and not, at the same time."

"Good way to put it. Let's just say it was complicated, so I'm probably closer to not being totally over it."

She nodded. "Mine wasn't complicated at all. It was very cut-and-dried. Black-and-white." He could see what looked like regret in her expression.

He wanted to know her story. And at the same time, he really *didn't* want to know.

"I guess I did it," she said, the green eyes brightening as she gazed at Summer in the crib in her pink-and-white pj's. "She's still fast asleep."

He gave her a few seconds to enjoy that, since transferring the baby to the crib without waking her seemed important to her. "So I guess we should have that talk. The 'further discussion.'"

I get the impression that fostering this baby means a lot to you, and I'm sorry, but I can't just hand her over. The note asked me to care for her. And even though I don't know who wrote that note, I feel obligated. That was what he'd have to say. He'd said so already but since he'd followed her here to "talk," he supposed she'd want to make her case now that Summer was taken care of.

"I'll make coffee," she said. "I have really good pecan pie, if you're interested. And a quiche lorraine. One of my sisters texted me that she'd dropped off two bags full of food after I called her earlier about getting my very first placement."

Sorry, Aimee, he thought. *But in about fifteen minutes, after a cup of coffee and a piece of pie, I'm going to be taking your very first placement home with me*. Talk about strange. She wanted the baby but couldn't have her. He didn't want the baby but felt that he had to take care of her.

"Sisters are like that," he said, following her out the door. "I've got one. She's three hours away in Cheyenne, but we talk a couple times a week."

"I have one sister I talk to a couple times an *hour*," she said with a smile. But it quickly faded. "And the other, I'm—" She didn't finish that sentence. "They're twins and having a double wedding next summer and—" She paused and bit her lip. She definitely seemed to be hurting over whatever was going on with that sister. "Well, let's go have that coffee and talk about Summer."

He had the sudden urge to take her hand and give it a squeeze in comfort, in solidarity, but he was something of the enemy here, he realized. And he didn't like that at all.

Aimee led the way to the kitchen, overly aware of the good-looking, tall cop following her. She usually tried to keep her personal life out of her professional life, but she was in uncharted waters here emotionally.

It felt like Reed knew too much about her already, but things kept slipping out, maybe in response to the careful way he listened. Or how she'd felt him looking at her when she held Summer, her heart about to burst from being *this close* to having her first foster child, even as she grappled with the idea that he might be taking the baby girl with him when he left.

She felt like he could see inside her. Was that the detective in him? Just his personality? Or maybe she just felt…vulnerable around him. Probably all three.

As she rounded the hallway into the kitchen, she stopped short, her gaze out the bay window, the detective almost bumping into her.

"Everything ok—" he started to ask.

She was still staring out the window, but it was clear from how he'd cut himself off that he was looking outside too.

Whoa. The storm had started early and had struck hard and fast in just the ten minutes they'd been upstairs. The wind was whipping the snow around to the point that whiteout conditions would start very soon. The snow itself was coming down hard. The storm wasn't supposed to get going to this degree for another hour, but already there was at least two inches on the ground.

"Uh-oh," he said, stepping into the kitchen to peer more closely out the window. There was a view of the gravel drive leading to the road out. The trees, so many still with leaves, looked like a winter wonderland. For a moment, the wind sent the snow rushing past the window, and they both instinctively stepped back. "There's no way I can take Summer outside in this, let alone drive her fifteen minutes to town—I live in the center of Bear Ridge, in the condo development by the park."

She bit her lip. She *could* invite him to stay till the worst of the storm passed. She didn't *know* Reed Dawson, but he was an officer of the law and had shown himself to be ethical and responsible and kind. Plus she *did* know quite a few Dawsons in town; they were everywhere. His cousin Ford, who was on the police force too, had been a classmate of hers growing up, and Ford was aboveboard; he'd probably vouched for Reed to join the PD, and that was one heck of a reference.

"You're both welcome to stay here," she said. "I have a guest room."

His intense blue eyes shot to her. She could see that he was thinking, the wheels turning as he considered his options. Not that he had many. The blizzard was running the show here. "I think I'll take you up on that. Till the storm passes. Maybe the worst of it will be over in a few hours and the plow trucks will be out clearing the roads tonight."

She nodded. Okay. So that was settled. Maybe she could even use the time to convince him to let her foster Summer. It just made sense on so many levels. For one, she had a leave of absence from her job. Could he get the time off so suddenly? His life would come to a screeching halt to care for a newborn full-time. Was he prepared for that? Had he even had time to think about it?

Hmm. If she played this right and did a good enough job of making her case, maybe he wouldn't be leaving with Summer after the storm passed.

"I'm still hoping," she said, "that I can convince you

to let me foster Summer *for you*. But if you're going to take her with you when you do leave, I need to accept that. This is all part of being a foster parent. It's not supposed to be permanent. I have to get used to that. I have to get used to everything and anything."

He was watching her, and it seemed clear he was taking in everything she'd said and processing it. "Must be hard. I've developed techniques so that I don't get attached in times like these."

She stared at him. "You have?"

He clammed up—clearly *his* turn to say too much. "I had to. We can just leave it at that."

She didn't want to leave it at that. She had so many questions. Was he talking about personal experience? What he'd experienced as a police officer? Both, maybe?

But she certainly couldn't pry after he'd made it clear he was done with that subject. "I'll make the coffee," she said, heading for the coffee maker on the counter. "If the power goes out, we'll be glad we got caffeinated."

"Definitely," he said. "And I'll take some of that pecan pie."

She smiled. This was better for both of them. Talking about coffee and pie.

"If the power does go out, you're set up?" he asked. "If not, I have an emergency kit in my SUV— flashlights, extra blankets, water, nonperishable snacks. Everything but a generator. Not a lot of baby stuff, though, I have to admit. Just the starter kit the doctor gave me. Hopefully that'll be enough."

She smiled. "When I prepared for every possible age of foster child, I made sure that no matter who came to live with me, I'd have whatever would be necessary—

the basics, I mean. So I have formula for Summer, bottles, a ton of newborn diapers, as you saw, several pairs of pj's. The works, basically."

"I'm sorry about all this," he said suddenly. "About the baby."

"It's certainly not your fault for caring about Summer and wanting to take responsibility. That's commendable."

He gave her a smile-nod and sat down at the table, his gaze out the window at the snow. There had to be three inches on the ground now, based on how it was piling up along the post of a mail box at the edge of her property.

"Pumpkin spice okay?" she asked, gesturing at the glass canister of ground coffee beans beside the coffee maker. "I just love it."

"Sounds great."

She got started on the coffee, relieved to have something to focus on besides the situation and Reed.

"I'll text my chief an update," he said. He pulled out his phone and typed away at the little screen. "In the meantime, I'll run to my SUV and grab my go bag. Good thing the BRPD always keep a change of clothes and necessities at the ready."

"I'm glad to hear that. I've got toiletries, of course, including a razor and shaving cream, but I don't think you'd fit into even my baggy sweats."

"Copy that," he said, going to the coatrack. He pulled on his coat and boots, then dashed out. Aimec peered out the living room window, facing the front yard. She could see the wind whipping the snow at Reed, who stood so tall and strong against it.

The front yard and parking area, small like the cabin,

definitely had a good three inches, despite how much was blowing around. Were it not for the mailbox, she wouldn't even be able to tell where the property ended and the road began. Reed went to the back of the vehicle, the hatch rising slowly against the blizzard. He reached in and grabbed a black duffel and the infant starter kit, then hurried back inside.

She took a face towel off one of the hooks by the door, put there for this very reason this morning, and handed it to him. Though, of course, she'd been the one she'd expected to use it.

He blotted his damp face with it. "Thanks. That helps." He had his boots off and coat hung up when she heard his phone ping in his pocket.

He pulled out his phone. "The chief agrees we should stay put," he said to Aimee. "Given Summer coming into the mix, he's giving me the next few days off to focus on finding who left her."

Her heart sunk. Which made her feel a little guilty. He certainly wouldn't need her to help with Summer if he had the time off from work. Then again, maybe that was a good thing. She should really just look forward to helping where help was needed, whether that was with Summer or a different child. Another placement would be forthcoming if she let her boss know that the detective would be caring for the newborn. She had no doubt there would have to be a meeting about that. But right now, the storm meant everything coming to a halt.

She headed into the kitchen and he followed her, sitting at the table.

"Do you have any leads?" she asked, taking out two mugs. She went to the refrigerator and got the cream and pie. Once the coffee was ready, she brought everything over on a tray and sat down across from him, each of them beside the window.

"So far, just that two of the five women who gave birth at area hospitals in the past five days have names that sound familiar. Given the storm, I'm not sure it'll be possible to investigate further till the worst passes. Outages, staff staying home—you know how it goes."

She nodded. "Well, Summer's mother trusts you. That's one thing we know."

"I do wonder who she is. And why she felt the need to leave her baby with me. Is she in trouble? Did she run out of money? Is she in a bad relationship?" He shook his head. "I'm trying not to speculate. But she did specifically ask me to care for Summer until she could come back. She said it would be only a few days. I'll just have to do that."

She paused in adding a packet of sugar to her coffee. *Have to.* Interesting choice of words. "I think it's wonderful that you're willing. It messed up my first placement but in the best way." As the words came out, she realized how much she meant them.

"I'm glad to hear you say that. Because I did feel bad. The way you held Summer upstairs, putting her in the crib, I could tell being her foster mom was very important to you."

"Well, in the meantime, she has two people who want to take good care of her."

He smiled and nodded, added cream and sugar to his coffee and took a long drink. A notification pinged on both their phones, and they reached for them.

Weather-app alert. "Blizzard conditions…will continue through the early morning hours. Heavy snow will continue into tomorrow morning."

The detective and the baby wouldn't be leaving in a few hours. Or even until tomorrow at the earliest.

Yesiree, nothing about today was going according to plan.

Chapter Three

For the past half hour, Reed had been sitting at the desk in Aimee's guest room, wishing he'd gotten the plus-size version of his phone so that he could actually see the files he'd called up on the BRPD database. He squinted at the tiny type of the list of cases in which he'd made arrests and/or testified in a trial. He shouldn't complain, though; he was relieved to be doing detective work instead of sitting in Aimee Gallagher's kitchen and chatting over coffee and pie.

Something about her—everything about her, actually—had gotten under his skin fast. That he'd ruined her plans for something so important to her. That she had some family issues. That she seemed equally vulnerable and strong.

That she was so…pretty.

They'd had their coffee and pie and checked five different weather apps, which all said the same thing about the blizzard. Their phones had both blown up, his from the chief and his cousins and the other detective checking on him in texts and voice mails. Her pings had been from her boss and a sister; he knew because she'd said so when she'd grabbed her phone to see who it was. They'd made a bit more small talk, then both said they should return the calls, so she'd shown him the guest room. He had the feeling she'd needed a breather from their situation as much as he did.

He'd been working on the case of baby Summer, looking through the lists of names, trying to remember if he'd run across a pregnant woman in the past nine months. He could think of a few in town, but he was pretty sure all had their babies well before a few days ago. *Had* he done or said anything on a case that would have led someone to trust him with a baby? Anything was possible. He just didn't know, and nothing was leaping out.

He was missing something.

He thought about the women who'd given birth in the past five days in the area, whose names sounded familiar. Tammy Newman had been a cook at a very prosperous cattle ranch here in town. She'd stolen a diamond ring that the ranch matriarch had taken off and left in the ranch cafeteria while she'd been sampling the day's soups. A visit to a jewelry shop a few towns over turned up the ring and Tammy selling it on video camera. Apparently, she'd turned her life around since hitting rock bottom—a baby on the way had helped with that, per her public defender's notes in her file—and was now a model citizen. According to his talk with the hospital administrator, she'd given birth five days ago to a very blond baby girl, ten pounds, two ounces, with a small birthmark on her forehead. Summer wasn't even ten pounds yet, had brown hair, and no birthmark.

The other woman, Robin, was the mother of a five-year-old who'd gone missing up on Clover Mountain. Reed had led the search team and found little Timmy Gomez—alive and well, thankfully—just past some thick brush, near a creek where he'd followed a woodland creature that sounded like a beaver. Timmy's mom had given birth to her second child three days ago. But he'd just followed up that lead and her baby was a boy.

Back to square one.

He stared out the window at the wind-driven snow flying around, thinking about anyone who'd been especially appreciative of his work on a case or any matter in the past year. He made a list of names in the notes app on his phone. He'd surreptitiously poke around and see if anyone had a newborn.

His phone rang, the display showing that the call was from his cousin and colleague Ford Dawson. Reed had gotten close to both Ford and his brother Rex over the past year. Reed generally avoided all the family's parties, from birthdays to preschool graduations to Sunday dinners since his own marriage fell apart, but he enjoyed spending time with his family in quieter ways, meeting up one-on-one to grab a bite to eat or have a drink. The two cousins knew his story and hadn't pressed him, which he appreciated. They, along with their four siblings, owned a popular guest ranch in town, and had a million little kids among them. There were other cousins in town too, with babies and toddlers galore. There must be something in the water in Bear

Ridge. He was happy for all of them—even if the sight of their happy family units was a bitter reminder of all that he had lost.

"What's this about a baby in your inbox?" Ford asked.

"That's old news," Reed said. "The new news is that I'm snowbound with the baby *and* the Family Services social worker who was going to be the foster mom."

"Was?" Ford repeated.

Reed explained the whole story, from finding Summer to the chief giving him the next few days off.

"Aimee Gallagher—I remember her from school," Ford said. "She was two years behind me, I think. Lives in that old cabin with the red door?"

"I'm in it now."

"Small place," Ford said. "Sounds cozy, as Danica would say."

Reed scowled. He heard the teasing lilt in Ford's voice at the possibility of romance. Ford's wife, a real estate agent, was also something of the town matchmaker— she even had online forms to fill out with "musts" and "deal breakers" and had brought together many happy couples in the past few years. She'd flat out asked Reed if he was interested in a fix up at the chief's anniversary dinner last month, and he'd said he was a lone wolf these days. Danica's response: *Ford once said the same thing. Now we're married with two kids.*

But she also hadn't pressed, which he was grateful for. Reed could clearly see there *were* happy couples out there, including many among his cousins. But he didn't want anything to do with getting his heart yanked out of his chest again.

"Aimee married her high school sweetheart," Ford

added. "*Middle school* sweetheart. Everyone was sure they'd be together forever. Probably the most surprising breakup in town."

Huh. Now he wondered why Aimee and her ex *had* split up.

"Danica's been after Aimee for years, to let her fix her up," Ford said, "but she's as interested in a relationship as you are."

Huh again. She'd said she was divorced ten years. That was a long time to be single. Then again, he certainly expected to be single ten years from now. And years from then too. And maybe she'd had relationships since then that hadn't worked out. He couldn't even imagine that for himself. He was never getting married again. So what really was the point of dating?

"God, what's happened to me?" Ford said on a chuckle. "Marriage to a matchmaker who's always talking about happily-ever-after, that's what. I'll shut up now."

Reed smiled. "Well, it's good to know something about the woman I'm snowbound with—someone who was a total stranger two hours ago." He'd seen her around town a few times—Bear Ridge was too small a town not to know everyone at least by sight, but their paths had never crossed. Until today. In a major way.

A cry came from the down the hall. Summer.

"Ah, the familiar sound of a crying baby," Ford said. "I'll let you go."

They disconnected and Reed got up and headed out to the nursery. But Aimee had beat him to it. When he entered the room, she was sitting on the edge of the rocking chair, gently rubbing Summer's back.

"I was about to say I've got it, that I don't want to put you out," he said. "But you really are all set up for this."

She looked up at him and nodded. "And I *want* to help."

"Maybe we can take turns, then," he said. "She'll need to eat every two and a half to three hours." The pediatrician had rattled off the basics, but he knew it all from first-hand experience. It wasn't too long ago that he'd been helping to care for a newborn. "I guess you can take this one, and I'll take the next."

She smiled a happy, warm smile, and he realized she was relieved he wasn't telling her that Summer was solely his responsibility, that he'd take care of this. If only she knew how relieved he actually was *not* to be sitting in that rocker, patting that tiny back, watching those bow lips quirk like Elvis, hearing the little baby sighs. And the scent of baby shampoo. Sometimes he woke up in the middle of the night with that in his nose.

"She's so little," she said.

"Yup," he said, having to look away. This was too reminiscent of another time, another life, another place. He and his ex, marveling over how seven pounds, three ounces could feel simultaneously so weighty and so fragile, worrying over every little thing, *thrilled* over every little thing.

She shifted Summer in her arms so that she was horizontal, swaying her gently back and forth. "Hey, I'm not half bad at this," she said, her smile tentative. "I don't have much experience holding babies. I—" She clammed up suddenly, and he wondered what she'd been about to say.

Stop wondering, he told himself. *You're out of here*

with the clear roads. And Aimee Gallagher will be some-
one you nod to if you see her in the grocery store or in
the coffee shop. No need to get personal here. In fact,
there was a need *not* to.

"I was thinking of making pasta for dinner," she said
quickly. "Linguini carbonara. I've got great Italian bread
too. Sound good?"

"You don't have to cook for me," he said. "I'm already
taking up too much of your life."

"I'm happy to make dinner. I love to cook. And it's
nice to—" Again, she clamped down on whatever she'd
been about to say. He was feeling a little bad for her, for
having to do that so much. He figured he wasn't particularly easy to talk to, but that had never bothered him,
since he'd made it a point not to get close to anyone.
They were in strange waters here, though. He didn't
want to make things any more awkward for her.

"Well, I'll take you up on that too," he said. "Italian is my favorite. I must order in from Pimoni's three
times a week. Maybe four."

She laughed. "That's my favorite restaurant."

He smiled but felt it fade as he watched her sway
Summer again, then stand to carry her over to the
changing pad. The last time he'd been in a nursery with
a woman and a baby, his ex-wife had been telling him
she was very sorry, but she'd had enough. And that
she was getting back together with Kayla's *real* father.

The knife, always embedded in his chest, twisted.

"I'll get back to the case," he said fast and practically
ran out of the room.

And he only had hours and hours to go, overnight too,
and who knew how much of tomorrow to get through.

* * *

Aimee stared at the door for a moment, wondering what had made Reed suddenly rush away. As they'd been talking—awkwardly—she could see a play of emotions on his handsome face every now and again, as though he was remembering something.

They were a match there. Both divorced with pasts they didn't want to think about.

The baby changed and dressed in fresh pj's that Aimee had in the dresser, she put Summer into the baby carrier and latched it into the stroller attachment she had in the closet. That would make it easy to maneuver her around. She wheeled the baby into the kitchen and put the stroller by the window, stepping back to see what the newborn would do. Not that she could do much, other than possibly look around or move her arms and legs. Summer's slate blue eyes were open and she looked curious and alert.

Aimee had done a little research on newborns as homework for her foster-parenting class, but she'd spent forty-five minutes, when she and Reed had been in separate rooms, reading up. Newborns didn't do much. They ate, pooped and slept. Parents and caregivers, on the other hand, had a lot to do. Bottle feeding every two to three hours. Burping. Bathing. Rocking. Talking. Singing. Changing diapers. Taking care of any diaper rash with ointment. Dressing. Washing bottles. Baby laundry. Grown-up laundry, stained with spit up. Holding. Repeat all. That sounded very good to her.

Her heart felt like it was bursting. She hurried over to the stroller and lifted the baby out, cradling Summer carefully in her arms.

"How precious are you?" she whispered. Summer was so beautiful. *How I wish I could have a baby of my own*, she thought. *I really wanted to have four of you by now.*

If that had happened, she'd still be married to her ex-husband, the man she'd fallen for in middle school. The man she'd thought she'd be with until they were old and gray, babysitting their great-grandchildren. *I'm really sorry, Aimee, but I want kids—my own kids.*

It had been ten years and it still hurt.

Don't think about it.

Not being able to have a child of her own didn't mean she couldn't have a child in her life. She'd finally gotten that through her head after all the time it had taken to grieve her marriage, grieve the truth of her situation.

From the note your mother left with you, she said silently to Summer, *it sounds like she loves you, but something is preventing her from caring for you for a few days. It also sounds like she doesn't have anyone in her life to turn to.* Aimee's heart went out to her, whoever she was. Aimee's parents were both gone but she had her sisters, even if she and Marin could not seem to get along.

Summer's mother must be all alone.

Her phone pinged with a FaceTime video just as she finished strapping Summer back into the car seat. She pressed Accept on her iPad, which was set up on a stand on the counter so that she could get started on dinner.

Her twin sisters' faces appeared on the screen. Right after Aimee had gotten the call from her boss about the placement, she'd called Ella to share the news. Ella had made her promise to call the moment she got home with the baby, and it had been a while, so she wasn't surprised her sister was calling again.

Ella looked excited. Marin—stony. As expected. Given the terrible argument she and Marin had had a week ago, how strained things had been between them since, she was surprised Marin was even on the call. Then again, the twins shared an apartment in town and were snowbound themselves, so Marin couldn't really make an excuse for not appearing.

Aimee hadn't been all that close to her sisters growing up; something about the age difference and how inseparable the twins were had put space between them that they'd worked hard to conquer as adults. Aimee had been six when the fraternal twins were born; Ella looking like their mom, Marin like their dad, Aimee a combination of both parents, with her mother's blond hair and delicate features, her dad's green eyes and height. Aimee was five-eight, her sisters both five-four, like their mom.

"Is the baby home with you?" Ella asked rapid fire. Her long wavy blond hair was in a low ponytail. "Let's see her! How much does she weigh? Did you feed her yet?"

Marin was silent.

Aimee popped up and wheeled the baby into view of the iPad. She heard two quick gasps.

"Omigod, Aimee, she's so beautiful," Ella said, hand to her heart.

"She really is," Marin said. "She's so alert!"

"And she's only three days old," Aimee said, so grateful that she and Marin were actually talking. Babies had a way of smoothing things over, even temporarily.

"So how is foster momhood?" Ella asked. "Are you okay? Overwhelmed? Have you changed your first diaper? Oh wait, I didn't even give you a chance to answer my first barrage of questions."

Aimee grinned. "Well, yes to everything. But things are up in the air and it's very likely I won't be able to keep her—"

"Not a surprise," Marin said, her expression back to stony.

"Meaning?" Aimee shot back, in spite of herself. She'd had a long talk with Ella about how things were between her and Marin, and Aimee had agreed that she should ignore any snide comments. But sometimes, she couldn't help herself.

"I just mean that nothing is a sure thing with a foster placement," Marin said. "Not that I know much about it, but I'd think at any time, anything could happen."

That's right, you don't know much about it. But you're right, anything can happen and did.

Aimee was about to explain when the door to the guest room opened and Reed came down the hall and popped his head into the kitchen.

"Hey, Aimee, I could go for another cup of coffee. Mind if I make a pot?"

Both her sisters' eyes widened with: *Who* is that? They were looking at Reed, who followed Aimee's gaze to the iPad, then back to her.

He froze for just a second. "Sorry, I didn't realize you were in the middle of a call." He gave something of a smile to her sisters and then disappeared fast.

"Um, is he part of the 'up in the air'?" Ella asked with a grin. "Tell us everything."

Too bad the kitchen didn't have a door she could close so that she'd have some privacy. She relayed the story, from start to finish, in a more professional way than she would have had Reed Dawson not been within earshot. He was probably behind closed doors in the guest room, but the cabin was small, and sound carried.

"Oh wow, Aimee, you were so excited about your first foster child," Ella said. "I'm so sorry."

"There will be others," Marin added dryly. "Isn't that pretty much what you told me about the *fiancé* you think I should dump?" With that, Marin got up and walked away.

Aimee's heart sunk. She didn't know how to fix things with Marin. *This is what happens when your sister confides a secret in you and then asks what you think she should do—and you tell her.*

Because you love her. Because you want her to be happy—in the long term. Because you know she's making a mistake.

Ella grimaced as she watched Marin storm away, then turned her attention back to Aimee. Her sister gave a shrug and sighed. This was hard on Ella too. Instead of her sisters asking her to be their maid of honor at their double wedding, the subject hadn't come up. Because (1) she and Marin were barely speaking, and (2) why would Marin ask her older sister to stand up for her when that older sister told her she didn't think Marin loved her fiancé? Didn't think she'd actually be happy in her marriage once the excitement of the wedding was over?

"Aimee, I am really sorry about the baby situation," Ella said. "I know how much you were looking forward to this. The detective will take the baby with him when the roads clear up enough?"

Aimee nodded. "There'll be other placements, like Marin said."

"I can see how disappointed you are, honeybun. But then again, you're still getting great experience with a foster baby while Summer is staying with you. And you get help too. In the form of that very hot cop," she whispered with a grin.

Aimee smiled and shot a glance toward the door, hoping the "hot cop" hadn't emerged to see if she was off her video call in time to catch that tidbit. "He is, isn't he?" she whispered back. There, she admitted it aloud. Despite that situation, there was no denying that Reed Dawson was very good-looking.

"What's he like?" Ella whispered.

"I want to hate him for getting in the way of my first foster placement, but that's pretty much what makes him such a great guy, you know?"

Ella wiggled her eyebrows. "Maybe we'll be having a triple wedding next summer, then."

Aimee felt her smile fade. "Hardly."

"Aims, listen. I know you've had a few disappointing relationships since the divorce. But you can't give up on finding your guy. He's out there. He may even be *in* there. Right now."

Aimee had to laugh. "I can give up and *have* given up on love. But not on the child I want. That's my focus now and I feel good about it."

"Well, fine. Call me tomorrow with details. Love you."

"Love you too," she said. "Tell Marin I said bye, okay?"

"I will."

With that, they disconnected, Aimee immediately wishing she had her sister's face back on-screen. *Unfamiliar* was down the hall, in the guest room. *Unknown* was her immediate future. Would Reed leave with the baby? Probably. No, not just probably—he definitely would.

She heard the guest room door open. A few moments later, he appeared in the kitchen doorway. "I poked my head out to see if you were done with your video call. Were those the twin sisters?"

She smiled. "Started that way. Then it became just *sister*. Marin stormed off thirty seconds in." Oh God, had she just said that? Yes, because she was upset about how things were between them and Aimee was a talker, always had been. It helped make her a good social worker, set people at ease with chatty warmth.

With Reed Dawson, though, she'd been nothing but awkward. Starting to say what was bursting in her chest and then stopping herself. Because she didn't want to get too personal with this man. Or feel close to him. Tomorrow, or maybe the next day, she'd go back to work at Family Services and she'd be the social worker assigned to his case. She'd do well to maintain a professional distance.

"You mentioned earlier you were having issues with one of your sisters," he said. "Family stuff?" He came inside the narrow room and went to the window where she'd parked the stroller, giving Summer a once-over.

"More like I opened my big mouth when maybe I should have kept it shut. About her engagement."

He raised an eyebrow. "Maybe we could both use another cup of coffee."

That got a smile out of her. "Definitely," she said. "Or a vat of wine. But since we're caring for a newborn, I think the caffeine would be more useful."

"Agreed," he said and then leaned against the counter. He glanced at Summer and started to move toward her, then stayed put. Because the baby was content and just looking at them and not crying? Maybe because Aimee was so attuned to strain these days with her sister, she was sure there was something going on with the detective and his feelings for his little charge.

Maybe he was resentful that he had to take care of her? He didn't seem resentful at all, though. More like... conflicted. *About what?* she wondered.

What she did know was that he sure took up a lot of space in the narrow kitchen with all that height. The broad shoulders. His outsize presence. Even his hair was attention-grabbing, thick and short and dark. He wore dark gray pants with a dark gray button-down shirt, no tie. If she didn't know he was a detective, she might have guessed it. Give the man a pair of aviator sunglasses and the look would be complete.

To stop staring at him, she turned to the coffee maker and made another pot of pumpkin spice. It wasn't as if either of them would get much sleep tonight, even taking turns waking up to feed Summer every two and a half hours.

She wanted to know his story. Maybe sharing hers would help him to open up.

But hadn't she just been thinking that remaining strictly professional was the only way to go here?

Chapter Four

Aimee handed Reed a mug of coffee and he sat down, which helped her equilibrium. He was less...everything when just half of him was visible, though what she could see was still mesmerizing. Like his face. And shoulders. And his chest in the gray button-down.

As she brought over a tray of cream and sugar and cinnamon sticks, she wondered if being so aware of him was a good thing. Was she maybe coming back around to the idea of dating again? Not that she and the detective would be a match, of course. But in general. She'd noticed handsome men around town or in the bigger town of Brewer, where her office was, but it was a one-second thing, an objective thing.

Eh, it's because he's here. In your home. Staying overnight. Of course you're focused on him. It's not a typical situation, that's all. She glanced at Summer, who'd fallen asleep.

Aimee made herself a cup of coffee and took a long sip, then went to the refrigerator and started taking out the ingredients for linguini carbonara. When was the last time she'd made a man dinner? More than two years ago, the last time she'd tried to have a relationship... until the subject came up about kids. She'd mentioned she was unable to have children, and things got very awkward from there.

If only it wouldn't be weird to mention it on the first date, at the first meeting, she'd be better off. It could be out in the open, so she didn't waste her time on someone who couldn't handle it. But since she'd given up on dating and relationships, it no longer mattered. She sighed inwardly.

"You don't like your sister's fiancé?" he asked, then took a sip of his coffee. He slid his blue gaze over at her and she felt it in her stomach. What was going on here? Why did he have her so "kerfuffled," to use her mother's favorite expression.

"I like him fine," she said, thinking about John McDonough. He was thirty, lanky, a tax accountant, and exceptionally organized and orderly. "Marin does too. But she doesn't love him."

"How do you know?"

Aimee felt a chill run up her spine as she remembered the conversation. "Because she told me so. Two weeks ago, which was just a week after he proposed, Ella came down with a really bad virus. She had to be hospitalized overnight. Marin and I were so scared, really shaken. And in the waiting room that first night, she poured open her heart to me. That she *cared* about John, that she *wished* she loved him, that she *wanted* to, but she didn't. She said that she was making a trade-off for the life she wanted—to be married by thirty, first child by thirty-two, second by thirty-five. Tears were streaming down her face." Aimee shook her head, recalling how she'd pulled Marin into a fierce hug and assured her she could break the engagement, that the right man for her was out there somewhere, waiting for her.

Aimee had understood more than Marin realized. She had loved her husband very much—they'd been together since middle school—but the yearning for what she wanted most of all had been all-consuming. Not only her marriage, but a family. Children.

Yes, she understood why Marin had accepted John's proposal. But she also thought she'd come to regret marrying a man she didn't love. And she'd said so in the hospital waiting room. Marin had nodded as though she'd agreed.

Reed took a sip of his coffee and waited for her to continue.

Aimee brought her coffee over to the table and sat down, staring out at the snow being whipped around outside, and wrapped her hands around her mug. "In the morning, when Ella's fever came down and we were told she was going to be okay, Marin took me aside and told me to forget everything she'd said the night before, that she was just scared about her twin. She insisted that of course she loved John. But…"

"You knew the truth."

Aimee nodded. "Marin kept her distance from me for a few days after that. And then one night, when I was having dinner at her and Ella's condo, they told me they'd decided on a double wedding next summer. Ella's fiancé came over because he just had to see her, and I could see how wistful Marin was, that she and John didn't have that kind of relationship. Fast forward to last week, and Marin seemed kind of down in the dumps while we were all looking through bridal magazines at dresses, and when Marin and I headed out together, I told her again that she could call off the engagement, hold out for her Mr. Right."

"And she didn't take that well," he said.

"Nope. She got so angry and yelled at me to mind my own business and to respect her choices. My sisters are twenty-eight. Ella's been with her fiancée for two years and he's the greatest guy on earth—golden boy, rock star, with a heart of pure gold. Ella's had many boyfriends over the years but when she met Ben, she knew immediately he was it. They got engaged after six months. Marin, on the other hand, was a late bloomer when it came to dating, and she always compared herself to Ella. She's had a few short-term relationships, but her relationship with John just kept going, and when he proposed after Ella got engaged, she was so happy. But she was happy to be *engaged*, period—not necessarily to John."

"I guess getting married and being settled is more important to her than how she actually feels about John. Maybe she's decided liking him is enough, that he'll be a good husband and father."

Aimee nodded. "That's what Ella said. But she wasn't there the night Marin opened up to me. It was so clear that she knew she was making a mistake. I just can't seem to forget it."

"Do they have great chemistry? A lot in common? Maybe there are plusses you can't see?"

"She said they had *no* chemistry. And that the sex was a work in progress, so *that's* not it. She also admitted they have nothing in common. She loves animals, he doesn't even like *dogs*. He loves old movies, she likes action flicks. She's a chatterbox with a big laugh, and he's reserved and shy and has told her to tone it down many times. I actually caught him telling her that twice, and I saw how she kind of shrank."

Reed reached out a hand and covered hers for a moment. She looked at him, so surprised by the kind gesture, by the show of support. She wished she could slip her hand into his and just sit there and stare at the snow, forget about everything for a half hour except how comforting his touch was. How nice this was—to talk.

She drained the last of her coffee and sighed. She had no business telling Reed Dawson her troubles—her sister's troubles, at that. She needed to flip the subject. "Is your sister married?"

"Happily and to a great guy," Reed said.

"Nieces and nephews? Is that why you're so good with Summer?"

He shook his head. "They've tried for a couple years to have a baby, but it's just not happening. They're thinking about adopting."

She inwardly gasped. "I—" *I can't have kids*, she almost blurted out. Thank God she stopped herself. This wasn't the time or place or conversation—or person—to share that with.

She popped up. "I'm finally gonna get started on dinner. Thanks for listening. I don't know what possessed me to tell you every detail of my life." *Almost* every detail.

He smiled. "I've been told I'm a good listener. So anytime, Aimee."

Dammit. He really was the great guy she'd told her sisters he was.

"Can I help with dinner? I can boil water."

She laughed and got out the big pot for the pasta and the sauté pan for the sauce. "I've got it, but thanks. Cooking will help distract me from…everything."

He looked at her thoughtfully, then over at Summer. Then back at her. "Well, if you need me, I'll be in my room trying to figure out who left that great little girl on my desk."

She really was great, Aimee thought, eyeing the sleeping infant as she carefully picked her up to mov her to the nursery.

And so are you, she said silently to Reed's strong, broad back.

Reed sat on the bed in the guest room, staring out the window at the snow whipping around like mad. He'd thought he'd come in here and go over his files for clues about who Summer's mother might be, but he couldn't concentrate. For the past twenty minutes, he'd read the same case file, none of it registering.

He'd changed into navy BRPD sweatpants and a gray Wyoming Cowboys sweatshirt, glad he'd stashed thick wool socks in his bag too. The chief had texted that the town plows wouldn't be out until the blizzard conditions were over—which wouldn't be anytime soon. All officers except Reed were taking turns being on call during the storm. At this point, there wasn't much anyone could do but lend a reassuring voice that the storm would end at some point and the plows would come out.

His phone rang and he snatched it up. His cousin Rex.

"I got the lowdown from Ford," Rex said. "How are things going?"

"As good as it could be. Considering."

"I know it can't be easy on you."

Understatement, Reed thought.

After Reed's world had derailed, Rex—who co-owned the Dawson Family Guest Ranch with his five siblings—had invited him to spend a week in a guest cabin, horseback riding, walking the river path, fishing, learning to shear sheep, hiking Clover Mountain. He'd promised that Reed could be antisocial or accept the constant invitations to home-cooked dinners or breakfasts at the café or diner and constant family get-togethers. Bear Ridge was overrun by Dawsons—second and third cousins to Reed in a family tree so tangled that he wasn't even sure how he was related to some of them. It was always someone's birthday; parties for the kids just about every weekend, it seemed. But Rex had assured Reed that he could avoid them altogether, if he wanted—that his family was there for whatever he needed, even if that meant leaving him alone.

The invitation to spend a week three hours north on a dude ranch run by family he barely knew had come at the right time. The Bear Ridge Dawsons had been so welcoming without being intrusive, the small ranching community so full of fresh air and quiet—except for the roosters and moo-ers and tractors—Reed hadn't wanted to leave. Rex and Ford, also on the force, had talked to the chief for him, and a month later, Reed had moved to Bear Ridge, the department's new detective.

That was just about a year ago. Bear Ridge and family and fresh country air had indeed done wonders for him. But every time he saw a baby, a toddler, a three-year-old, all he felt was that old ache at the reminder that he was long forgotten by the little girl he'd loved as his own child.

But Reed was holding up better than he expected in the responsible-for-a-newborn department.

"Having Family Services and a foster mother as my cabinmate makes it easier," he told his cousin, realizing how much it was true.

"I'm glad to hear that because I'm also calling to invite you to Chloe's birthday party Saturday afternoon," Rex said. "She's turning three."

Three. The same age Kayla was now. Reed's former stepdaughter's—daughter's—big brown eyes floated through his mind, her fine sandy-blond hair. *Da* had been one of her first words.

Once upon a time, he'd been someone's daddy.

Now he was…

Don't think about it. Think about Rex instead. The cousin he'd been lucky to run into a few days after his world turned upside down. The cousin who'd made getting out of Dodge as easy as saying yes. Reed wasn't about to say no to the invitation. Rex had had his back in too many ways. Reed could certainly show up with a nicely wrapped stuffed animal, sing, "Happy Birthday" and make chitchat for an hour and a half before hightailing it out of there. For Rex, he could do that much.

Plus, Rex had been through the relationship wringer

himself. A few years ago, he'd been a burned-out US marshal with a rogue witness he was supposed to meet in a Bear Ridge nature preserve, when he found a stray dog pawing a dirty old bottle in the water. Turned out the bottle had a message inside—a *fifteen*-year-old letter to Santa from an eight-year-old foster child who was asking Santa for a family, her greatest Christmas wish. Rex had been so moved he'd vowed to find Maisey Clark, needing to know if she ever got her wish. He'd found her right in his own backyard, so to speak. Then a single mother of a six-month-old baby girl, Maisey ran the Dawson Family Guest Ranch's day care center. In one fell swoop, he got himself a family—and he'd adopted that sweet stray dog too.

Yeah, Reed would attend Chloe's birthday party.

No matter how much it stung.

Chapter Five

As Aimee browned the prosciutto in butter and olive oil in the sauté pan, she glanced out the window at the raging snowstorm, hoping the power wouldn't go out. The stove was electric—she couldn't cook during a blackout. If the power did go, they'd be stuck with peanut-butter-and-jelly sandwiches by candlelight. Which sounded a little too romantic, actually.

She usually only cooked once a week, on Sundays, making batches of her favorites to take for lunches and to defrost for dinners. Pastas, burritos, quesadillas. But once upon a time she'd cooked every night, captivated by being married, sharing a home with her husband. He'd been a terrible cook and so she'd happily taken on the role as sole chef. He'd always cleaned up and taken care of the dishes. How had they gone from "middle school couple of the year" and married at twenty-two to divorced at twenty-four? The shock that her husband hadn't stood by her, that he'd given her up when he'd learned she couldn't give him children, had brought her to her knees.

She'd lost her parents only a couple months earlier to a car accident, and the loss upon loss—her parents, her husband and marriage, her dreams—had sent her retreating. But it turned out that her sisters, then just eighteen, newly graduated from high school, had needed her and so she'd rallied for them. Aimee had moved back to the cabin they'd inherited from their parents, and the sisters had lived together until five years ago, when the twins wanted to move out to share a place in town, walking distance to work. Ella was a second-grade teacher and Marin was a vet tech. But even when they were no longer living together, the sisters had stayed close. Until now.

Aimee got out a bowl and whisked together eggs and cheese, then added water to the pasta pot and set it to boil. For just a moment, with her mother's old apron on, cooking a favorite dish, a baby now asleep in the nursery, she could pretend that all her dreams had come true. That she was visiting her childhood home, that her parents were alive and out picking up dessert, that her husband was working refinishing the back deck. That her sisters would come over and they'd all share a meal, then play with the baby in the living room. Her family intact. Her marriage intact.

Well. That reality wasn't possible anymore. She'd had a long time to get used to the big changes in her life. And she'd moved on. Getting certified as a foster parent had been a goal of hers for the past five years, and she'd begun the steps when she'd felt ready to take on the big responsibility of bringing a child into her home, however temporarily. She was creating the life she wanted.

And since her last few relationships ended when it was revealed she couldn't have children, she'd accepted that she was going to be alone. Her sisters had tried to tell her there had to be men out there who couldn't have children of their own either, or who wouldn't care that she couldn't and were open to fostering and adoption. But Aimee was too cynical for that these days. Fostering was her only chance at having a child in her life. It had brought Summer to her—even if she would be leaving tomorrow.

Murphy's Law. But Aimee was so sure that she was meant to do this, to be a foster mother, to adopt eventually, that she'd have to roll with the punches, even when they knocked her out for a few hours. Like saying goodbye to Summer would.

And her very handsome guardian.

Her phone and the iPad pinged with a FaceTime video. Her sister Marin. Aimee quickly put the linguini in the boiling water, then answered, bracing herself. Maybe Marin was calling to smooth over how things had gone earlier.

"So I've made a decision," Marin said, her light brown hair up in a loose bun, her hazel eyes stony. "I know that originally, we all thought you'd be our maid of honor. But clearly you can't stand up for me if you don't think I should marry John. So I'm going to tell Ella we should just each have our own maid of honor. I'm thinking about asking Claudia."

Aimee felt a stab in the region of her heart. Claudia was Marin's best friend. "Marin, I—"

"You what? You suddenly realize I'm an adult and can make my own decisions? If you can't respect that I'm marrying John, I don't want you standing up for me."

"I'm just operating on what you said, Marin. What you told me with tears streaking down your face in that hospital waiting room. I love you. Of course I want you to be happy."

I don't love him. But I want...what Ella has. What Claudia has. I want that so badly. I want to plan a wedding. I want to be married. I want a family...

"Then, respect what I'm saying," her sister snapped and then disconnected the call.

Aimee's entire body sagged. She gave the linguini a sad stir and wanted to fling the metal, slotted spoon hard at the wall.

"Sorry," a male voice called from the hallway.

She glanced up and there was Reed, standing in the hall just outside the kitchen.

"I accidentally overhead all that," he added. "You okay?"

She shook her head, and then the sobs came, ugly-cry city. He hurried over and took her hand. The comfort, the physical proof that not only wasn't she alone right now but that someone was actually holding her hand when it had been a long time since she'd received such a simple, necessary, kind gesture, had her sobbing harder.

Reed gently tugged her against him and put his arms around her. She sagged against him, leaning her head against his shoulder.

She could feel him reaching out an arm to grab a tissue from the box on the counter, and she wanted both arms back around her. She'd had no idea how much she missed a big, strong hug, like her father's, like her husband's, like all three of her last relationships that had fizzled out years ago. She couldn't even remember the last time someone hugged her like this.

But this was Det. Reed Dawson, who'd be taking a piece of her heart with him tomorrow or the next day. She shouldn't really be getting her comfort from him. It would just make saying goodbye to Summer, watching as Reed carried her out the door and out of her life, all the harder.

She lifted her chin and sucked in a breath. "I'm okay now. Sorry you had to not only hear all that but deal with me ugly crying."

He gave her a gentle smile. "I don't think you could possibly ugly cry. You're too beautiful," he said, then froze. "I mean…" he began, seeming a bit flustered for the first time since she'd known him. He handed her the three tissues he'd plucked from the box instead of finishing what he'd started to say.

She didn't know how it was possible, but the hug, the compliment, the flustered detective warmed her heart just enough for her to lift her chin. *Beautiful, huh?* she thought with a secret, wobbly smile. With her red-rimmed eyes, clogged nose and tear-streaked face, she knew she was anything but. But she'd take it.

"I'll just finish up the sauce," she said, despite not feeling much of an appetite anymore. "The pasta needs another few minutes."

"Put me to work." He rolled up the sleeves of his sweatshirt, her gaze drawn to his muscular forearms, the masculine hands that had held her just a moment ago.

Summer being asleep made dinner prep easy. Aimee

had moved her into the nursery and had checked on her a couple of times.

"Hmm, you can set the table," she said, pointing to the top two cabinets and the drawer with the silverware. "Grab whatever looks good for a drink from the fridge."

"On it," he said, taking out two plates and the silverware.

She tested a strand of linguini. Perfect. She got that drained, finished her sauce and then added the pasta into the pan and stirred. It smelled amazing. She got the garlic bread out of the oven, put everything in two serving bowls and brushed against Reed as he took a pitcher of iced tea from the fridge.

They sat down at the table, both their eyes widening as they glanced out the window. The blizzard raged on. There had to be half a foot of snow on the ground, the wind whipping it around to create bands of whiteout.

"We're lucky the power has stayed on," she said.

"Definitely. Caring for a newborn by flashlight doesn't sound fun."

"*Is* it fun for you, even with regular electricity?" she asked, tilting her head, realizing she really wanted to know how he felt. Was he enjoying this experience with Summer? Or was it an obligation? She couldn't quite tell.

"No," he said, his attention on the big helping of pasta he put on his plate. "Not for me."

Her gaze darted to him. Well. No hemming and hawing there. "So, it's strictly an obligation, because the note was personally addressed to you."

"Right," he said.

"You don't like babies?" she asked.

"How about those Wyoming Cowboys?" he said in a perfectly neutral tone, taking a piece of garlic bread.

She had to smile. "Okay, fair enough—none of my business. I guess I'm just so enthralled by Summer. By having a baby in the house, in my care. Even if she's actually in your care."

"You're a foster parent," he said. "This is what you want."

But not what you want. Again, she wondered why. But she could tell he did not want to be asked, so she'd drop it. For now. If caring for Summer was a burden, maybe she could talk to him again about letting her foster Summer for him. The ol' sitter-for-the-sitter idea.

"This is delicious," he said, twirling linguini on his fork. "So good. Better than Pimoni's."

She felt herself beam. "That is quite the compliment. Thank you."

"Thank *you* for cooking." He held up his glass of iced tea toward her, so she clinked it with her glass and they sipped.

They dug into their pasta, Aimee so aware of him across from her. She wondered what he was thinking. Probably about the case—Summer's mother and who she was. If the snow would ever stop, and when, so that he could get back to his own life.

"What do you think will happen with your sister Marin?" he asked. "Think she'll marry the fiancé?"

Huh. So he'd been thinking about *her*. And her situation. The man was kind. With very strong arms. And so damned handsome, which she was faced with every time she looked at him—which happened often in the small cabin. It was a dangerous combination for a woman who couldn't afford to develop feelings for him.

"Sure sounds like it. Maybe I do just have to accept what she's saying, respect that she's made a choice. Like I had to with my own marriage."

Oops, she'd done it again. Said too much. She kept her eyes on her plate, hoping he hadn't caught that. But he was a detective, so of course he had.

"What do you mean?" he asked. She could feel him staring at her.

"How about those Cowboys?" She sent him an awkward smile and took a fast drink of her iced tea.

He smiled back. "Everyone's entitled to make their own choices—you don't get to decide for her. But sometimes you're perfectly entitled to say, 'Hey, loved one who I care about—your choice sucks.'"

She laughed and shook her head. "How do you manage to always make me feel better?"

"Years of experience," he said, biting into a piece of garlic bread.

"Yeah, I know from that. How'd we get to be in our thirties?"

"Right?" he said with a smile before taking a bite of his pasta.

"It's strange, but I'm glad you're here, Reed," she said, looking across the table at him. "At first, I hated that you were, since it meant you were interfering in my first foster placement. But it turns out you're nice to have around."

His expression veered from surprised to touched. "I could say the same about you. And not just because we'll be taking turns at waking up all night long."

Her heart soothed, she smiled and dug into her linguini, her appetite back. And as they somehow got into a discussion of the kinds of loud sounds that woke them up in their usual lives—neighboring roosters a quarter mile away for her, car horns and police scanners for him—she realized she shouldn't think about the fact that she was beginning to like the detective a little too much.

Reed had a baby monitor on his bedside table turned up high—but he wasn't asleep when he heard the cries. It was just past midnight and he was in bed, though on top of the down comforter, his list of possibilities for who Summer's mother was beside him on his phone's notes app.

A few hours ago, when Summer had woken from her nap, Aimee had leaped up and asked if she could go tend to her and he'd said sure, relieved that he didn't have to, actually. Which he'd already admitted to her. He'd been grateful that she hadn't pressed. He didn't plan to talk about Kayla or his past. He had just a few more to go, per the note. Summer's mother would come back, he'd assess the situation with Aimee in her role with Family Services, and they'd go from there.

It was his turn to care for Summer, so he got up and headed out of his room and next door to the nursery. Aimee was standing at the changing table, sprinkling cornstarch on Summer's bottom before putting on a fresh diaper—and softly singing "Twinkle, Twinkle Little Star."

"'Up above the world so high, like a diamond in the sky...'"

He froze in the doorway, every word of that lullaby, every line slamming into his head, his heart, his stomach.

His ex-wife had been singing "Twinkle, Twinkle Little Star" when he'd come into the nursery the last night he'd seen Kayla. It had been after midnight then too; he'd just gotten home from his shift, which had run hours late. She'd turned at the sound of his footsteps and stopped singing, her expression stony, chin lifted. And then she'd gutted him.

Now, heart in his throat, Reed stared at Aimee's back as she lifted Summer from the changing table and continued singing. "'Twinkle, twinkle little star, how I wonder what you are...'"

"I can't do this," he said.

Aimee whirled around, surprise on her face. "Reed?"

"I can't do this," he repeated, shaking his head.

"Can't do what?" she whispered, the worry and concern in her eyes adding to the hell tearing him up inside.

He *couldn't* do this. But he wouldn't abandon Summer either. Not when she'd been left in his care. Was it the baby at this point who was triggering him or Aimee *and* the baby? Seeing them together was a double reminder of everything he'd lost. And then that damned lullaby.

He closed his eyes for a moment, letting his head drop back. He didn't want to talk about it. Any of it. But he was the one who'd opened that door and he owned Aimee an explanation.

Words weren't coming out of his mouth, though.

"Reed, I've got this, okay? If you need to go back to your room and decompress from...what's got you so torn up, go. I'll feed Summer in the meantime—I knew she was going to wake up any minute, so I already prepared her bottle." She pointed at it on the table by the rocker. She sat down, holding Summer, and held the bottle, the baby suckling away.

"'Twinkle, twinkle, little star,'" she continued in a somewhat strained whisper, her gaze on the baby, no idea that she was ripping his heart out. "'How I wonder what you are.'"

"The last time I saw Kayla," he said, his voice tight, "my ex-wife was singing that song. In a nursery just like this one. Kayla was almost two then. She's three now."

Aimee's eyes widened with compassion—and curiosity. "Kayla?" she asked in almost a whisper.

"My daughter. My stepdaughter, technically. Now I'm nothing to her." He took in a breath and crossed his arms over his chest.

He could see the questions in Aimee's eyes, the concern on her face. *Just get it out*, he told himself. "I came home late from my shift—hours late. In Cheyenne, where I used to live," he added, not even sure he'd mentioned that to Aimee. "I went into the nursery to kiss Kayla good-night as quietly as I could. My wife was there, sitting in the rocking chair like you are, holding the baby like you are, singing that song like you were."

"Oh, Reed," Aimee said, her eyes misting. She was looking at him intently.

The terrible story rushed up inside him and he felt like if he *didn't* get it out of him, he'd choke on it. He hadn't talked about that night and the aftermath with anyone but Rex. And that was a year ago.

"There was a suitcase next to the chair," he said, recalling it—large and red, the one she'd taken on their honeymoon. That night, he'd learned she'd be using it to leave him. "She told me she'd filed for divorce that afternoon and that she was getting back together with Kayla's 'real' father. That I was gone so much, worked so many hours, that he had been able to slip into their lives and make his case for a fresh start." He closed his eyes again for a second, the vivid memories feeling like yesterday and a million years ago at the same time.

Now he saw tears welling in Aimee's eyes. The story *was* sad as hell. His fault too. All of it.

"I just remember staring at her in shock, unable to process what she was saying. Divorce? She was getting back together with Kayla's biological father, who'd left her when she told him she was pregnant? *What?* And then she'd said, 'Don't look like this is shocking news, Reed. I've tried to talk to you time and again. You don't listen. You don't change. Kayla and I are packed and leaving now. I was just waiting for you to come home to tell you.'"

"Omigod, Reed," Aimee said. "This just gets worse and worse."

He nodded. *Yeah, it does. And the worst is yet to come.* He saw himself standing in the doorway a year ago, could feel the panic gripping his chest, the help-lessness.

He swallowed past the lump in his throat. "I just stood there and said, 'But you can't leave. We can work this out. Kayla is my *daughter*.' And she said—I'll never forget it because she seemed sad instead of cold as she'd been a second before—'No, Reed. She's not. You always said you'd adopt her, but you never made time for that because your job took precedence over everything. But it's fine, because she's young enough to forget you.' Then she stood up with Kayla in one arm, took the suitcase and walked out. I never saw Kayla again."

"Oh, Reed. I'm so sorry. How long ago was this?"

"Just over a year ago. I didn't contest the divorce, didn't try to argue for shared custody. I had no rights to Kayla because—as much as I hate to admit it—my ex was right about why I didn't adopt her. Why didn't I? *Why?*" That had consumed him for months. He had put his job first. Ahead of the little girl he'd felt was his in his heart.

"Let's get out of the nursery," she said, standing up. Summer was done with the bottle and Aimee left it on the small table beside the chair.

His legs felt like lead, but he did want to get the hell out of this room.

Aimee had Summer vertical against her chest and was patting her back for a burp. He trailed after her out of the room. She walked over to the sliding glass doors that looked out onto the back property of the cabin, the whipping snow illuminated by the moon.

"I'm gonna go make some coffee," he said. "Even though it's so late."

She nodded and didn't follow him. He was glad for that. He walked into the kitchen and braced himself against the counter. Getting all that out hadn't made him feel better at all. In fact, he felt sick.

He slowly made the coffee to give himself time to decompress. It was at least a half hour later when he went back into the living room. Aimee was walking around the room, softly talking to Summer, telling her about snow and what it was and where it came from. He sat down on the sofa, both hands wrapped around the mug of coffee.

"I'm going to put her in the infant bouncer in front of the doors," she said. "She can watch the snow fall and whip around." He knew that Aimee was being her always thoughtful self as she settled Summer in the bouncer, facing outside, the seat slightly rocking. No lullaby, though there was a button to play songs. They could both see the seat and Summer's profile, but she wasn't front and center, everything about her poking at the raw spot in his chest.

Aimee came over to the couch and sat on the end, giving him some much-needed space.

But she was still too close. Too close and too far at the same time.

Chapter Six

Aimee had known from the first time she met Reed Dawson that he had experience with babies. And given his very straightforward response earlier, when she'd asked if he was enjoying caring for Summer and he'd said no, she'd also known there was a story there. She hadn't been expecting *this*, though.

"I'm so sorry for all you went through, Reed." She turned a bit toward him on the sofa, curling her legs up behind her. "My goodness, how harrowing."

He glanced at her with a nod. She could still see the strain in his face but he seemed calmer. "Good word for it. And just when I think I'm dealing with it fine, that it's part of my past and that I've moved on because I've *had* to, something will happen that makes me feel like it all happened yesterday."

"Like me singing, 'Twinkle, Twinkle, Little Star.'" She'd remove that from her repertoire of nursery songs.

"I can imagine. Being responsible for a baby again. The nursery setting. The song. Of all the songs in the world, how'd I pick that one?"

He looked over at her then, and the urge to slide over and wrap her arms around him, to comfort him, was overwhelming. But she stayed put. She had a feeling if she even tried, he'd feel uncomfortable and bolt.

So she figured she'd ask her burning question. The one that had been echoing in her head the past half hour. "If I can ask, Reed—how did you end up marrying a pregnant woman in the first place?"

He sipped his coffee and put it down on the coffee table. "I was chasing after a suspect. He jumped a fence, so I jumped it too, but I came down hard on my ankle. She was the nurse at the ER. While she was wrapping my foot, I could see tears in her eyes. When I asked her if she was okay, she blurted out that her boyfriend broke up with that day over lunch when she told him she was six weeks pregnant. Later that day, I stopped by to thank her for taking care of my ankle and brought her a little gift, both pink *and* blue booties. It just sort of took off from there."

She could definitely see him doing that. "Wow, so you were there for the entire pregnancy."

He nodded. "I proposed after just a month of dating. I knew she was the one, and I thought of that baby as mine from the get-go. I was there for the delivery, for those magical first days and sleepless nights, where you just marvel over the tiny new being you're responsible for, who you love so much you think you'll burst. In my heart, my head, everything in me, I was that baby's father."

"When did things start to go wrong?" she asked.

He sighed and shook his head. "It's hard to say. My ex wanted to stay home with the baby, so that made it a little easier for me to continue my long hours. Plus, I was the sole breadwinner, and I wanted to be a good provider for my family. I tried to shorten my days, not work so many nights, but it just didn't work out that way. I missed her first taste of solid food, her first word, her first steps. We started arguing—she kept saying I was more married to my job than to her. I thought I was doing okay balancing work and my family. I had a hard time seeing her point of view—out of selfishness, I realize now. She was telling me what she needed and I didn't listen."

"I'm so sorry," she said again. She scooted over closer to him and took his hand and gave it a squeeze. "Sometimes when you're in the middle of something, it's hard to see the big picture."

He stood up and paced to the windows, looking out at the storm. "At the time, though, I was thinking that I couldn't change my hours, that the job was what it was. That she had to understand that. I was so damned stubborn."

He shook his head again and paced a bit more, then came back to the sofa and dropped down.

"That final night, I followed her to the front door of our house," he continued. "She stood there with our two-year-old and their things packed in that damned red suitcase and she said, 'You're not her father, Reed. And keeping up a relationship with you will be too confusing for her. As I said, she's young enough to forget you. This is goodbye.'"

Aimee winced three times during that last part. She

grabbed his hand and held it. She had so much to ask, so much to say, but she knew he wasn't finished and she wanted him to get it all out.

He took a long sip of his coffee. "I should have adopted Kayla, but there was never time to take off to start the proceedings and get it done and I suppose I thought it was just a formality. I'd always planned to do it, though. And then it was too late."

"What a painful situation," Aimee said gently. "I've dealt with cases with similar issues." Like cops, Family Services saw it all. You couldn't be unaffected just because you weren't personally involved—the case itself made you involved.

He nodded and was quiet for a moment. "I met with a lawyer to ask if I had any case for visitation. But she confirmed for me that I had no rights. Just like that, I lost my daughter. And now mother and *real* father are married and the happy family lives in the family home I agreed to give up in the divorce."

"And you haven't seen Kayla since the final night?" she asked. How hard that must have been all these months.

He shook his head. "If I hadn't run into my cousin Rex a couple days after, I would have gone out of my mind. He invited me to spend a week in a cabin at the guest ranch, staring into nature. I never left."

"The move to Bear Ridge was clearly the right one," she said.

He nodded. "But now there's Summer. And you. And 'Twinkle, Twinkle Little Star.' It's...*a lot*."

She reached out a hand and touched his face, then

opened her arms and wondered if he'd let her comfort him, hold him, the way he had done for her before dinner.

He pulled her to him and held her tight.

Oh, Reed, she thought, something shifting in her chest.

Reed woke up on the couch to the sound of Summer crying. The baby monitor was on the coffee table but the nursery door was ajar and he could hear her loud and clear. Aimee was asleep at the other end of the couch, curled up and covered by the chenille throw.

A while ago, Aimee had put Summer to bed in her crib and had come back out to the living room. He'd surprised himself for not wanting to disappear into his room after telling her everything, after opening himself up the way he had. He hadn't wanted to be alone in the dark with all those memories that had gotten dredged up. He had a feeling that Aimee, given her training and experience as a social worker, instinctively understood that. So they'd sat on the couch with the hot chocolates Aimee had made, keeping the conversation light, talking about their favorite things, from food to movies to the entrées at Pimoni's, where, Reed recalled, he'd promised to take her if it ever stopped snowing.

Now it was close to 4:15 a.m. The sky was dark but he could see the snow had stopped.

Hallelujah.

He'd say there was six to eight inches of snow on the ground, but at least nothing more was falling from the sky.

Reed stood up and went into the nursery. Summer was fuss-crying in her crib. He scooped her up before she could wake up Aimee, who'd taken the last two wakings, even though they were supposed to take turns. The dinner at Pimoni's was supposed to be a thank-you for that.

Not a date.

He looked down at the infant cradled along his arm. She looked up at him, slate blue eyes alert.

I'm supposed to take care of you, he said silently. *That means more than feeding you and putting you down for naps. It means holding you close, like this, singing to you in my terrible voice, rocking you. I owe you more than just an obligation to babysit. You're a brand-new human and you need everything.*

With that, he took Summer into the kitchen, got the bottle Aimee had premade at the last feeding and plunked it in a container of hot water to heat it up a little. I'm a pro at the one-armed hold, he told Summer silently. Because I've had a lot of practice.

As he took baby and bottle back toward the nursery, he glanced over at Aimee on the couch. Still asleep— good. She definitely needed the rest.

In the nursery, he sat down on the rocking chair with the bottle and watched Summer drink. Memories of Kayla still pinched, but getting the whole story off his chest must have dislodged something, because the pinching wasn't as severe. The dull ache was still there, how terribly he missed Kayla and no doubt always would. But this was a start. He resolved to see Summer as more than an obligation that ripped his heart. He'd see her as a tiny being who needed him. And he'd go from there.

Starting at five, the plows would be out. He had no doubt Aimee had a reliable plower who'd clear the long drive to the cabin.

And then he'd be able to leave, which would make things easier. Because playing house was doing a number on him. He liked Aimee Gallagher too much. Cared about her. Wanted things to work out for her with being a foster mom, with her complicated sister.

But just hours ago, as he'd had her in his arms, holding her, taking the comfort she'd offered, he'd realized he'd *wanted* her—a place his mind had refused to let him go this past year. If they'd known each other longer than a day, if the situation wasn't so…fraught emotionally for both of them, maybe he would have kissed her. Maybe she would have kissed him.

And maybe there would have been much more happening on that couch last night. But his first foray into romance couldn't be with a woman he already cared about, a woman who had a lot going on and didn't need a man push-pulling with her.

But a relationship, a real relationship, with dating and building attachment and the possibility of a future, was out of the question. He might be able to better handle being around babies and toddlers without constantly thinking about Kayla. But falling hard for a woman again?

He wasn't going there. Ever.

Chapter Seven

"Look at that, Summer!" Aimee said, holding the baby by the window in the nursery at six thirty in the morning. "The snow stopped! And do you hear that? That is the joyous sound of a snowplow rumbling down the road. That means we can come and go in a little while."

As she left the nursery and headed for the kitchen and coffee, her heart sank just as fast as it had soared with the appearance of the sun and the blue sky. Reed would be able to leave this morning—and he'd take Summer with him.

She thought he might be awake and on his phone or going through his databases and cases at the kitchen table, but he wasn't there. Still sleeping? Probably. She'd slept right through Summer's last feeding and had woken up on the couch, covered with the chenille throw—and *she* hadn't pulled it over her.

Goose bumps trailed up her inner arms as she remembered their after-midnight chat—not the heavy-duty one, but the one after, when she'd put Summer in her crib and had come back out to find him still on the couch. She'd been surprised that he'd been up for more conversation at all, but he'd said yes to hot chocolate with oatmeal cookies and they'd spent a long time chatting about their favorite everything. For cookies, his was good old chocolate chip. He could eat the chicken Milanese sandwich at Pimoni's every day for lunch, which she already knew, and he loved Marvel movies and action flicks, and fishing on the Bear Ridge River, alone preferably, because it was such a good thinking activity. His favorite color was navy blue. His middle name was Hughes, his mother's maiden name. She'd also learned his parents were traveling the West Coast in an RV, their retirement dream, and were currently in Southern California.

She hadn't felt so close to a man since before her marriage had exploded. On her couch, post 1:30 a.m., as they'd sipped their cocoa and nibbled their cookies and talked and talked, she'd found herself eyeing Reed's broad shoulders. His powerful chest. The way his eyes just slightly crinkled at the sides when he smiled, which was often during that lighter conversation. She'd even thought about the two of them kissing. And *more*. But those very pleasant thoughts must have lulled her off to sleep because the next thing she knew, the sun was up and out and Summer was squawking in the nursery.

She did notice that Reed had not stayed on the couch with her. That he'd taken care of Summer and then gone back to his room. Alone.

It was better that way. Because given where her

thoughts and nerve endings had led, she was worried that she had honest-to-goodness fledgling feelings for the detective. And if he *was* even open to romance just a year after his divorce, once he found out she couldn't have kids, anything that might happen between them would come to a grinding halt, like things had with the last few men in her life. Somewhere down the line, Reed would be ready to have a family again. Given what he'd been through with Kayla, it seemed likely that having a biological tie to his child would be important to him.

A bit unsettled by where her thoughts were taking her now, Aimee put Summer in the infant stroller while she set about making a fresh bottle. After she fed the baby and got a good burp out of her, Aimee carried Summer around the living room, showing her the photographs on the mantel. "These are my sisters, Ella and Marin," she told the infant, whose eyes were actually on Aimee's face, not the photos. "They're planning a double wedding for next summer. June brides."

Aimee had been a June bride.

"The blonde is Ella and the hazel-eyed one with the light brown hair is Marin. Marin is barely speaking to me these days," she added, her heart pinching. "They're twins. I'm the older sister. Six years. When I was a kid I was so jealous of their bond. I guess they both always looked up to me as the older sister, but even though we were close, it wasn't on that same level as the two of them."

She'd felt it less when she'd moved back to the cabin after they'd lost their parents. Her sisters, just eighteen, had been so grief-stricken, in such need, despite being brand-new adults. Now, of course, Aimee could look back and see how very young they all were. Marin, especially, had trailed Aimee constantly, almost as if she was afraid to let her older sister out of her sight. Aimee had gotten so close to them then, and though they all led their own lives, they'd remained close, celebrating all holidays together without fail, and birthdays, including their parents'.

She showed Summer the photos of her mom and dad, her heart in her throat. What she wouldn't give to have her parents back, to talk to her mom about her marriage, about not being able to have children, about getting certified to become a foster parent. To be wrapped in one of her dad's great bear hugs and assist him in assembling his famous weekly lasagna, which she missed to this day.

Since the photos were getting her all emotional, she walked Summer over to the sliding glass door, overlooking the back deck, which was piled high with snow. That would take forever to shovel and she wasn't looking forward to it. Maybe she'd hire the teenagers who lived at the neighboring ranch to do the job and save her back.

A half hour later, Aimee had shown Summer just about everything in the cabin, except of course, for the guest room, since Reed was in there behind a closed door. She had the baby back in the stroller in the kitchen as she thought about what to make for breakfast. Cheese omelets and a side of bacon, she decided, figuring the smell of sizzling bacon would lure him out.

It worked.

Back in his charcoal pants and button-down shirt and looking very much like a detective again, Reed came into the kitchen. "Snowplows wake you up, or did Summer?"

"Summer actually, by ten minutes or so. I love both sounds, though, so I didn't mind in the slightest."

He smiled. "Yeah, after a blizzard, there's no sweeter sound like the grinding and scraping of very large machinery."

She glanced out the window. Blue skies. Sun. No snow—except the eight-ish inches on the ground. "I almost can't believe it's really not snowing anymore. The storm went on and on."

She bit her lip at the idea of him and Summer leaving at some point this morning. She wasn't looking forward to that at all.

"Same," he said. "When I noticed that it stopped, I almost felt like something was missing before I realized it was the whipping snow." He sniffed the air with an appreciative expression, smiled at her, and then went over to Summer and ran a light hand over her soft brown, wispy hair. "Summer and I bonded a bit last night at her last feeding. That's thanks to you, Aimee."

"Me?" she asked, glancing at him in surprise. "What did I do?" She grabbed the tongs to flip over the bacon.

"You listened—without judgment, without interrupting, without saying much other than to be supportive. It all helped. I'm hardly at the point where it's easy to hold Summer and feed her and even look at her sweet face, but talking about what happened last year—it helped."

Aimee felt a rush of warmth to her chest. She was so touched. "I'm glad you opened up. It was time for you, I suppose. Helped along by a very cute baby too." She grinned at Summer, who was looking at Reed, her blue eyes alert.

"I feel bad that she can't have any bacon," Reed said, glancing at the pan.

Aimee laughed. "Or the Swiss cheese omelets I'm about to make us. Hungry?"

"Starving. I've been up for a while, actually, working on figuring out who Summer's mother could possibly be. I keep coming up empty. It's very frustrating. I definitely need coffee." He went over to the pot and poured himself a mug, adding his cream and sugar. "And I'll tell you what. Since you made dinner last night and got the bacon and coffee going, I'll do the honor of making the omelets. They're one of the few things I'm pretty good at."

"Be my guest—literally." She took her coffee cup over to the table and sat down. "I know you've been focusing on your local cases," she said as he cracked four eggs into a mixing bowl. "But maybe it's worth looking into cases from Cheyenne. Maybe the mother isn't someone you met recently."

"I think that's a good idea. I've exhausted the possibilities for around Bear Ridge. The chief and Ford have both been making calls for me on the subject too and they've also come up with no one. So yeah, I'll turn my focus to Cheyenne."

"Think you might have to drive there?" she asked.

"Internet and phone should cover me," he said, taking a sip of his coffee. "I definitely don't want to step foot in that city ever again, which is a shame because Cheyenne is a great place."

She gave him a thoughtful nod. If that's how he felt

about his hometown, he would definitely need more time to let the past go and heal.

She watched as he whisked the eggs and added a pinch of salt and pepper. She was kind of mesmerized as he did the most quotidian things of adding some butter to a sauté pan and then pouring in the eggs, letting them set as he got out the Swiss cheese from the refrigerator. "Besides," he continued, "if Summer's mother is from Cheyenne, she drove to Bear Ridge to drop her off with me and is likely still around. I can't see someone who'd just given birth making that long trip right away, with a storm closing in—and she did say she'd be back for the baby in a few days. I'll look at all the possibilities."

She nodded and sipped her coffee and then played a few rounds of peekaboo with Summer so she'd stop watching Reed. Stop being so aware of him.

By the time they'd finished their breakfast—and Reed was right, he made a very good omelet—put Summer down for her nap and cleaned up the kitchen, both the town plows and the service Aimee used every winter had come and gone.

He glanced out the window. "My plan is to head over to the BRPD now with Summer—for two reasons. One, her mother might come back today. I know she said a few days, but the separation may have caused a change of heart and perhaps she'll come back for Summer at some point today. And I can make use of the databases there and the monitors, instead of my tiny phone screen." He squinted for good measure.

She'd smile, but she could barely keep her eyes from misting. She turned away so he wouldn't see.

He was leaving. And taking Summer, as he'd always said he would.

As Reed stacked the last of the pots and pans in the dishwasher, he turned to Aimee and said, "So since it stopped snowing, I owe you dinner at Pimoni's tonight, as a thank-you for everything you did for me and Summer."

The misting stopped and her heart lifted a bit. She *hadn't* seen the last of him or Summer. She'd figured his mention last night of taking her to Pimoni's had been more of a "someday" thing. She knew this wasn't a date—nor did she want it to be—but she sure was happy about it.

"I never pass up a chance for Pimoni's," she said. "Especially when it's free."

He smiled. "Pick you up at six thirty? I'll feed Summer right before and take along your infant stroller so she can fall asleep during dinner."

Goose bumps trailed up her spine. "Sounds good."

It did. Too good. And she was a little too aware of how excited she was about going out with Reed. Because she'd see Summer again? And she could make her case for fostering the baby while Reed worked on the case of who her mother was?

Or because of the chance to get a little dressed up, post-blizzard-friendly even, and sit across from Reed Dawson at their mutually favorite restaurant, which was definitely considered romantic, with candlelight between them?

Maybe both.

Reed, Ford and Rex were in the break room at the Bear Ridge Police Department, standing around the coffee station, each with a mug in their hands. Reed eyed the box of donuts the regular front-desk clerk had brought in. Betsy, a tall, strong, former cop, and mother of five in her fifties, was oohing and aahing over Summer in her stroller at her desk. Reed plucked a chocolate coconut with a napkin and took a bite.

The two Dawson brothers looked a lot alike, tall and muscular with dark hair and blue eyes, like Reed himself. Ford was the eldest of his six siblings at thirty-six. Reed admired both men. They were both hardworking, kind and fair to everyone, and hard-nosed when they had to be. Dawsons *were* everywhere in Bear Ridge and that included the BRPD with three of them now, but no one found that to be an issue because each of them could be counted on at any time, and the rest of the force and the town knew that.

Reed had arrived at the station just fifteen minutes ago, and though the other detective and the rookie were out, the Dawson brothers and Betsy had all rushed him to see the baby and ask a million questions. Reed answered what he could, but everything was up in the air until Summer's mother could be tracked down.

"It might not be related to a case, you know. What about relatives?" Ford asked, then took a sip of his coffee. "Obviously someone on the more distant side, but someone who met you somewhere along the way, someone you made an impression on. If you're family, it would explain why she knew she could trust you."

"Or maybe it's the girlfriend or wife of a relative," Rex said, taking the pumpkin donut.

Reed nodded. "Good suggestions. I'll give that some thought. I don't have a big family, which is why my brain didn't even go there. Everyone seems accounted for. But maybe not. I can also ask my sister what she thinks."

"You're lucky you've got someone like Aimee to help you out with Summer," Ford said. "I know you said she's newly certified as a foster mother, but four hands with a newborn is much better than two."

Especially with your history. Ford didn't have to say it, but both Dawson brothers knew his story and how hard it had been this past year for him to be around babies and toddlers.

"To be honest, I'm not entirely sure I should take advantage of her help," Reed said. "Summer was to be her first placement and I messed that up for her. She was really looking forward to it. And being snowbound, she bonded with Summer. But is it better to let her move on so she can get another placement?"

"I think while you're looking for the mother, you should let Aimee be the foster mother, even unofficially," Rex said. "You're still taking responsibility for caring for Summer, but you've got serious backup from someone who really wants that role."

"Actually, aside from a few speedbumps, taking care of her hasn't been too bad for me," Reed said. "Not like I expected. Maybe time really does work its magic."

"It does," Ford said.

Rex nodded. "We both know that."

"I know honoring that note is important to you," Ford continued. "But a newborn is hard work. Yeah, they sleep like sixteen hours a day, but it's the every three hours in between that gets you."

Hmm. That was true. Having Aimee's help, especially in the middle of the night, had eased things for both of them. And she *had* bonded with Summer. Perhaps he should accept her help, let her get this experience with her first placement. He'd talk to her about it tonight at dinner.

"And besides, it's not like you have a fully equipped nursery in your bachelor pad," Rex added.

That was another major consideration. He'd brought some of the necessities with him when he left Aimee's place this morning. Diapers, ointment, bottle and formula, burp cloths, a pacifier, a couple of changes of pj's. It was not ideal, though. And Aimee's nursery *was*.

"Well, I've got to hit the road," Rex said. "Reed, I know you've got the next couple of days off till the mother returns, so I might not run into you. I'll see you Saturday at the party, though, right?"

Ah, right. His daughter's third birthday party.

"You should bring Aimee and Summer," Ford said. "It would be nice to see Aimee again."

Jeez. First Reed was attending a child's birthday party at all and now he was bringing a date? And a baby?

Not that it would be a *date*. Just like tonight wasn't a date.

He would bring Summer, and Aimee *was* the foster mother. So that helped settle *that* in his mind. Not a date. Not at all. Just like tonight wasn't.

"Besides, bringing someone will stop Danica from cornering you about a fix up," Rex said with a grin shot at Ford. "Our unofficial town matchmaker works the singles at every family party."

Rex had a good point there.

"You can mention I'm taking her to Pimoni's tonight for good measure," Reed said—then realized he shouldn't have brought that up. It *did* sound like a date, when it most definitely wasn't. "As a thank-you for everything she did for me and Summer. It's not a date."

Ford and Rex gave each other a look, like they didn't believe that at all.

"Anything happen last night?" Rex asked, a gleam in his eyes.

Ford was also looking at him expectantly.

Reed gave an exaggerated eye roll. "Nope. Just a lot of middle-of-the-night feedings, burps—from the newborn—and diaper changes."

The brothers laughed. "Very romantic," Ford quipped.

But Reed's smile faded as he realized he'd *wanted* something to happen.

Chapter Eight

After Reed left with Summer, Aimee called her boss, Mariana, to update her on everything. She explained that she hoped to help Reed with the newborn until the mother returned and would make her case for that tonight during the thank-you dinner. Mariana, who'd also become a friend over the past five years, had immediately said, "Hmm, the thank-you dinner sounds like a date." She'd also said that Aimee should take the rest of the week off, as planned anyway, in case Reed did need her help.

"There might be a new placement for all we know," Mariana had added, "so let's just see."

Aimee hoped so. Having Summer here for the night had made her even more sure that she was meant to be a foster mother.

Once she saw on the Bear Ridge Community Facebook page that the town's schools would be closed today for a snow day, she called her nearest neighbors, who had two teens, to ask if they'd like to earn some money shoveling the back deck. They immediately agreed, knowing that she'd pay them well and in hot chocolate. Reed, she'd discovered, had shoveled the walkway and a path to the driveway before he'd left, which of course he hadn't mentioned.

While the teens shoveled, making quick work of the pounds of snow, she looked in her closet for the perfect outfit to wear tonight. Something casual but still…nice. Something a little more festive than she'd wear to work. So not a dress, exactly, but not a pantsuit with a scarf.

Her phone rang and she snatched it up.

"I'm dying to hear everything," Ella asked. "Is he still there? If not, I'm coming over."

Aimee laughed. "Come on over. He actually left a little while ago."

"Be there in fifteen!" Ella said.

Aimee smiled and disconnected. She gave up on her outfit choices, figuring she'd leave that to Ella, and went into the kitchen. She made two take-out cups of hot cocoa with mini-marshmallows and put a wad of cash into two envelopes for her teen shovelers. They were leaving just as her sister arrived.

Ella burst in, her long blond hair up in a loose bun with a hairpin through it. She hung up her jacket. "Okay, spill."

Aimee grinned. "There's a lot to tell, actually."

Her sister's blue eyes widened. "Ooh."

They went into the kitchen and Aimee poured them two cups of coffee. She told Ella everything except the personal details regarding Reed's past. She'd just mentioned that he'd gone through a rough divorce. Mostly, she focused on how wonderful it had been to take care of Summer.

"If there's one thing I know for sure, it's that I am meant to be a foster mother," Aimee said.

Ella leaned over and pulled her into a hug. "You definitely are. You are so maternal. I don't know what Marin and I would have done if it wasn't for you when Mom and Dad died. Technically, we were all adults. But eighteen is really so young. So was twenty-four."

"The three of us were all there for each other," Aimee said, taking a sip of her coffee. She bit her lip. "Marin FaceTimed me last night, telling me she didn't want me to stand up for her in the wedding as her maid of honor."

"I know. It's the other reason why I came. To tell you that of course you'll be *my* maid of honor. And I'm sure Marin will calm down and change her mind."

"About her fiancé?" Aimee dared to say.

"That, I don't know. But it's her choice, her life, Aimee. You might be being a little too mom-ish here."

"I just can't seem to forget what she told me that night."

"But maybe it really was her reacting to a very scary night. All her fears poured out. And then in the light of day, maybe she was back to herself, strong, solid Marin, and all those worries went away, and she felt certain that John is what she wants."

Getting married *is what she wants*, Aimee amended silently.

Aimee thought about what Ella said, though. "I guess." Ella's points made sense, but it was *what* Marin had said that had Aimee so convinced her sister was making a mistake. Like: *I don't love him.* The light of day and a good prognosis for Ella wouldn't change that. Marin had simply buried her truth again.

But this wasn't Aimee's choice. Or life. And she did have to respect that Marin had made a decision. She sighed. "I'll call her later and apologize."

Aimee would try to feel good about Marin's decision. She had a long time to do that. Over the next months, she'd likely get to know her future brother-in-law better and maybe she'd see all the good things in their relationship instead of always hearing Marin's word echoing in her head.

I don't love him. I just want what Ella has...

"Good," Ella said. "Because then I can get all superficial and talk headpieces and dresses and shoes and venues again." Her gorgeous one-carat, solitaire diamond ring sparkled in the sunshine coming through the windows of the cabin. "So, will you see the detective and Summer again? It sounds like you three got kind of close all snowbound together."

"Actually," Aimee said, taking a sip of her coffee to savor the news. "We're going to Pimoni's tonight—he wanted to thank me for coming to his rescue during the blizzard and helping out."

"Ooh, a date?" Ella asked.

"Definitely not. Just a thank-you. Reed is...complicated. He's only been divorced a year."

"A year is a meaningful period of time," Ella said. "It's a date."

Aimee smiled, those goose bumps trailing up her spine, and shook her head.

Her sister was peering at her. "Do you want it to be a date?"

"I like him. Let's just put it that way. And he's incredibly good-looking."

"Oh, Aimee. You have no idea how happy I am to hear you say that. This is the first time in ages I've heard you be even remotely positive about dating again."

"Every time I date, I end up squashed," Aimee said. "Hurt—bad. But Reed Dawson is…"

"Is…?" her sister prompted.

"…everything I've ever looked for in a man," she said, the truth of that statement hitting her hard. "Oh God. I more than like him."

Her sister was grinning. "So what are you wearing to dinner? I love your iridescent gray, floaty dress with the sash. So pretty."

Aimee did too. "It's too much, I think. I need something between date and work."

"Let's go check out your closet."

Thank heavens for sisters, Aimee thought.

With Summer in her infant carrier, Reed rang the doorbell at Aimee's cabin at six thirty that night, excited to see her after the long day apart. After spending so many hours in close quarters in her company, he chalked that up to having developed a bond with her—that's all.

But when she opened the door and his mouth almost dropped open, he knew it was more than that. Bond plus attraction equaled trouble here.

She wore a fitted, V-neck black sweater, which clung to her curves, slim black pants, a small gold-heart locket around her creamy neck and black leather boots. Her blond hair was loose past her shoulders, and her red lips were beckoning to him. "I'll just grab my coat," she said.

He swallowed as he watched her put on the red wool coat that he'd met her in. There was no need for hats and gloves and scarves, like yesterday, since the temperature was in the midforties.

As she came out and locked the door, he heard a car engine start and glanced toward the sound. A dark gray compact car was parked under a stand of evergreens across the road and down a ways. He stared at it and could just make out a woman behind the wheel in sunglasses—with red hair.

Like the description of the woman who'd dropped off Summer in the BRPD.

Like the description of the car that had peeled away moments after he'd gone inside and found the baby on his desk. He wasn't able to make out the license plate from here.

Reed was about to hand Summer to Aimee and run over when the car peeled off again and disappeared. "I'm 99 percent sure that was Summer's mother in that little gray car."

Aimee gasped. "Really?"

He nodded. He'd call the chief about sending the rookie out to look for the car, but the last thing Reed wanted was for a cop car to scare the mother away. The woman was around, clearly keeping tabs on him and Summer, which was a good thing. She'd be back. The note said "a few days," and now that he knew she was watching them, he was more confident that she'd return for Summer when she was ready—which would depend on what had spurred her to leave her infant daughter with Reed in the first place.

"I guess she followed you here," Aimee said. "I wonder if she was parked in the BRPD lot today."

"Could be. Maybe she was thinking about coming in to pick up Summer? Or she just wanted to be close by to her baby? I wish I knew who she was and what's going on with her."

Aimee nodded. "Same. Any luck today in narrowing down her identity?"

They walked to his SUV, the driveway still coated in snow, and he settled Summer in the back. "No. No one popped up as a strong possibility. I've moved on from looking at old cases to looking into distant relatives. My sister mentioned a branch of second cousins that our family had a falling out with around ten years ago, but she was pretty sure the ages don't work—a female cousin who'd be late forties with a young teenaged daughter. She couldn't remember their last name, though. They weren't Dawsons. I'll call my mother in the morning and see if they ring a bell for her."

He went around the side of the SUV to open Aimee's door for her, the scent of her light perfume intoxicating him for a moment.

The drive to the restaurant took a bit longer than normal since the roads were slushy and Reed was being extra careful with the baby in the back seat. Pimoni's, in an old stone cottage-like building that looked straight out of a fairy tale, was as inviting as ever. The lot was half full, folks eager for a night out and someone else to do the cooking after being snowbound.

The hostess led them to a rectangular table for two in

the back, as he'd requested, so there'd be more room to park the stroller. Pimoni's at night could be a little too romantic, as it seemed now with its dimmer lighting, the candles, the frescoes on the salmon-colored walls and the just-audible Italian opera.

The waitress came to take their orders—the entrée of chicken Milanese for him with rosemary roast potatoes, the shrimp scampi for Aimee. Summer had had her bottle in Reed's condo just before he'd left to pick up Aimee, and she was awake and alert, her gaze sometimes on him, sometimes on Aimee.

"How was today—having Summer with you?" Aimee asked, dipping a piece of Italian bread in the little dish of olive oil between them.

"I had my moments," he said, "where I'd feel that ache. But for the most part, I was okay. Summer's her own baby, right? I shouldn't look at her and see or think of someone else."

"She's a *great* baby. We got lucky with how easy she is." She froze for a second. "You, I mean. You got lucky."

That made him feel like hell, actually.

"I did get lucky—especially in that you were assigned to be Summer's foster mom. And speaking of, what do you think of basically continuing in that role until the mother is found or returns?"

He saw Aimee's face light up. "I'd love that."

"It makes sense. And like my cousin Rex pointed out today, it's not like I have a fully equipped nursery in my bachelor pad. So I'd like to move back into the guest room for the next few days, if that's okay."

Especially now that he knew that Summer's mother

was watching Aimee's house, he felt right about staying there.

Aimee smiled and held up her sparkling water. "Of course. Count me in to help out as foster mother. I adore that baby. And you don't have to worry about me getting too attached. Knowing it's not a permanent situation from the start will help with saying goodbye when the time comes."

"What made you decide to become a foster parent?" he asked. He'd assumed it was her job and all she'd seen as a Family Service social worker. But it had suddenly occurred to him that it was a little surprising that Aimee, at thirty-four and clearly interested in parenthood, *didn't* have kids of her own.

The beautiful face that had lit up just moments ago dimmed. Unfortunately, right then, the waiter reappeared with their entrees.

"Let's eat," she said. "Because if I answer your question, I might not have an appetite and how incredibly good does my shrimp scampi look?"

Uh-oh. He reached across the table and gave her hand a fast squeeze. "It does look good. I'll trade you a bite at some point."

"Deal," she said and took a bite. "Ah, so good."

He took a bit of his long-awaited chicken Milanese. "Same here."

They ate and swapped stories about their days, Aimee telling him that her sister had stopped over to get the details and that talking to Ella about the situation with Marin had been sort of helpful. She shared how Ella thought she had to accept that Marin's choice, but that Aimee was still struggling with it. A tough situation to be in, for sure. And he told her about how everyone oohed and aahed over Summer and took turns holding her. He'd been afraid the rookie was going to drop her and actually held his hands under the guy's arms, which everyone had found very funny.

He hadn't missed the look that had passed between his cousins, though. A look that had said: *Reed cares about this baby.*

But that was a good thing. A moving-on thing. Summer wasn't permanent in his life, after all, just as Aimee had noted she wouldn't be in hers. In a way, he should be thankful that he'd found himself in this strange situation, because he could feel it changing his life as the seconds ticked by.

Aimee offered him a bite of her shrimp scampi, and he almost leaned forward to take the mouthful straight from the fork in her hand before catching himself and realizing that that would be a little too erotically charged. Instead, he took the fork itself and gobbled up the bite, then offered her a forkful of his dinner.

"Scrumptious," she said. "Next time I'm in for lunch with my sisters, who also love this place, I'll get the sandwich version."

"With the excellent shoestring fries," he said. "Here, try this rosemary potato."

He held out his fork, which she took. He watched her slide it into her mouth, the red lips making him suddenly lick his own.

"Oh! I didn't know you were married, with a baby!"

Reed's head swiveled at the sound of a familiar voice to find the McAllister family, Dan, Linnea and young Brady, whose pet cat he'd found before the storm, standing to his right. Lineea's face was all lit up as she gazed at the baby. "Isn't she just precious! And what a good baby, just looking around so alert! How old? Just a few days, right?" She didn't give them time to answer before continuing, "And to think, Detective, you drove us around to find our cat before the storm hit when you had much more important things to do. We can't thank you enough."

"Mommy, Whiskers is important too," Brady said.

Reed managed a smile. "He sure is. I'm glad he's home safe."

"Well, you enjoy your dinner with your beautiful family," Dan McAllister said, giving Aimee a smile before ushering his own family away.

To think that, once, being out to dinner with his beautiful family had been his reality. Now here he sat with a completely different woman, a completely different baby, who weren't his at all. That Linnea McAllister had mistaken them for a family seemed almost…ridiculous. Of course they weren't a family. He'd never be part of a family again.

"Oh boy," Aimee said, looking a bit stricken, her cheeks flushed. "Though I suppose we do look like a couple out to dinner with our perfect, noncrying baby."

Now Aimee looked *completely* stricken.

"You okay?" he asked, reaching across the table to touch her hand.

She bit her lip. "To answer your earlier question, the reason I wanted to become a foster parent is to help children who need homes, temporarily or otherwise."

He nodded silently, knowing there was more and wanting to give her room to say it at her own pace. He could tell by her expression that she was struggling to get the words out.

She paused and lifted her fork, then put it down. "I can't have kids of my own," she whispered. "It's why my marriage broke up. We were childhood sweethearts, got married at twenty-two. We both wanted to start a family right away. Have four kids. Maybe five. But month after month we were disappointed… And finally, I found out why." She turned away and blinked hard.

Now he reached both hands across and took hers. "I'm so sorry, Aimee."

She took in a breath. "It took me years to get back into the dating scene. I hoped I'd find someone who would be okay with adopting. But my past three relationships lasted all of two or three weeks each. Every one of them ended once I blurted out the truth."

"That sounds really hard," he said, shaking his head. "I'm so glad you found the foster-parent route."

"Ha, until you came along and messed it all up." She was half smiling and half very sad.

"I have an idea. Why don't we get the rest of our dinner wrapped up to go and take it back to the cabin? We can continue talking in private."

Tears misted her eyes and he wanted to leap up and grab her into a hug. "That sounds just right."

He waved down the waiter and explained what they needed as Aimee got Summer under the fleece stroller blanket, her soft wool cap on her head.

Once they were back in the car, she said, "You're just too easy to talk to."

"I could say the same about you, Miss."

She sent him a wobbly smile. "I'm glad you're coming back. Both of you."

He was too. Despite how incredibly dangerous it seemed.

Chapter Nine

When they got back to the cabin, Aimee put Summer down in her crib, well aware of Reed in the doorway. He stood there in a gesture of kindness and comfort, she understood. In case she broke down. In case she simply got sad over her situation, the way she had at the restaurant. The woman who'd stopped by their table at Pimoni's with *her* beautiful family had gotten to her.

She couldn't stop thinking what that woman had said to Reed: *I didn't know you were married, with a baby...* Or what her husband had added: *Enjoy your dinner with your beautiful family...*

An ache had spread in her chest. Her most fervent wish, if she let herself go there, was to be part of exactly what they'd been mistaken for. A family.

Her husband. Her child.

Would she ever have a family? Maybe she'd eventually adopt a child, but would she have a life partner? A husband? She wanted that. She'd thought she'd made peace with having to give up the idea of a husband and pursue single motherhood. But now...

She suddenly understood why Marin had accepted John's marriage proposal when she didn't love him. *Her* most fervent wish was to be married, like her twin would be. She wanted the excitement of getting engaged, wearing a diamond ring, planning a wedding. Marin *liked* him fine, he ticked off enough boxes on what was important to her. He was a compromise that she could live with in order to get what she wanted. Of course Marin had said yes.

Aimee still thought her sister was making a mistake. But at least she understood Marin better.

Aimee looked down at Summer, sleeping in the crib, her fist up toward her cheek as usual, her little chest rising and falling in her sweet yellow pj's. Her yearning was so overwhelming that she had to turn away.

"Should I heat up our doggie bags?" Reed asked. She had the feeling he'd posed the question specifically to help get her out of the nursery and away from what was making her so emotional.

The two of them were good at reading each other.

"You know what?" she said, turning and heading toward the door. "Yes. Let's finish dinner. Things are what they are, right? I have to *accept*."

"I don't know, Aimee. Sometimes, yes, you have to accept. And sometimes you have to fight like hell for what you want."

She stopped in her tracks, tilting her head. "I can hardly fight to have a baby."

"But you can adopt. And you're on your way, right?

You're certified as a foster mother. You're here with Summer, gaining very valuable experience with a newborn."

I'm here with you, falling harder by the second.

She touched his forearm as a thank-you. "Let's go eat. Comfort food and a comforting cop are just what the doctor ordered."

He smiled at that and led the way into the living room. "Make yourself comfortable—he says as if this is his house." Reed shot her another smile. "But really, I've got this."

"Stop being so indispensable. It's gonna be hard when it's time for you to go." Understatement, she realized. It's gonna *hurt* when he left.

There. She'd allowed herself to think it, even though she hadn't meant to. She had to watch out. This wasn't her man. This wasn't her baby. This wasn't her family.

She dropped down on the couch and stared out the sliding glass doors at the beautiful trees illuminated by the moon.

Reed brought over a glass of sparkling berry-infused water and her half-finished shrimp scampi, then went back for his chicken Milanese. He sat down beside her and clinked his glass with hers. "To going through a lot and coming out the other side," he said. "A bit beat-up, but standing."

She smiled. "I will definitely toast to that." She clinked her glass with his.

He smiled back and she suddenly couldn't take her eyes off his handsome face. *I'm falling in love with you*, she realized, butterflies letting loose in her stomach. Danger, danger.

The thought unsettled her but excited her. She hadn't thought she could feel this way about someone anymore. And he knew her story. Maybe something would happen between them, maybe it wouldn't. But she wouldn't make the first move.

"Last rosemary-roasted potato?" he asked, holding out his fork.

Aimee laughed. "I'm stuffed. But thank you. It takes a kind man to give up his last potato."

"Especially a Pimoni's potato." He slid the fork into his mouth, and now she really couldn't tear her gaze away from those lips of his. How she wanted to feel them on hers. Or on her neck. Her collarbone.

Their plates empty, they put them down on the coffee table and sipped their waters, looking out now at the trees.

She tucked her legs up behind her and turned to face him. "You know, you might have messed up my first placement, but again, I'm really glad you're here." Did she even mean to say that aloud? "Today, I was thinking about how I could have handled Summer alone, if all had gone as planned, but it was so nice having a partner. I thought I was full speed ahead on single motherhood, but I'm coming to realize—"

Oh God. What was she saying? Why was she telling him this?

Because he was so easy to talk to. Because he listened without judgment. And he always made her feel heard and supported.

Besides, if something were to happen between them, her cards were already spread out on the table, faceup.

He knew her story. He knew what she wanted, really wanted.

"That you want it all," he said, finishing her line for her. "A baby and a husband. And you should have it."

She bit her lip. "What about you?"

"I don't want anything," he said. "So that's easy."

She tilted her head. "Nothing?"

"I want you, Aimee," he said, then froze, his cheeks kind of flushing. "Oh man. I did not mean to say that out loud."

"But I'm glad you did," she whispered.

"Doesn't help you, though, Aimee. Doesn't get you what you want. Romance, love, marriage, babies, family— all of those couldn't be further from my mind. I can't see going back there ever, let alone anytime soon."

Disappointment socked her in the stomach and she could feel her shoulders sag. "Well, now we know what we both want. Where we stand."

He let out something of a sigh and nodded.

"Last night, today, tomorrow—that's could count as a 'few days,'" she said. "Summer's mother may come back for her tomorrow. And then the two of us won't have any more reasons to be sitting on my sofa."

He turned his head to look directly at her, leaned against the pillows. "Meaning?" he asked, and she could tell by the desire in his eyes that he was pretty sure he knew where she was going with this.

"We could…have tonight," she said. "And tomorrow will be a new day, each of us knowing what we want and where we're headed."

"Just to make sure I fully understand you. Are you

proposing a one-night stand?" he asked with a smile, but then his expression turned more serious.

"I am," she confirmed. "No strings. No expectations. Just two people who are very attracted to each other, who've been through a lot, separately and together, in the past couple of days."

"Sex is magic," he said. "I know it can do wonders for the spirit and the body. But it can also *wound*," he added. "And given what you're looking for, Aimee, I don't want to do anything that might hurt you with the cold light of day. So as much as I want you, I'd rather take a cold shower than ever make you feel bad."

Oh, Reed. She took his hand and held it. He turned their entwined hands over and kissed hers.

"We should probably just leave any kissing to *that*," he said with a light smile.

"I think we should have tonight. Just tonight. Two people who fully understand each other." She slid closer. "Like I said, no strings, no expectations."

Even closer...

Until she got very bold and straddled him, her arms outstretched, hands on both his shoulders.

"Oh God, Aimee," he said, his eyes darkening. "If you're sure."

"I'm sure," she whispered. She leaned forward to kiss him, but he beat her to it, his torso pressing up as his lips descended on hers, warm, strong, soft, hard.

She kissed him back with everything she had. His hands were in her hair, then on her arms, then up under the back of her sweater. The feel of those hands on her bare skin had her letting out a breathy little moan. And then she felt her sweater being lifted and up over her head and flung to the side.

"So sexy," he whispered, his gaze on her bra, her cleavage. She was so glad for her preference to wear sexy undergarments—tonight, it was a black lace demi bra and matching panties. His mouth was on the tops of her breasts, his hands reaching behind her to unclasp the bra, which he also flung off. And then his hands and mouth and lips and tongue were all over breasts, her nipples, causing her to press closer but needing to arch her back, to move against him.

With her eyes open and on him, she slowly unbuttoned his shirt and he shrugged out of it. She almost gasped at the sight of his chest, rock hard, a line of soft hair trailing down to his toned stomach and beneath the waistband of his pants. Her hands flew to the button and he groaned.

She stood up and shimmied out of her pants before she helped him off with his own. Now they were both in their underwear. His black boxer briefs were so hot. But she wanted them off.

Before she could blink, he had her lifted in his arms and was carrying her to her room, kissing her along the way.

He laid her down on the bed, his mouth still on hers, then down her neck, along her collarbone, onto her breasts again, his hands everywhere. She arched against him, barely aware of the moans escaping her lips. She inched down his boxer briefs until they were low enough for him to kick them off, her hand wrapping around his erection, his groan delighting her. He opened his eyes and looked at her, and she was overcome for a moment by the desire and tenderness she saw in his expression. It touched her deep inside her heart, her soul. This was more than sex for him, no matter what he'd said. Even if it was just for tonight.

Then he was slipping her panties down her thighs, and suddenly, they were naked. He slid down her body, his hands and mouth exploring every inch of her, Aimee barely able to contain herself, her moans and heartbeat loud, her breathing fast. "I have a very old condom in my wallet," he said. "But it's all the way in the living room. Have any unexpired ones in grabbing distance?"

She smiled. "Drawer of the bedside table. A gag gift in my Christmas stocking last year." She reached over and found the box, ripping open the top and grabbing the little wrapped packet. When she had it open, she slid it on him, his groans thrilling her, the way his body stiffened with need and desire only adding to her anticipation.

He was propped up on his elbows, both hands on either side of her face, looking directly at her. "You are so beautiful. So sexy."

Oh, be still my heart, she thought. She'd never wanted a man more. Never.

And then she felt him thrust inside her, and she could barely think anymore.

They moved in such harmony, their mouths fused, his hands in her hair, hers digging into his back, which he seemed to like quite a bit. He flipped her over and she rocked against him, her back arched, her head back, sensations building until she exploded.

And then he turned her over onto her back and stretched her arms over her head, moving so fast against her, inside her, that she knew she was about to explode again. They reached climax at the same time, breathing so hard, so fast, Reed's head buried in her neck, kissing her electrified skin.

"That. Was. Everything," he said.

She'd thought she was falling hard an hour ago? That had nothing on now.

Reed woke up to find Aimee fast asleep beside him, her beautiful face so peaceful, her long blond hair flowing behind her. Immediately, flashes of their time together on this bed hit him, one after another, and he was so tempted to kiss her awake for round two.

But there couldn't be a second time. They had an agreement. One night only, a one-time thing at that.

If I were ready to fall in love again, he thought, wishing he could stroke her hair away from her face, *I'd want nothing more than to make love to you every night.* But he wasn't there—he felt millions of miles away from there. And he honestly didn't know if he'd ever be ready. If he'd ever want to risk caring about anyone the way he did for his wife and their daughter.

The agreement he and Aimee made—one night, no strings, no expectations—helped him feel better about taking what she'd offered when she was in a vulnerable state of mind over what she'd revealed to him.

But he wondered if, in the morning, she'd regret sleeping with him. If—

Creak. Creak-creak.

Reed froze and listened. Sounded like footsteps— but outside on the front porch. That must have been what had woken him up in the first place. Out here in the country, it could be a bear. A family of raccoons. Or a burglar.

He gave a quick glance at the time on his phone on the bedside table. It was just 10:37 p.m. He heard another noise, another creak, and pulled on his underwear, then hurried into the guest room to quickly dress in his sweats and socks. He grabbed his boots and went to the back door in the kitchen, stepping into the boots as he looked out through the glass, glad the lights were off in here so he could see outside.

There. A woman moving toward the side of the house, where the sliding glass door were. Aimee's plow service had snow-blown a path around the house so that the various valves and meters could be reached, and the woman was scurrying along that.

A woman with long red hair under a wool hat pulled down low. In a long black puffy coat.

Summer's mother.

Reed opened the kitchen door as quietly as he could and followed her. She stood on the back deck, peering into the living room, hands cupped around her face.

She clearly wanted to see her baby.

I know how you feel, he thought, that old ache hitting him even now.

He stood just a few feet away. "It's me, Reed Dawson," he called. "Please don't run away. It's cold out. It's late. Come in. Even if you're not ready to be reunited with your baby. Come in and talk."

She'd frozen at the first words, and had turned her back to him so she wasn't in profile anymore, but let him finish before bolting around the side of the house.

Three, two, one, he thought, expecting to hear a car engine start any minute. Bingo. And then it peeled away fast.

Interesting. He had no idea who she was. There was nothing familiar about her. He couldn't get a sense of her age, between the dark night and the way she'd been bundled up.

Who was she? What kind of trouble was she in? And what was her plan for reuniting with her child?

"Reed?" Aimee called from inside the house. She stood in the living room in a long sweatshirt and yoga pants, looking around and finally spotting him outside. She opened the sliding glass doors. "What's going on? Did I hear you talking?"

He took another sweeping glance around the property of the cabin. Back to silence and stillness. He came inside, stepping out of his boots. "Summer's mother was out there, peering in the windows. She was in the disguise she wore to drop her off—unless she really does have long red hair. I'm assuming it's a wig."

Aimee's eyes widened. "Did she say anything?"

"I followed her and saw her cupping her hands around her eyes to look through the sliding glass doors. I told her to come in, get out of the cold and that even if she wasn't ready to reunite with her baby, we could just talk. But she ran."

Aimee sat down on the sofa, her hands clasped under her chin. "I wonder what she's up to. Did she come out here just to see if Summer is okay? But she's not ready to take her back?"

He half sat on the arm of the sofa. "Maybe she's in

some kind of trouble? A bad relationship? Maybe with the baby's father."

Aimee nodded. "That sounds plausible. Maybe she needs a safe place for Summer, but she's dying to see her, so she's skulking around at night, hoping to catch a glimpse?"

"It's good she wasn't here a few hours ago," Reed said. "Or she would have seen a prelude to the bedroom."

Aimee blushed and he wished he hadn't said it.

"Well, it's good thing that won't be happening again," she said, biting her lip. "No worries about someone in a likely difficult situation unexpectedly getting an eyeful."

He nodded. In a way, knowing that Summer's mother could be out there, watching, trying to see inside the cabin, gave them a very good excuse for sticking to their plan—one night, no strings, no expectations.

"I don't regret what happened earlier," she said, tucking a swatch of hair behind her ear. "If you were wondering."

"I was, actually. And I'm glad you don't. I don't either."

She stood and took in a breath. "Well, I'll turn in, then. I've got the next waking."

But things between them were clearly strained because of the sex, the intimacy of it all in contrast with the agreement. He felt it too. The complicated *if only*.

And the light of day was many hours off.

He nodded and watched her head down the short hallway to her bedroom, wishing she'd turn around and come back. Just to talk. Just to have her company. To be with her.

Which worried him. He'd known that sex with Aimee Gallagher wouldn't be just about physical release. And he'd been right.

Chapter Ten

The morning also took its time coming. Reed had a hard time falling asleep with both Aimee and the mysterious redhead on his mind. Just when it seemed he'd fallen asleep, baby cries woke him up in the middle of the night, blaring into his ear from the monitor on his bedside table. But when he'd walked into the nursery and picked up Summer, all his stress and questions fell away. The tiny tyke had that effect on him now. He just concentrated on her, taking care of her, focusing on her needs, and he forgot himself.

At 6:00 a.m., he woke to the smell of coffee, which he needed STAT. Aimee wasn't in the kitchen. He could hear her singing softly in the nursery, its door almost closed, so he figured he'd give her privacy. He took a long, hot shower, trying to block out the memories, the vivid images, of making love to Aimee as the water sluiced over him. What he would give to have her with him in here, naked and soapy…

How to stop wanting her was the question.

He topped off his coffee and then FaceTimed his parents. The adventurous couple, both sixty-six, were early birds, always up at the crack of dawn, and they would certainly not be sleeping in while traveling the West in their RV. He was comforted by their sweet faces beaming at him, a palm tree behind them at their camp-ground. They were in California now.

His mother's dark hair was chin-length, with a fringe of bangs. His dad still had a thick head of hair himself, salt and pepper. It gave Reed hope for himself thirty years from now.

"Reed, you look tired," his mother said, peering at him. "I thought small-town life was supposed to be easier on you as a detective."

He smiled. "It is. Sort of. But I'm working on a case that's keeping me up at night." He told them about the baby. About Aimee. About the blizzard that snowbound them together for a night. He left out the very personal details, of course.

His parents, both very expressive, had run the gamut of reactions, from shock to concern.

He filled them in on his sister's vague memory of second cousins and a falling-out over a decade ago. Had it been about a female in her twenties with a young child?

"Oh yes, Sandrine Wheeler," his mother said. She turned to her husband. "You remember Sandrine—my cousin Wendy's daughter. One of them, I should say. Sandrine had three husbands, last I knew. But yes, there was an argument about how Sandrine was neglecting her little girl. Not anything you'd call someone like your Aimee for. Sandrine had a loving personality. But big enough things like poor nutrition, not taking her to the doctor when she clearly had strep throat. I actually took the girl to my PCP once because I was worried."

Sandrine Wheeler. Cousin Wendy's daughter. Little girl. Neglect. Reed had immediately jotted the info in the little notebook he carried about when his phone was occupied.

And despite this interesting insight from his mother, her use of "your Aimee" hadn't gone unnoticed.

"How old was the girl?" Reed asked.

"She was eight—I know because I had to tell the doctor her date of birth, and I had to call three relatives for that because her mother was who knew where."

Eight. Reed froze. That meant she'd be eighteen now. "Do you recall her birth date?"

"Just the month—June, not the date."

He jotted that down. "Did she have red hair, by any chance?"

"Oh no, she had brown hair. Such a pretty girl. And an elfin chin—just darling."

Summer had an elfin chin. Maybe most babies did—although Kayla hadn't.

"What's her name?" he asked, shaking away thoughts of Kayla. "The girl?"

"Mae. Her last name was Pickett, her mother's second or third husband."

Mae Pickett. Had he ever met a Mae Pickett? Possibly. The name didn't ring a bell. Nor did Sandrine Wheeler.

"And Sandrine—how old would she be now?"

"Hmm, let me think," his mom said. "She was early twenties, so midthirties now at the latest."

"Did I ever meet them?" he asked. Neither of them sounded familiar.

"Oh, definitely. I'm sure they were at the big family events—family reunions, weddings. I don't know that you met them personally, but you were in the same rooms at the same time for at least a few occasions. I seem to recall there was a big wedding not too long before the falling-out with Sandrine and her branch of the tree."

So he might have met Sandrine and Mae ten years ago. He had a lot of questions—but he'd look for answers in the police databases and his own case files, now that he had names.

"Mom, you've been an incredible help. Thank you. I think you've solved what good old-fashioned detective work and databases couldn't get to the bottom of."

"Your mother has a memory like a steel trap," his father said, nodding his head, which had his mother looking proud.

Reed smiled. His parents were good people, happily in love, and he was grateful for them.

"So what happened to Sandrine and Mae?" Reed asked. "Any idea?"

"Well, Sandrine left her husband and moved in with another boyfriend way across Cheyenne from where we all lived. She told us to go to hell after we confronted her about how she was raising Mae, called us busybodies. We lost track of her. She was always kind and sweet to Mae, if not exactly a responsible parent, so I figured Mae would get by okay. As for Summer, I hope that sweet little baby will be reunited with her mom—if she's a good parent. You'll let me know what happens, right?"

"I absolutely will."

They talked a bit more about his parents' trip and then they said their goodbyes.

Reed took a slug of his coffee and did a search of his case files from Cheyenne with the names *Mae*, *Pickett*, *Sandrine* and *Wheeler*.

The only name that appeared in his cases was Mae. Twice. But only one was the right age. Mae Stone. Not Pickett. At first, he thought it might be a dead end. But he did remember that case. Three years ago, a fifteen-year-old girl, Mae Stone, had called 9-1-1 because her father, Ted, hadn't come home the night before. Reed had gone over to her house, a very tidy mobile home, and interviewed the girl. Based on her information, Reed had found her father deceased in his car in the parking lot of the big-box store where he worked as an assistant manager, a pair of pale pink headphones in a bag on the passenger seat with a card that said on the front "I'm So Proud of You, Daughter." Inside, he'd written a note about how proud he was that Mae had gotten all As on her report card that term. He'd had a cardiac arrest at age forty.

Reed had brought the gift and the card over to the house and had broken the news to the girl himself. She'd sobbed, hugging the card to her chest. He'd stayed until her paternal grandmother had arrived; the two fell into each other's arms. He'd told the two he was so sorry for their loss and that every time Mae wore those headphones, she'd feel her dad's pride in her. That was the last he'd seen or heard of that girl. He checked the database for a photo of Mae Stone, but nothing came up, which meant she wasn't in the system, had never been arrested.

But Mae Stone wasn't Mae Pickett. *Pickett* was the last name of Mae's father. Not Stone.

He scanned the case file again for Mae Stone's date of birth. June 17.

June. Like his mother recalled as Mae Pickett's birth month.

He FaceTimed his mother back and asked if she could recall anyone with the last name Stone in Sandrine or Mae's life. His mom said no. No Stone, then made a joke how Reed certainly was leaving no stone unturned.

His father belly laughed at that.

Reed smiled and disconnected.

Mae Stone would be eighteen. Same age as Mae Pickett. Same birth month. And though he'd been the detective who'd relayed the sad news of her father's passing, maybe she remembered that he'd been gentle, had given her the gift and card.

Maybe.

The name Mae, and the age, were the only links that added up in his Cheyenne cases. But how could Mae Pickett be Mae Stone?

He supposed they didn't have to be. There were probably dozens of girls in the state who were named Mae and who'd been born in June. Mae Stone might have no connection at all to his distant cousins.

But that felt too coincidental.

Good thing it was his job to find out.

* * *

Aimee was making pancakes when Reed rushed into the kitchen. He noticed Summer in her infant stroller by the window and went over to drop a kiss on her forehead, which surprised her. He didn't even seem to notice that he'd done it. He was fine holding Summer, rocking her, running a gentle finger along her cheek. But had he ever kissed her forehead?

She was about to mention it, in a casual way, to point out that he was making major progress in terms of how babies affected him and the hole in his heart, but he started telling her about video calling his parents.

She felt her eyes widen as he got to the part about his distant cousins and one name turning up in his case files: Mae Stone. That she was the right age, with the same birth month as Mae Pickett, but with the wrong last name.

Aimee flipped the pancakes, glancing at Reed. "What a sad story about Mae's dad. I'm glad it was you who was there for her and not a less compassionate detective. If Mae is Summer's mother, there's the connection why she'd leave her newborn with you."

"I'm going to call Cheyenne hospitals to ask about any Maes who gave birth three to seven days ago," Reed said.

"And check marriage records," Aimee suggested, sliding the pancakes onto a plate. "Maybe Sandrine Wheeler married Ted Stone?"

"I thought about that, but Mae Stone referred to her father as her father, not her stepfather. It's a good idea to check marriage records, though—you never know."

"You never do," Aimee said. "And call Cheyenne

high schools and see what you can find out about Mae Stone and her past and family history."

"We'd make a great team," he said, then immediately winced.

Because of last night. Because they had made a great team then. And also with caring for Summer. And figuring out the complications of her mother's identity.

"But do all that after you have breakfast. I make great pancakes, if I do say so myself." She could tell the smile she was pasting on her face was forced. She didn't have to wonder if he'd notice. He would.

She set the plate on the table and headed to the fridge for maple syrup and butter. She watched him sip the orange juice she'd poured. Those lips had been all over her last night.

What she would give for a big hug. Just to feel cocooned in his arms.

They both sat, Reed digging into his maple-syrup-laden pancakes and declaring them as good as Aimee had said.

"If Mae is Summer's mother," Aimee said, "she's just eighteen. So young."

He nodded. "I wonder who the father is. *Where* the father is. Could Mae be trying to get away from him?"

"Very plausible." She sipped her coffee, hoping there was a less fraught reason for Mae to have left her three-day-old baby on the desk of the detective who'd once been kind to her.

If Mae Stone was even the person they were looking for.

Reed's phone pinged with a text from his cousin Rex.

Maisey wants me to remind you that you have to bring
Summer to Chloe's birthday party tomorrow afternoon.
And Aimee. See you guys at one. There will be a lot
of pizza.

"Something about the case?" Aimee asked when he
put down his phone.

"Actually, no. By any chance, would you like to go to
a three-year-old's birthday party with me tomorrow? It's
being held in the day care center at the Dawson Family
Guest Ranch. The three of us are invited."

Hmm. Tomorrow? That he was asking her this late
meant he'd been hemming and hawing about bringing
her. That he'd decided to take her, especially after their
night together, told her that he wasn't running from her.
Interesting. "I'm invited too? How nice. I'd love to go.
Which cousin's child is this?"

"Rex."

A three-year-old's party. The same age as his Kayla
was now. She wondered if that would be hard for him,
despite how far he'd come. She liked the idea of being
there for that reason alone.

"Count me in for the party. We can pick up a gift on
the way."

"Great," he said, pouring more syrup on his pancakes.

She wondered why he'd invited her to the party. A
family party. It certainly wasn't a date. And she was
certain that he'd make it through fine on his own, even
faking it, if he had to.

But he had invited her. And not just because his family had; he could have easily made an excuse and just taken Summer.

Maybe there was hope yet for her and the detective.

A big maybe, but she'd take it.

Chapter Eleven

At noon, Aimee knocked on the guest room door. Reed had been behind closed doors for the past few hours, making a million phone calls about the dual Maes, talking to relatives in Cheyenne about Mae Pickett, and hospitals, schools and neighbors about Mae Stone. Aimee had been on baby duty, and now she was turning Summer over to Reed so that she could meet her sister Marin for lunch.

After breakfast, Aimee had texted Marin that she'd had an epiphany and could they talk? Marin had taken her time responding. Aimee had been able to give herself a sparkly red pedicure and let it dry before the three dots appeared and stopped and reappeared on the screen. But it was a yes, and Aimee was picking up lunch for the two of them to have in the break room at the veterinary clinic.

Reed opened the door, and for a few seconds, she

was overwhelmed by her reaction to the sight of him. So good-looking. Filling the doorway with his broad shoulders and height and outsize presence. "Heading out?" he asked.

She nodded. "I can take Summer with me if it's easier for you."

"No worries, Summer and I will be fine. And we're definitely getting closer to the mystery of who Summer's mother is."

Aimee nodded. "Summer's due to wake up anytime now. I'll be back in about an hour since Marin doesn't have long for lunch."

"Good luck, by the way. I hope it goes well," he said, putting his phone in his back pocket and stepping out of the room.

"Me too."

Five minutes later, she was en route to the vet's clinic, which was located just a few doors down from the Bear Ridge Diner. She knew Marin loved their BLTs. Aimee got two to go and two bottles of pomegranate sparkling water. She was right on time when she arrived at the clinic. Their waiting room was pretty crowded, two people waiting in line at the reception desk, one with a cat carrier, one with a beagle on a leash. The seats were full of folks with very well behaved dogs and more cat carriers, and Aimee even saw a rabbit in one carrier. More than a few of the dogs glanced up at her, sniffing the air, and she realized they probably wanted the bacon. She texted Marin she'd arrived.

A few minutes later, a door opened and Marin poked her head out, waving her in once she spotted her.

"Wow, busy day?" Aimee asked, following Marin down a hallway. There was some barking and voices.

"Every day, all day," Marin said, her long, light brown hair in a low ponytail. She wore dark red scrubs, her name embroidered on her shirt pocket. "Normally I'd get an hour for lunch, but another tech had to leave, so we're all covering."

"Thanks for meeting with me, then. I extra appreciate it."

"Well, it's no fun being in a cold war with you, Aimee," Marin said as she led the way into the break room. It was empty, which was good since they could talk privately.

Aimee sat down at a round table by the windows and set out the containers and bottles. "No, it sure isn't."

"So what was this epiphany?" Marin asked before taking a bite of her BLT.

"I'm going to be really honest here—"

"You know what? I wish you wouldn't be. I'm not looking for more honesty, Aimee. Either stand up for me and support my decision, or don't."

Aimee winced. Her sister was hurt and angry, not to mention embarrassed that she'd said anything to Aimee at all that night she'd revealed her true feelings.

"Honest about me, I meant," Aimee said.

Marin eyed her, then swiped a french fry in the little mound of ketchup she'd squirted in her container. "Oh."

"I know what it feels like to want something so badly it's a physical ache. Getting engaged, planning a wedding, having a ring on your finger, starting a family—that's your dream, Marin. And you're making that happen with John. I want you to be happy and I've realized that you will be because you'll have what you want most of all."

Even as she said it, there was an upside-down element in what she was saying. But maybe that was her cynicism talking. Maybe Marin *would* be happy. Maybe she wouldn't be in love with her husband, but she'd have what she wanted. In any case, Aimee *did* understand why Marin was marrying John.

Marin's shoulder sagged with relief. "I do care deeply about John. Yes, we're not perfect. Yes, I wish we were more *this* or *that*. Yes, I wish I could have every little thing I want. But marrying him is what I want."

"I understand now," Aimee said, but that tiny voice was still screaming: *I wish you could marry a man you did love.* She'd keep that screeching voice to herself from now on.

"So you do want to be my maid of honor?" Marin asked, her eyes a little misty.

"Of course. You're my precious sister."

Marin started to cry then and grabbed Aimee into a hug. "Good. You're *my* precious sister. I've hated how things have been between us."

"Me too. It's miserable when we're not okay."

Marin nodded and took in a breath. "Ella and I were making plans to go to bridal salons in Brewer on Sunday. I know I speak for both of us when I say you have to come."

Aimee smiled. "I *do* have to. I wouldn't miss that for the world."

"So, tell me what's going on Reed and the baby," Marin said, then took a bite of her sandwich.

Aimee finally opened her container and took a hearty bite of her BLT. She felt tons better about the Marin situation. Even if… But lately, *even if* seemed to be the story of her life.

"Well, I've managed to fall in love with the guy," she said, surprising herself with her honesty. "But it's not gonna happen between us."

Marin put her sandwich down, looking at Aimee very seriously. "Why?"

"He's not open to a relationship. I might be more hopeful if things weren't so complicated, but they are. He's only been divorced for a year and he doesn't even know if he wants children. Whereas I want a child, a family, so badly that it's a physical ache."

Marin reached over to squeeze Aimee's hand. "But now he's staying with you. That has to mean something."

"I think it just makes things easier for him. Two people, one with a wish and one with an obligation, to care for the baby. Plus I have a decked out nursery and he doesn't. But it looks like he's getting close to finding out the identity of Summer's mother. I don't know what will happen once mother and baby are reunited."

"Well, all I can say is that I hope everything works out between you and Reed. He sounds like an amazing man."

"He is." She let out a wistful sigh. "He's everything I've ever wanted in a man. In a husband. In the father of my future child. And wouldn't you know…?"

Marin was quiet for a moment. She picked up her sandwich, then put it back down. "What makes him everything you want?"

"He's such a good person. I knew that immediately, based on how he reacted to finding a newborn on his desk. Given his past—and his job—taking care of Summer hasn't been easy for him to do. But beyond that, I'm constantly amazed by how kind and compassionate he is. How easy he is to talk to. How he always has the right and insightful thing to say to make me feel better. How he always wants me to perk me up when I'm sad. I've really shocked myself with how open and vulnerable I'm been with him. And same for him—he's revealed some really personal stuff. Oh—and he's a good cook."

And amazing in bed. That part she didn't mention. She'd keep those wonderful, delicious memories to herself.

Marin smiled, but she seemed a million miles away, maybe thinking about her own relationship.

Not that Aimee *had* a relationship. She had a friend in Reed Dawson, that much she knew, and that was vital in itself.

"And he invited me to his cousin's three-year-old daugher's birthday party tomorrow afternoon. The three of us are going—him, me and Summer."

Marin's eyes widened. "First dinner at Pimoni's and now a family party? Oh, Aimee, I'd say you're in a relationship."

She'd held out some hope for the same reason and she was aware of the little burst of happiness that spread in her chest…along with the blinking neon danger sign.

On the way to the birthday party the next afternoon, Reed updated Aimee on where he was with Summer's mother's identity. The redhead in the sunglasses and black puffy coat hadn't been spotted around the cabin again, but Reed now had a very good idea who she was.

"From what I can tell, Mae Pickett stopped existing

when she was fifteen. Marital records show that Sandrine Wheeler *did* marry Ted Stone when her daughter was thirteen. Sandrine flew the coop and abandoned them both around a year later with the contents of Ted's bank account, but it also turns out that Ted adopted Mae and they had a real bond."

Aimee gasped. "So Mae Pickett is Mae Stone! Did her paternal grandmother take her in when her father died, then?"

He nodded. "Unfortunately, her grandmother passed away earlier this year. That was the last anyone saw of Mae. There are no records of her graduating from high school this past June. There are also no records of her giving birth in any Cheyenne or area hospitals."

"What? How is that possible? She *is* Summer's mother, right?"

"I think so. I still have so many questions. I'm not sure if she remembered meeting me at the wedding or family reunion or if she connected the name Dawson to cousins and then put two and two together. Or maybe us being related didn't play into her decision at all, and she picked me just because I was kind about her father. I just don't have any answers yet."

Aimee winced. "She's so young. And clearly alone. I wish she'd knock on the door and let us help her."

"I know. Me too. Maybe she will. I think I made it clear when I spoke to her outside the cabin that she could do exactly that. We just have to wait it out since finding her first probably isn't going to happen."

As Reed turned onto Main Street, Aimee pointed at the toy shop that had recently opened. There were so many children in Bear Ridge, thanks in part to the huge

Dawson family, that they were able to keep a small-town toy store in business.

Reed parked and put Summer in the infant stroller, the sidewalks clear from any snow residue because of the strong sun and temps in the high fifties. A gift in itself. They headed inside the shop, Aimee beelining for the toddler section for toddlers. Reed was busy looking at puzzles, board games, dolls, and easels and water-based paint sets when he froze, the ol' knife twisting in his chest.

There was a toy stroller with Big Bird from Sesame Street sitting inside.

He'd bought Kayla a toy stroller—with Big Bird, who she adored, in it—when she was eighteen months. It was her favorite thing to play with, to wheel Big Bird around like Mommy and Daddy wheeled her around in their stroller.

Now he was going to another girl's third birthday party when he'd been unable to even wish his own little girl a happy third birthday.

She's not your daughter, Reed...

He could still hear her saying those words.

As easily as that, everything you loved could be taken from you. He shivered.

He felt Aimee's eyes on him, then her hand on his arm.

"You okay?" she whispered, concern in her voice.

He sucked in a breath. "I'm fine." But he did want to make this quick and get out of the store.

"I saw something that would be perfect for the birthday girl," Aimee said. "Back in a jiffy and you can tell me if you agree."

Aimee to the rescue. If he had to spend much time shopping around, he knew that the acidic ache in his gut would get worse.

She returned a few moments later with a dress-up costume in size 3T—a police officer, like her father. It came with a hat, vest and pants, plus a badge, and even a pair of toddler-sized cardboard aviator sunglasses with "mirrored" lenses.

Reed nodded. "That's great."

They went to the counter, Aimee asking to have it wrapped. They left with a brightly wrapped gift, a colorful lollipop and card stuck under the bow, Reed barely able to remember even sticking his credit card in the reader.

Even outside in the cool fall air, the acid churned.

One step forward, two steps back.

The Dawson Family Guest Ranch was a gorgeous, rustic-meets-luxe property on hundreds of acres. Being out here, where he'd decompressed a year ago, where he'd walked for miles in the fresh country air, ridden horses, skimmed stones in the river, hiked up Clover Mountain, eaten a lot of great chili in the ranch café, restored his equilibrium and focus now, just as it had back then.

There had originally been just six guest cabins, but the ranch was so popular, not just in the area but in the country, that several more groupings of cabins had been added, including "VIP" accommodations. The party was being held in the lodge, inside the day care center that Rex's wife, Maisey, had been running since before they'd even met. The center was closed to guests of the lodge for the duration of the private event.

Reed held open the door for Aimee, who wheeled in the stroller. There had to be at least sixty or seventy people milling about, sipping drinks, noshing on appetizers. And countless kids playing with all the great equipment and toys in the large, colorful space. He recognized a former bull-riding champion, nationally famous, who'd married into the Dawson family this past summer. Logan Winston had walked away from the spotlight to be there full-time for the seven-year-old son he'd recently discovered existed. Reed had heard plenty of folks talking about that around town, that they didn't get it. Reed did.

"Glad you made it!" Rex said as he approached, the birthday girl in his arms. He hoisted her up. "Chloe, do you remember meeting Reed? He's Daddy's cousin."

"Happy Birthday, Chloe," Reed said.

"I'm a big kid now!" Chloe said, her brown curls bouncing past her shoulders. She was one cute kid. And she looked so little like Kayla, had such different coloring, that the acid stayed back.

"And you must be Aimee," Rex said, extending his hand.

Reed smiled. "Aimee Gallagher, my cousin Rex, the one responsible for my being here in Bear Ridge."

"We've definitely seen each other around town," Rex said.

They shook, and then Aimee introduced Summer.

"She's so cute!" Chloe said, peering in the stroller. She began yanking her dad's hand. "Daddy, let's get pizza!"

"As the birthday girl wishes," Rex said with a bow.

He grinned at Reed and Aimee. "I'll see you around the party, I'm sure. Gift table by the buffet. And thank you again for coming."

"I could go for pizza now," Reed said. "Hungry?"

"Always for pizza."

They wheeled Summer over to the buffet, Reed dropping off the gift on the table along the way. They were bombarded with hellos and handshakes and oohs and aahs over Summer. Many had heard about the situation, while a few others assumed, like the McAllisters, that the newborn was *their* baby. Reed stopped correcting after a while.

They sat down in padded folding chairs under the wall of huge arched windows, Summer napping in the stroller. Kids of all ages, but mostly under ten, ran around everywhere. Reed decided to focus on his pizza, which was delicious.

Aimee had just finished her slice of pizza when two former classmates from Bear Ridge High pulled her away to chat and catch up.

"Well, Summer, it's just you and me," he said, giving the baby's soft, wispy hair a gentle caress. He looked around, astonished that he was truly here. At a kiddie birthday party.

He realized he was actively *trying*. To let go of the past. To move on.

Children's music played from a speaker, but as long as "Twinkle, Twinkle, Little Star" didn't come blaring out, he'd be just fine. He could do this. He eyed the kids playing pin the tail on the donkey on a pint-size easel nearby. Another group was lined up for the curvy slide, one for all age ranges. The birthday girl herself was about to race past Rex with a cupcake wobbling in her hand, and just as she reached where Reed was sitting, the cupcake fell—chocolate-frosting-down on Reed's shoe.

She stopped, her face crumpling, big hazel eyes on Reed. "I dwopped my cuhcake."

For just a second, he saw Kayla in front of him, a year older than the last time he saw her, her fair hair longer, in an orange dress with multicolored tights, what used to be her favorite look. Kayla had loved chocolate cupcakes.

This girl wasn't Kayla. Every toddler he saw wasn't Kayla.

He really was starting to let go. Sometimes it would still pinch. And sometimes he'd be all right. One day, his previous life would feel very distant.

"Hey, that's all right," Reed said with a smile. "Let's go get you another." He grabbed a few napkins from the table beside his chair and scooped the cupcake off his shoe.

The girl brightened and beelined for a long table against the wall where the baked goods were plentiful. Another cupcake in her tiny hand, she started to run off, then corrected himself to go slower, and Reed had to smile.

"Ooh, Reed," said a female voice. "Just the single man I was looking for."

He turned to find Danica, Ford's glamorous wife, heading his way. The town matchmaker. At least he could use his built-in excuse that he'd brought someone to the party.

"I've been meaning to ask you what you're looking

for in a relationship," she said. "I know you said you weren't in the market yet. But there are more single women than men in Bear Ridge, so I'm being pushy."

Huh. So she hadn't seen him come in with Aimee. Rats. "That's fine," he said with a smile. "I'm still not in the market, though."

"Darn. I'll put you on my someday list, then. What are your absolute musts and deal breakers? What's your ideal romantic partner?"

"Oh, that's easy," he said.

Her blue eyes honed in on his. "Really? Most people have to really think about it."

"My ideal date would be divorced, like me, and therefore equally cynical about love and the world." He paused, and not because Danica was half frowning. Aimee was divorced, but was she cynical? Hardly. He cleared his throat. "No single mothers. That's an absolute. She'd need to be okay with zero assurances that I'd want children in the future too."

"That is very specific, Reed," Danica said with something of a knowing smile. "But something tells me you're quite serious."

"I am."

"Well, when you're ready, let me know. You'll be a major catch."

He noticed the "you'll be" instead of the "you are." In other words, he had too much baggage right now. Well, he happened to agree with that.

He would not be dating in the near future. He couldn't even see it in the far future.

But he had been aware that when Aimee had returned from lunch with her sister yesterday, he'd dropped everything he was doing to hear that it had gone well and she was now *both* her sisters' maid of honor. They'd hugged, and having her back in his arms had felt so good. And when she'd said she was going to then take Summer to her sisters' condo for dinner and to show off Summer, Reed thought, *But you were just gone for an hour and a half.*

He glanced around for her and saw her talking to Daisy Dawson, the only female among the six Dawson siblings. She was the guest relations manager at the ranch, and he recalled his shock when he'd heard that she and her husband had met when he'd come to stay at the ranch to try to steal it out from under the family. The Dawsons had been through quite a lot in life and love.

Reed was no exception.

But he was done with it all—the love part.

"Aimee Gallagher!"

Aimee was on her way through the crowd of happy children and chatting adults, to find Reed and Summer, when a female voice called her name. She turned and smiled at the tall, glamorous redhead with the sharp swish of bangs. She wore a winter-white pantsuit with pink cowboy boots.

"Savannah Walsh!" she said, rushing up to give the woman a hug. Savannah was an old classmate. She'd been a year ahead of her, but they'd been in a few clubs together. Savannah hit the big-time as a manager of rodeo performers, including one of the biggest names in Wyoming: Logan Winston.

"Catch me up, Aimee. What have you been doing for the past almost-two decades?"

"Well, let's see. Married and divorced by age twenty-four. I'm a social worker with Family Services, newly certified as a foster parent. I just got my first placement—a newborn a couple of days ago. It's a long story."

Savannah's eyed widened. "Wait. We're going to have to go through all that word by word. Did you say married and divorced by twenty-four? Same for me but twenty-five!" She grinned and held up a palm. "Congrats on being a member of a club no one want to join."

Aimee laughed and high-fived her. "Yeah, I know a couple of those clubs."

"And a foster mom—that's so wonderful," Savannah said. She bit her lip, quite uncharacteristic of the confident superstar Aimee remembered. "I've been thinking a lot about if I want children. I didn't think I did. I've gotten incredible satisfaction and fulfillment from my career. But lately…"

"You've been thinking about it?"

Savannah nodded. "Me, a mother. I can't quite imagine it. But I feel it—the stirrings of maternal instincts that I've never felt before. I see a baby now and I actually feel something."

"And is there a significant other to help make this happen?"

"That's the problem—no. You want to hear something a little nuts? Sometimes I think I'll never feel about any guy the way I did about my secret high school crush."

Aimee grinned. "Ooh, who is it? Is he still in Bear Ridge? Single?"

"Actually, I just found out that he's divorced—with six-month-old triplets."

"What? Six-month-old triplets and divorced? How did that happen?"

Savannah shrugged. "That I don't know. I'll have to ask my sisters—they know everything."

Ask them if Reed Dawson and I will work out...

"Maybe you two can reconnect while you're here?" Aimee suggested.

"Honestly? Hutch Dawson is the only thing I've ever been afraid of. I see him from a distance and I turn around, my heart pounding. No one who knows me would believe it." She grinned and shook her head.

"Dawson? Is he related to the Dawsons who are throwing the party?"

"He's a cousin."

Aimee smiled to herself. "Dawsons are everywhere in Bear Ridge. A Dawson is staying with me for a while. Do you know Reed? He's a detective who moved her from Cheyenne last year."

"I've heard the name, but I've never met him. I'm not in town often enough—my work keeps me way too busy and traveling. But I'm coming back for Christmas for two weeks—I'd love to get together."

"It's a date," Aimee said. "And maybe you'll connect with Hutch and the triplets then too."

"If only I knew what I really wanted," Savannah said with a sigh. "Hutch and I were total enemies back in the day. Who knows if he'll even talk to me? And I don't really know if I do want a child or if I just need a change in my life. Why can't life be a little easier to figure out?"

"Right?"

"Savvy!" called someone who began tugging Savannah over for a hug.

"Go," Aimee said with a smile. "Call me when you're home for Christmas."

Savannah gave Aimee's hand a squeeze and was swallowed into the crowd.

Wow, that was interesting, Aimee thought as she weaved her way past a group of little kids playing choo choo train. They sure had a lot in common. Early divorces. Ten years single. But Aimee wanted a child more than anything whereas Savannah wasn't sure she did at all.

She headed over to the buffet where there was a coffee station and made herself a cup of coffee with pumpkin spice creamer. Fortified by the caffeine, she looked around for Reed and found him sitting on a couch near the door, Summer in his arms, feeding her a bottle.

Her heart moved in her chest for both baby and man.

And that was against the rules on both counts.

Chapter Twelve

At 2:40 a.m., Reed was in the nursery with Summer, giving her a bottle on the glider. Aimee was asleep in her bedroom and he already missed her. After the birthday party, they'd gone into town and shown Summer all around Bear Ridge, from the downtown shops to the park with the little dunk pond. Despite the nice fall temperatures, with a bit of lingering snow, it was easy to imagine the Christmas tree and Santa hut that would go up on the town green in just a couple of weeks. They'd passed by the playground, and Reed stopped and watched the kids playing, one kid in his Halloween costume, his cape flying behind him as he ran around.

It had been the first time he'd been able to take delight in kids on a playground without thinking of what he'd lost. Instead, he'd thought of Summer and what she had to look forward to.

Aimee had been there beside him and had commented on it, as she had at the party, where he'd had the same experience. A year had done its job, worked its time-magic, but he knew that caring for Summer, aided by Aimee, had helped a lot.

They hadn't talked about their night together. In keeping with the agreement—no strings, no expectations— they had both acted like the night hadn't happened.

But he thought it of constantly, and he wondered if she did too. They'd had dinner together—he'd cooked— and they'd talked about the party and who they knew in common. She'd gotten kind of quiet and then said that she was going to head to her room and turn in early, that she'd take the first waking. He could tell that she needed some space from him and he knew right then that she *had* been thinking about the time in her bed. And what they'd agreed to.

She'd also told him she'd be going out in the morning to meet her sisters for a trip to Brewer to visit bridal salons. He was absolutely fine with being on his own with Summer. But Brewer was almost an hour travel time round trip and she'd be gone for several hours, between shopping and lunch. He'd miss her. A lot.

How could he want to spend every minute with someone he was actively trying not to fall for? And if he had to try so hard...

He'd been so tempted to knock on her door, but he had no justification for it. He was the one who had put the roadblock in anything happening between them. Not Aimee.

"Waah! Waah!"

Reed looked down at Summer, who was suddenly letting out fussy wails, her face reddening a bit. She was almost done with the bottle. He shifted her so she was vertical against him and patted her back, finally getting a big burp. The crying and fussing stopped.

He looked down as she looked up and a burst of affection spread in his chest.

"You're all right, Summer," he said. "Literally and figuratively."

"Aw," came a voice from the doorway. He glanced over and there was Aimee in her very sexy T-shirt and loose yoga pants, barefoot, her blond hair loose down her shoulders.

"This is all thanks to you," he said. "I guess I was changing without realizing it until a baby landed in my life." Huh. That was true. He'd been changing all along. Day by day, hour by hour. He just hadn't been aware.

Her sweet smile lit up her face. "I'm really glad. That means that in the future, when you're ready, you'll welcome the idea of your own child."

"I don't know about that," he said, frowning. He still wasn't comfortable with the idea of a child of his own. But that he could sit here with an infant in his arms, a baby girl, and actually feel bonded and content and protective instead of ripped to shreds was good progress and all he'd want to achieve. "There would be a wife in the picture in that scenario. Ideally. And I'm not looking for a wife. Probably ever again."

She stared at him for a moment and then stepped into the nursery. "So you're just going to condemn yourself to a life of being alone?"

"*Condemn* seems like a really strong word, Aimee. I'm just saying I've been married, it was a disaster in the end, and I'm not interested in ever going through that again."

Disaster was an understatement. He'd had a few buddies back in Cheyenne who were divorced. But even the worst stories he'd heard didn't come close to what he'd been put through. He knew it wasn't a competition. Pain was pain. But Reed had lost everything.

No, he wouldn't be getting married again.

"Well, you likely wouldn't go through anything like you did in your marriage," she said, picking up a squishy stuffed bunny from a chair by the door and holding it against her chest. "Like you said, you've changed. You probably wouldn't go about your life in the same way, with your job and your hours."

He certainly didn't want to have to defend how he felt. Or even talk about this. "Well, that's all moot, so how about those Cowboys?" He tried to put a less severe expression on his face, but he didn't like this conversation and didn't even know how they got here, at 2:53 a.m.

Her face fell a bit and he wondered if the conversation had really been about their chances. If they even *had* a chance. His gut twisted. Dammit. He had to be gentle but honest in his responses to Aimee's questions. He had to be careful.

He'd told her straight-out that he didn't want to hurt her, and that was why he'd made sure there had been an agreement between them, a solid understanding, before they'd slept together. Sex had to be about release for the both of them. Not romance or love or even companionship.

Yet you invited her to the family party. You're bringing her into your life.

He mentally kicked himself.

He didn't know how to handle this. There seemed to be so many moving, emotional parts, and he wanted to do right by Aimee. Summer was important to her. He had to be careful there too.

This needed to be a friendship, a partnership in caring for this newborn whose mother was out there for who-knew-what reasons.

That settled, for him, at least, he got up and placed sleeping Summer in the crib.

He glanced at Aimee, standing there completely vulnerable on the ABC-123 rug, the stuffed bunny to her stomach, a sliver of moonlight illuminating the uncertainty on her beautiful face.

I'm sorry, he thought. *I wish I could give you what you want. I wish we could start something*—continue *something,* he amended. *But I can't. And I won't hurt you.*

Which he was pretty sure he was doing anyway, right then.

"Good night," he said as he shut off the light in the nursery.

"Good night," she whispered.

He stepped out and she was right behind him, the bunny still in her hand. He went left, she went right.

Each to their separate room, as it had to be.

In the morning, at nine thirty sharp, Aimee picked up her sisters at their condo and drove the half hour to Brewer, a bigger town with a more vibrant downtown than Bear Ridge. There were two bridal salons, one more boutique-like with a small selection and the other large, with hundreds of gowns, and the twins had made appointments at both. They were starting with Your Day, the boutique.

She wished she could think just about gowns and headpieces and beaded bodices or flowing satin, but she had Reed on her mind.

She couldn't stop replaying the change in him last night. She'd thought he was coming around, but the more comfortable he got about being around kids, the less comfortable he got about a romantic relationship with a woman. Namely her.

The two issues were separate, she supposed. She knew he'd always carry around the loss of Kayla, even if it didn't weigh on him the way it once did. But Kayla hadn't chosen to leave him, Kayla hadn't decided to forget him. Kayla hadn't broken his heart. His ex-wife had. And that was what he was afraid of—getting pushed off a cliff again and so bruised and battered he had to change his entire life just to find some peace.

He'd told her straight-out that he was a lone wolf and planned to stay that way. She had to accept it. Even if he'd told her that sometimes she had to fight for what she wanted. She also had to know when fighting wouldn't get her anywhere—and would drive a wedge between her and others. Like with her sister Marin, she had to let him be, accept his decision. She didn't have to like it. But she could support it and be there for him with Summer. And she would.

Just like today she was there for Marin and Ella equally. Instead of fretting in her bedroom after leaving the nursery last night, Aimee had gone through the bridal links her sisters had texted her. It wasn't like she could sleep, anyway.

Photos of beautiful wedding gowns. Of beaded head-pieces and delicate veils. Of beautifully decorated and appointed venues, including the lodge at the Dawson Family Guest Ranch, which had a ballroom and balcony with views of Clover Mountain. She'd gone through photo after photo, getting more and more wistful. Reed might be adamant that there wouldn't be marriage in his future, but Aimee was discovering that she'd never given up hope that she'd find the man who'd love her and accept her for who she was.

As Aimee and her sisters walked up the three steps to Your Day Bridal Salon, a gown in the window made her stop in her tracks.

It was so beautiful—exactly what she would want if she ever got married again.

Simple and satin and strapless, no beading, just floaty and elegant.

"Is it awful of me to say that I know what I'm not looking for?" Ella asked as they headed inside. "I definitely don't want a dress like you wore to your wedding, Aimee. Was that mean?"

Aimee laughed, thinking about the huge white monstrosity. "Not in the slightest. That dress was my former mother-in-law's taste, not mine. She was buying and she sort of browbeat me into it, all that pouf and lace and puffs."

Marin was being unusually quiet. Aimee wondered why—then realized her own future MIL might be more involved in Marin's wedding choices than Marin wanted.

"Don't forget the bow on your butt," Ella said, grinning.

Aimee gave her a playful punch in the arm. "How could I? At least I couldn't see it myself."

She didn't love the dress at the time, but the old Aimee had been more about pleasing others than in listening to her own voice. She'd gotten better at that with age and time and with the help of the therapist she'd seen for six months after her husband left her.

The twins had decided to each pay for the other's dress as a gift, so there shouldn't be a mother-in-law putting in her two cents. Aimee knew that Ella adored her MIL-to-be, a very warm-spirited person who loved to cook big, elaborate Sunday dinners and had made Ella feel like part of the family from her third date with her now-fiancé.

Marin, however, had described her MIL-to-be as reserved, and after Aimee had met her at the engagement party, she'd go as far to say that the woman was kind of cold. She'd overheard her sisters talking before that party, and Ella was saying how she felt guilty that she loved the idea of having a mother figure in her life, someone she could get very close with and confide in. No one would ever replace their mother in her heart, Ella had added, but she was so happy that she'd have a special bond with her MIL.

Aimee had hugged Ella, deeply moved by that.

Marin had been *very* quiet, and Aimee had wondered if her sister and future MIL had any kind of relationship at all. Her fiancé also had a reserved sister, and when Ella had mentioned that Marin was lucky to get a SIL since her own fiancé didn't have siblings, Marin had said she didn't think they'd get all that close.

Marin didn't love John *or* his family.

But her sister was holding a gown up to herself and walking toward the three-way mirrors, her face lighting up, her eyes filling with happy tears. "This is the one. This is my dress!" The gown was gorgeous—kind of antique-looking and delicate, with lace and off-the-shoulder straps.

Ella looked over. "Oh, Marin. It's gorgeous. It's so you!"

"It is, right?" Marin said. "I just love it. But you can't love the first dress you see and try on, right? That's never the one, is it?"

"Consider yourself lucky if it is," Aimee said. "I tried on at least twenty dresses and still didn't love the one I ended up with."

"I wonder what Jeralyn will think of it," Marin said, biting her lip and eyeing her reflection. "She'd probably like something more traditional, more a gown like you wore, Aimee."

Both Aimee and Ella made horrified faces.

"No MILs are allowed to have opinions today," Ella said. "This is about what *we* love."

Marin nodded and seemed fortified by that. But then she said, "I know, but maybe I should text John a photo of it?"

"Absolutely not," Ella insisted. "Aimee, confiscate Marin's phone."

Marin smiled but there was no mirth in her eyes.

"Ooh, I adore this one," Ella said, grabbing a very pretty beaded, strapless white princess dress. "I love the tulle. Or do I want something more like this?" she added, taking a dress more like the one Aimee had fallen for in the window. "Like a 1940s movie star."

"Try on a bunch," Aimee said. "And Marin, you try that dress on," she said, pointing to the beauty she held. "Once you see yourself in it, you won't give John or Jeralyn another thought."

Marin's eyes lit up and she headed for the dressing room, where a saleswoman met her and said she'd select some headpieces that would go beautifully with the dress.

When she came out, both Aimee and Ella gasped.

Marin's eyes filled with tears. Because she knew it was *the* dress or because she wouldn't buy it?

Aimee's heart pinched. She had to let Marin find her way here.

"I love it," Marin said, staring at herself in the mirror, eyes still misty. "But I think I should try on all different kinds of gowns."

"I've got six to try on already," Ella said, barely able to lift her arm. The saleswoman hurried over and took them, leading the way into a dressing room. "But, Marin, that is your dress."

Marin looked at herself again and then went back into the dressing room.

Ella came out in a pretty dress, but Aimee could see on her face that it wasn't even close to the one. "Nah. Next!"

Aimee smiled. Finding Ella's dress would be fun. Marin's, on the other hand...

Before she went back into the dressing room, Marin said, "Oh, Aimee, I almost forgot. Ella and I were talking last night, and we'd love it if you and Reed and baby Summer came over for dinner tomorrow night. We'll invite our grooms and it'll be like a dinner party."

Aimee bit her lip. "I'm not sure Reed will want to go to a family thing with me. He's kind of backing away." *Do not let the ache in your chest appear on your face*, she ordered herself. *Today is about your sisters and their dresses, not your crummy love life. Or lack thereof.*

"Um, you just went to a party with his family," Ella called out from the dressing room. "He's coming to yours!"

She did like the idea of getting his take on the dynamic between Marin and her fiancé. And Reed was so special to her that she would like her sisters to meet him, even if, when Summer's mother came back, they'd go from the intensity of these past few days to being casual acquaintances waving hi across Main Street or chitchatting small talk in the line at the coffee shop.

The ache was back. And she didn't think she *could* keep it off her face.

"He's coming and that's that," Marin said, the gown left behind in the dressing room. "He owes you for having to meet a thousand Dawsons and trying to keep their names straight."

Aimee laughed. "It does feel like there are thousands of them." In the first ten minutes, she'd been introduced to a Caden, a Camden, a Cole, a Caleb, and a Cody and had been unable to remember who was who a minute later.

Ella came out in another dress that was beautiful but still not the one. "He's coming to our dinner. No discussion."

Aimee narrowed her eyes. "Are you two trying to

matchmake? To get Reed and me together in a romantic-ish setting, like a dinner party with your fiancés?"

"Yes," they both said in unison.

Like Aimee had thought many times before, *Thank God for sisters*.

Chapter Thirteen

After everything he'd settled in his head about him and Aimee, attending a dinner party with her sisters and their fiancés seemed like a move in the wrong direction. Like they were a couple going to an everyday-type family function—and as if Summer was a baby who was theirs instead of just being the child they were caring for temporarily. But he couldn't bring himself to say no or make an excuse, considering she'd gone with him to his family event. What helped was that she'd given his going a purpose—to get his take as a detective on Marin and John's relationship.

"Maybe you'll see something that I don't," she said from the passenger seat of his SUV en route to the twins' condo with Summer. "Maybe John looks at Marin with deep love or holds her hand under the table." She shrugged.

"Are the two fiancés friends?" he asked.

"I don't think so. They're happy enough to chat about

sports or the rodeo when the four of them are together, but I think that's the extent of it. They're very different. John is kind of buttoned-up, and Ben is more a free spirit, fun-loving—he's a teacher like Ella but high school math."

They arrived at the condo, in the same development as Reed's. The three six-story units were meant to look like rustic lofts to attract a new and young workforce, and though Reed hardly considered himself that, he had been drawn to the buildings and interiors, with their exposed brick and arched windows, when he'd moved to town.

"Thanks for coming with me," Aimee said as she rang the doorbell.

"Of course. Summer gets a night out too." He held up her carrier. "People fussing over her. She likes that."

Aimee smiled and then the door opened, the twins and their fiancés welcoming them in and taking their coats. There was handshaking and introductions and oohing and aahing over the baby. So far, so good, Reed thought. Everyone was friendly and smiling. Ella and Ben said they had to get back to the kitchen—they were tonight's chefs and had made pasta, which Reed was always up for. Marin and John led the way into the living room. The place looked a lot like Reed's but was a roomier two-bedroom and more nicely decorated.

The first thing Reed noticed about Marin and John's interaction: Marin sat down on the sofa, and John chose the easy chair perpendicular to it rather than sitting beside her. Reed and Aimee sat on the love seat, Summer in the corner, alert and watching.

The second thing Reed noticed: John talked a lot,

going off on pedantic tangents. And Marin noticed. He'd seen her wince a few times as though she were a little embarrassed at how he was going on about hedge funds and the way both companies and people mismanaged their investments.

The third thing: John *didn't* look at Marin with love. In fact, he looked at her as though waiting for her to say the wrong thing so he could pounce with a correction, which he did a time or two.

Aimee looked like she wanted to bop John over the head.

This was all before they sat down to eat.

Marin and John did have that "couple look" the way some did—there was something matching about them. Both had light brown, straight hair, Marin's past her shoulders. Both were tall and fit, both wore glasses. John wore khakis and a navy sweater; Marin was in slim cut jeans and a navy sweater.

Laughter pealed from the kitchen.

Laughter was not pealing from the living room.

"Come and get it!" Ben called from the kitchen doorway, gesturing toward the dining table.

Now, Ella and Ben, on the other hand, looked like complete opposites but seemed in total harmony. Ella was blonde and Ben dark-haired, Ella wore a colorful print dress with hot-pink leggings and Ben wore all black. And yet they finished each other's sentences and giggled a lot, and that was just from kitchen eavesdropping.

The four of them stood, Aimee scooping up the carrier.

"Is she much of a crier?" John asked, grimacing. "I

was on a plane last month with a crying baby. Practically the entire two-hour flight. Isn't that the worst?"

"Summer's an easy baby," Aimee said, smiling at her before turning her attention back to John. "She's not very fussy at all."

"Even if she were," Marin said. "Babies *do* cry. I mean, it's what they do best," she added on a chuckle.

John seemed to be thinking about that. "I'd think what they do best is learn."

That was the third or fourth time he just had to one-up Marin in some way.

"The pasta's getting cold, people!" Ella trilled from the dining room as if she was used to breaking up little nothing discussions.

Once they were all seated at the rectangular table, a plate of porcini mushroom ravioli in a parmesan cream sauce in front of them all, they dug in. There was a big wooden bowl of salad and baskets of Italian bread. Reed's stomach rumbled. The food looked Pimoni's-level-good.

"So what's this I hear about Ella trying on thirty-two wedding gowns at two different shops and passing on every one of them?" Ben said with a grin as he took a piece of bread and dipped it in the infused olive oil.

"Apparently, same with Marin," John said. "I suppose we guys have it a lot easier with the tuxes."

Ben nodded. "Thank the Lord."

Ella scooped salad onto her plate. "Although Marin did fall madly in love with a gown not five seconds after we walked into the first shop."

"Oh really?" John asked, eyeing his fiancée. "Did

you send my mom a photo of it? She'll definitely want to see it."

"No," Marin said, pushing a piece of ravioli around on her plate. "I figure I'll narrow down my choices to five and then get opinions."

"Or you could just buy the one you love," Ella said. "You'd be done. I have another thirty-two to try on, at least." She laughed, but Marin was biting her lip.

John looked from Ella to Marin, ravioli-laden fork paused in the air. "I know my mom is going to want to see the dress before you buy, Mar. You know how she is."

Hmm. At least he was acknowledging it. Aimee had told Reed about the mothers-in-law when she'd gotten home from the shopping trip. Which had had him re-calling his own mother-in-law, whom he'd adored. A kind, loving woman, she'd thought of Reed as a little too much of a "saint," as she'd called him, for marry-ing her pregnant daughter after she'd been abandoned by the father. He'd lost her in the divorce too.

"Maybe I *should* go back and buy the dress in the morning," Marin said. "It's so beautiful. I tried it on and I just knew." She looked over at John. "If your mom doesn't like it, I'll be so disappointed."

"I know, honey, but you know how she is," he said for the second time. "You could send a photo of it to Jenna. She'll give you her honest opinion."

"Your sister and I don't have the same taste, though," Marin pointed out.

John nodded. "It's good to get others' opinions, though."

Oh boy. They were talking about a wedding gown. The *bride's* wedding gown. Which should be the bride's decision. That Marin's fiancé wasn't even pretending to take her side against his mother was a big problem. Butting in to overrule her opinions, both big and small, would carry through the marriage for *decades*.

Ben brought up the upcoming rodeo, and thankfully, the conversation turned to that.

If John noticed that his fiancé had gotten quiet, Reed couldn't see any sign of it. He didn't look in her direction once. He talked a lot about his favorite rodeo event, bull riding, and how Logan Winston, national champion and hometown hero, had "abandoned" his fans last summer and walked away from competing.

"I know his former manager," Aimee said, forking a piece of ravioli. "Savannah Walsh? I ran into her yesterday and she mentioned that Logan is building a free rodeo school in town—it'll be primarily for kids and teens."

"That's amazing!" Ella said. "I've seen so many students who can't afford extracurricular activities and outside interests, so I'm really happy to hear this."

John twisted his lips. "It's nice and all. But Logan Winston is a superstar bull rider—he could build the school and still compete. He has years left in him on the back of a bull."

"I heard the reason he quit the rodeo was because he found out he has a son he didn't know about," Ben said. "He gave up the spotlight to be a full-time dad—that's champion material right there."

"Aw," Ella said. "I agree." She leaned over to kiss her fiancé on the cheek.

John shrugged. "Well, I guess you go from that to Summer's mom dumping her on a cop's desk and, yeah, he looks pretty good in comparison..."

Marin's cheeks flushed. "I wouldn't use the word *dumped*, John. She left the baby, healthy and appropriately dressed, on his desk with supplies and a note that she would be back in a few days. Obviously, something is going on in her life and she needed the baby in safe hands."

"Are you close to finding out who she is?" Ben asked.

Reed nodded. "I think we'll be hearing from her very soon."

"Jeez," John said to him. "Your entire life was uprooted. You could have just turned her over to Aimee as the foster parent, but you chose to take care of her like the note asked. You must really love babies."

Reed almost laughed. "I like babies fine. But I have Aimee's help. I couldn't have done this without her."

He looked at Aimee across from him. She sent him a thank-you smile, which went straight to his heart. It struck Reed as interesting that there was underlying tension between him and Aimee, but he was pretty sure that an outside observer would never know it. And supposedly there was no tension between Marin and John, but you'd need a machete to get through it.

Luckily, Summer did start crying about twenty minutes after dessert had been served, and it gave them a great excuse to leave a bit earlier than they might have.

Once they were back in the SUV, engine started, Reed shook his head. "I've conducted my investigation—Marin and John aren't exactly soulmates."

Aimee smiled. "*You* believe in soulmates?"

He mock narrowed his eyes at her. "You know what I mean. Simpatico. Kindred. Birds of a feather. Peas in a pod."

Like us, he could easily say.

The truth of that hit him hard in the stomach.

"I just can tell you, with certainty, Aimee, that Marin and her fiancé are not any of that."

Aimee sighed hard. "I just wish Marin cared. I wish she wasn't willing to overlook so much. If she'd stand up to him—and his mother—I wouldn't worry like this. I'd know she could handle them."

"I wouldn't want that dynamic," Reed said. "But if Marin believes, truly believes, that this is her *one* chance to have what she wants—a wedding, a marriage, children— then yeah, she's going to overlook other things she wants. Like real happiness." He reached over and gave her hand a squeeze.

"Thanks again for coming with me," she said.

"I'd do anything for you, Aimee."

She looked at him, surprise in her green eyes, but didn't say anything.

He would do anything for her, he knew. But only to a point. And she knew it. That was what she hadn't commented on.

Back at the cabin, Aimee fed Summer on the sofa, while Reed worked on his laptop across from them on the love seat, still trying to piece together the last nine months of Mae Pickett Stone's life. She looked over at him, and he seemed frustrated.

"Dead end after dead end," Reed muttered. "I think Mae must have taken off when her grandmother died earlier this year. She was grieving, had nowhere to go, was scared what would happen because she wasn't eighteen then. So she met someone and got pregnant? And then what? That is the question."

"I wish we—" she began to say, then realized that Summer wasn't taking the bottle. "Reed, Summer won't eat. She keeps turning her head. And she feels warm." She put a hand to the infant's forehead. She was definitely warmer than usual. Aimee set the bottle on the coffee table and carried the baby to the nursery, putting her down on the changing table while she grabbed the forehead thermometer from the basket on the shelves just above.

Summer had a fever.

She started to fuss, her cheeks flushing, but then she looked pale too.

Aimee picked her up and held her vertically. Was she overreacting or did Summer feel even hotter suddenly? She paced, rocking Summer in her arms. The baby wasn't crying. In fact, she seemed listless.

Oh no. Something was definitely wrong.

She hurried into the living room. "Reed, I think we need to take Summer to the clinic. She's burning up and seems lethargic."

Reed was already on his feet and rushing to the door to get his coat and boots on, then came over and took Summer so Aimee could do the same. They hurried out to the SUV, with the baby in the carrier. "She's going to be fine. Babies get sick. Just like Marin said—babies cry, it's what they do. They also get sick with scary viruses that all babies get."

Aimee was panicking, though. Her heart was beating out of her chest. She got in the back seat with Summer so she could keep an eye on the baby. She called the clinic to report that they were coming with a listless newborn with a fever.

In fifteen minutes, they'd arrived at the clinic and were ushered right into the exam area, the ER doctor and two nurses taking Summer behind a curtained-off section. Reed and Aimee were allowed to stay, which Aimee appreciated. They sat on the hard chairs just outside the curtain.

Reed reached over and took her hand—and held it. Aimee squeezed and he squeezed back. "She's going to be okay. She will be because she has to be. Her mom's out there, waiting for the right time to be reunited with her."

Aimee wished she knew what the story was, why Mae Stone had left Summer in the first place. Was she even a good person? They had taken that for granted because of how the note was worded, but what if they were wrong? She was out there, watching, that much Aimee knew. But for what? And why? What was she waiting for? Had she been watching them tonight? Had she followed them to the clinic?

She shared her train of thoughts with Reed, who rushed out to the parking lot to see if a little gray car was there.

He came in and nodded. "The car is there, at the far end of the lot, but it's empty. She's lurking somewhere, maybe even inside the clinic somewhere. She must have been watching the cabin and realized when we rushed out that something was wrong. What I don't get is—if she's watching, why not come get her baby? She clearly cares what happens to Summer."

Even with five years' experience at Family Services under her belt, having seen just about every possible type of scenario, this was a first, and she couldn't figure out what Mae was doing and why. "And where is she now?"

Reed shook his head. "I did a scan of the parking lot and didn't see anyone in the shadows."

Aimee let out a breath. Mae would come out of hiding when she was ready. They'd just have to wait. In the meantime, they'd both promised to take good care of Summer—promised Summer herself—and they would.

Finally, the doctor came out from behind the curtain. He'd diagnosed Summer with a common virus, nothing major, and said she might or might not develop cold symptoms. They should give her infant fever reducer on a schedule and otherwise keep her comfortable, plus keep her hydrated by making sure she ate every two and a half hours.

When the nurse gave them the discharge papers, Summer in her carrier on the exam table, Aimee fell into Reed's arms and he wrapped them around her. He didn't hesitate, which she'd not only noticed but appreciated. This wasn't about romance right now. It was about compassion.

"She's okay," she whispered.

"She's okay," he repeated, his voice strong. "Let's get her home."

Home. She liked the sound of that. But this was all temporary. Soon, probably very soon, Reed and Summer would both be leaving.

Taking her heart with them.

In the parking lot, Aimee asked where Reed had seen the car, if it was still there. Reed looked but shook his head. Mae was already gone. Had she been in the clinic? Had she been listening? Wouldn't a nurse have asked her who she was?

"Wait—there," he said, pointing. A small gray car was turning out of the exit.

"I guess we just have to wait her out. She'll come when she's ready."

What is your story, Mae Stone? What's got you staying away from your newborn? What has you watching us? Aimee wished she had answers but she knew they'd come eventually. Right now, they had a sick baby to tend to and keep comfortable.

Reed settled Summer in the back seat. Aimee got in the back again, but the experience going home was much less fraught than the drive over had been.

When they pulled up at the cabin, Reed glanced around for the small gray car but said he didn't see it. Aimee looked too. Nothing. Mae was like a cat.

Once inside, coats and boots off, Aimee took Summer in her arms over to the sofa. She attempted to give her a bottle again, but Summer wouldn't drink.

"I think I'd like to just hold her and gently rock her and let her sleep in my arms," Aimee said.

"If you get tired, hand her over, and I'll do the same." He sat down beside her, running gentle fingertips along Summer's still-hot forehead. "Poor baby. But you're gonna be okay. Doc said so. And we say so."

The doorbell rang and Reed said he'd get it. Aimee figured it was Marin, coming over with the cardigan Aimee had accidentally left at their condo. Obviously, she didn't need it returned so immediately, but Aimee figured her sister would use returning it as a reason to ask how she thought the dinner party went—not well—and to defend her fiancé, if need be.

Aimee wasn't up for that right now. At all. She had a feeling that Marin had suggested the dinner in the first place as less a matchmaking thing for Aimee and Reed, and more so that Aimee could see that things were "just great" between Marin and John, when in fact, they were…unsettling. The night had backfired on her sister, and it had been plain for everyone to see. Marin couldn't feel good about that. Or maybe Marin would just ignore the whole thing as she had many times before over the past month.

Reed opened the door.

It wasn't Marin with Aimee's sweater.

It was a teenaged girl. With a dark pixie haircut and blue eyes Aimee could see from the sofa.

Aimee gasped.

The girl might not have long red hair, but she *was* wearing a long black puffy coat.

It was Mae. Summer's mother.

Chapter Fourteen

"Mae," Reed said gently to the girl on the porch, taking in her every detail of her.

Now that she was standing so close, no sunglasses, no wig, he easily recognized her from the mobile home, when he'd had to break the news to her that her father had died. Her hair was longer then, but the color, and her vivid blue eyes, the delicate features, the elfin chin as his mother remembered—all the same.

She looked past him to Aimee, who was now standing, Summer in her arms. Aimee walked over so that she was beside Reed.

"Come in," Reed said. "Please."

Mae seemed nervous, but she came in.

Reed shut the door. "Let me take your coat."

Mae stared hard at Summer, her eyes welling with tears. "Is she okay?" she asked, taking off the puffy coat. Reed took it and hung it on the rack. "I actually came over a few hours ago and rang the bell but no one answered. And so I waited. And then you got home but then rushed right out with the baby so fast that I knew something was wrong. I followed you to the clinic."

"Summer's fine," Reed assured Mae. "She has a fever and a common virus that infants get, but the doc expects her to be fully recovered by late tomorrow."

The girls' shoulders visibly relaxed. "You're calling her Summer? Like I wrote in the note?"

Reed nodded. "It's a very pretty name."

Mae gave a wobbly smile. "I like it a lot. Summer." She nodded to herself, her eyes on the baby.

"Would you like to hold her?" Aimee asked with a soft smile.

Mae nodded. "Just for a few seconds."

Aimee carefully transferred her. Mae touched the back of her hand to Summer's forehead. "She does feel hot."

"She'll be okay," Reed said. "Doc assured us."

Mae looked down at the beautiful infant in her arms. "You're a beautiful, good baby," she whispered, then took in a breath. "You can take her now," she said to Aimee.

Aimee nodded and took her back. "Why don't we all sit down? Would you like something to drink, Mae?" Aimee asked. "Or eat? I have a full fridge if you're hungry."

Mae shook her head. "Nah, I'm fine."

Aimee led the way into the living room and sat down carefully on the sofa, shifting Summer against her chest. Reed gestured for Mae to follow, giving her the opportunity to sit beside Aimee, close to Summer, but she chose the love seat across. Reed down sat next to Aimee and gave her arm a quick, soft squeeze.

They all seemed to be holding their breath. Mae included.

"I'm glad you came out of the shadows, Mae," Reed said.

"How'd you know who I was?" she asked.

"I figured that, based on the note you left," Reed said, "we'd crossed paths at some point, probably from a case of mine. But I had trouble pinning down your identity. At first I thought you were from Bear Ridge, but when I kept hitting dead ends, I shifted my focus to Cheyenne, to relatives and to cases there. My sister mentioned that we had distant cousins there, and my mom remembered a Sandrine Wheeler with a daughter named Mae Pickett."

Mae sighed. "I don't even remember that girl—Mae Pickett. My life was so different then. When my mom married my dad, everything got better, but she walked out on us. Even though I was a teenager, he adopted me because we really bonded—he was there for my homework, projects, father-daughter dances at school. He even took me to visit the state university to show me that I could go there if I kept up my grades. That I could be anything I wanted."

"He sounds like a great dad," Aimee said.

Reed was overcome with admiration for Ted Stone—he'd stepped up and then some, not only taking care of Mae but assuring her of a parent by adopting her.

Mae nodded, her eyes welling again. She looked at Aimee, then turned to Reed. "He was. And when he didn't come home that last night, I knew something bad had to have happened. I called 9-1-1 and you came. You looked so familiar to me, but I couldn't place you."

"I was wondering about that, if you'd recognized me from family events we might have both attended."

"I didn't at first," Mae said. "And a half hour later, you came back with the bad news, losing my dad was all I could think about. I remember crying hysterically, and clutching the headphones and card to my chest, and you were so kind to me. You said really nice things and you stayed the whole time until my gram was able to come."

Reed had felt so bad for the teenaged girl in the mobile home that night. He remembered sitting with her on the sofa, holding her hand as she cried.

"It was only when I was packing up to go home with Gram that I realized why you seemed familiar," Mae said. "I met you at a family wedding back in my old life. I'd dropped my glass of punch and the glass shattered. I was afraid I'd get in trouble, but you were passing by and told me not to worry about it and got me another glass of punch. I guess we're distant cousins or something?"

Reed nodded, barely remembering the punch incident.

Mae sniffled and wiped tears from under her eyes. "So when I knew I had to leave my baby for a few days, I decided to leave her with you. It took me hours to track you down to Bear Ridge, but I did and drove the three hours here. I figured with how nice you were to me, and being related and all, that you'd take good care of my baby. And you did."

Reed gave Mae a gentle smile. "I took your note very seriously." He glanced at Aimee, who was watching and listening so intently that her shoulders were practically up to her ears. "Mae, can you tell me why you felt you had to leave Summer with me in the first place?"

Mae bit her lip and took a deep breath. "When my gram died back in January, I was only seventeen and I was afraid I'd get put in foster care or something like that. I had some money from when my dad died so I took a bus to a town that had a rodeo, thinking I could get a job and I did. I worked in the concessions area, selling T-shirts in one of the big stands. I figured I could just start over and then get my GED and then maybe I'd get to the state university like my dad hoped. I had all these dreams but—" Mae suddenly gasped, staring at Summer.

Reed looked down at the baby to see what had prompted the gasp; she had opened her eyes a bit.

"Her eyes are still blue like mine," Mae said, her voice shaky. "I hear they change eventually."

"If they do change," Aimee said, "that will take a few months, but they might stay beautiful blue, like yours."

Mae gave another wobbly smile and nodded. "My dad had blue eyes too. Even though he wasn't my real dad, I liked that we matched." She smiled a bit, lost in thought for a moment. "He always talked about us moving to California and swimming in the Pacific and having a little house with palm trees. I planned to save up enough money from the rodeo to buy a plane ticket."

Reed's heart went out to this young woman who'd been through so much. He was glad she'd held on to her dreams.

"And then I met Jack," Mae went on, and Reed sat up straighter. This was the part he was waiting for most of all. "He was supercute and bought, like, three T-shirts at my stand before he got the nerve to ask me out, he said. He was hoping to break into bronc riding and loved the rodeo. I thought he really liked me but…" Her eyes welled again. "He stayed over one night at the room I was renting in a boardinghouse, and in the morning, he was gone. I didn't even know his last name. Didn't get his number. He left me a note saying he had a great time, but he was trying out other rodeos to break in. I never heard from again. And two months later, I found out I was pregnant."

"Oh, Mae," Aimee said, so much compassion in her voice. "You must have felt so alone."

"I did. I was so scared. I had no one. I'd made a few girlfriends and they helped find a free clinic. I went every month for checkups and all that. But the night I went into labor, I was by myself. I took an Uber to the clinic and all of a sudden, like, five hours later, I was a mom."

"And you're just eighteen," Reed said. "So young."

She nodded. "I stayed at the clinic for two days. The nurses there were really nice. They told me if I wanted to keep my baby, they could recommend programs for me, and that if I wanted to think about adoption, they could direct me there too. But I didn't know what I wanted. And then I thought about you."

"Why's that?" he asked. Finally, he and Aimee were about to get the answer they'd been after from the get-go.

"I needed time to figure out what I wanted to do— needed to do—for my baby. I thought if I could just leave her with someone I could trust for a few days… I could find out how it would feel to be without her, you know?"

"Oh, Mae," Aimee said. "You wanted to know if you could bear to give her up for adoption?"

Mae's eyes filled with tears. She nodded and seemed choked up. "When I got to Bear Ridge, I went to the police station and wrote out the note and then went in and left Summer in her carrier on your desk. I was so afraid the lady at the front desk was going to stop me, but she was really busy with the phones. I just said I had something to leave for you and she waved me through."

Reed nodded. "We had a temp that day."

"I got lucky, then," Mae said. "The regular person probably would have noticed I was leaving a baby carrier on someone's desk."

There was no doubt of that, Reed thought. Betsy, their regular front desk attendant, noticed everything.

"So after I left Summer, I was a shaking mess," Mae said, biting her lip. "I got a room at a cheap motel on the highway and I just sat on the bed for hours. It felt so weird to be without the baby. I wanted to go back and get her right away, but then the blizzard happened. And it gave me a lot of time to really think. I thought about having very little money and nothing to offer my baby. About how I was raised and how I'd want to do better than that—be a really good mother for my kid." Tears streamed down her cheeks.

Mae wiped under her eyes. She was quiet for a few seconds.

"And then, when the roads cleared up enough late the next day," Mae said, "I googled your home address and I figured I'd go park in your condo development and say my goodbyes in my head to Summer. But on my way over, I saw you leaving the police station and you didn't have Summer. So I followed you."

Another mystery solved. That was how she'd known where Aimee lived.

"I parked down a ways behind a stand of trees and googled the address and found your name—Aimee Gallagher," she said, looking at Aimee. "And then a search of that told me you were a social worker with Family Services. I didn't know what that meant." She turned to Reed. "I got really scared that you were turning her over to the state. I thought I'd made a terrible mistake leaving her with you. I wasn't sure what to do."

"Ah," Reed said. "That's why you were staying in the shadows."

Mae nodded. "But then I realized you were actually *staying* at the cabin with the baby. I saw you two kissing once. So I figured you were a couple. And I started to relax. I was happy that the baby was in two sets of good hands. It helped me accept, 100 percent, that I needed to give my baby up for adoption. I know I can't be the mother she needs. I wish I could be, but I can't—it isn't what's best for her."

"That's very brave and honorable of you, Mae," Reed said.

Aimee nodded. "She'll always know you loved her so much you wanted her to have a stable home."

Mae gave another wobbly smile and looked at the two of them. "Will you two adopt her? That's what I want for her. For Summer."

Reed almost gasped.

Aimee actually did.

"Mae, I'm a certified foster mother," Aimee said.

"Helping to take care of Summer these past few days has been so wonderful, so special and meaningful. I *love* Summer, and it would be a dream come true for me to adopt her. If you're sure this is what you want to do, I would be so honored and happy to be her mother. And just to let you know, we can make it a private adoption so that there won't be any issues regarding the state and Family Services. I know a few attorneys I can call to get the paperwork started."

Reed heard the hope in Aimee's voice. He looked at Mae, willing her to say: *Yes, let's do that.*

Two people here would get exactly what they each needed.

And Reed could go back to his life as a lone wolf.

Mae bit her lip and lifted her chin. "The thing is, it's really important to me that she be adopted by a *married* couple."

Aimee's heart sank to her stomach.

Married. Aimee certainly wasn't that.

"A stable home with two parents," Mae continued, looking for a moment at Summer in Reed's arms. "A caring, loving mom and a caring, loving dad in a solid marriage. Something I never seemed to have at the same time at any point growing up. That's what I want for my baby."

Aimee didn't know what to say. She certainly couldn't argue with Mae about what she wanted for her child. It was an entirely reasonable thing to want, and there were plenty of loving, married couples who would adopt Summer in a heartbeat.

Aimee always knew Summer would be leaving. But

a minute ago, when she believed that Summer could truly be hers, that she could adopt her, she'd been overcome with happiness.

Now her dreams were dashed.

Snap out of it, she told herself. *Buck up immediately. An eighteen-year-old girl making a huge, emotional decision is sitting here in the room with her newborn. This is about her, not you.*

She still wanted to cry.

"Mae, if that's what you want," Aimee said, "if that's what important to you for Summer, then rest assured there are so many loving, married couples out there who will want to adopt her. You'll have your pick of wonderful parents." She could hear her voice crack a bit and cleared her throat.

She could also feel Reed's eyes on her, but she kept her gaze on Mae.

Mae tilted her head and seemed confused. "But I want you and Detective Dawson to adopt Summer."

Now Aimee's gaze shot to Reed. His eyes widened. Aimee swallowed.

She hadn't seen this coming. Then again, nothing since the day she'd met Reed Dawson had been remotely expected.

"First, call me Reed, Mae," he said.

Aimee waited for *second*, but Reed wasn't saying anything.

"I realize that you're not married," Mae said. "I mean, you're not wearing wedding rings. But from what I've seen, just sneaking around and peering in the living room windows, the two of you are deeply in love and care so much about Summer. I want you two to adopt her," she repeated.

Reed opened his mouth, but again, nothing came out.

Aimee was at a loss for words right now herself.

"Mae," Reed finally said. "I have a good idea. I think we all need to sleep on this. It's late, it's been a really rough day, and we could all use some space to think."

Aimee nodded. "You're welcome to stay here."

Mae shook her head. "I think that would be too much."

"Then, why don't you stay at my place tonight?" Reed said. "You'll have it to yourself—and the fridge and cabinets are stocked. Aimee and I will talk and we can all get together tomorrow."

"That sounds good," Mae said. "You'll keep Summer here with you, right?"

Reed nodded. "Of course."

Mae stood up. She lifted her chin again as if determined about her decision.

Reed walked over to Aimee, who also tried to keep a pleasant expression for Mae. "I'll take Mae over to my condo—she can follow me in her car, and I'll get her settled, then come back."

"Okay," Aimee managed.

Mae smiled so sweetly at her and Reed. "I just know you two are the right parents for Summer. You both are my hope for her."

Aimee watched Reed swallow—hard.

This was Aimee's dream.

But she and Reed weren't even a *couple*.

Chapter Fifteen

Reed was grateful that his housekeeper had come today, so his condo was in tip-top shape for his special guest—bedding changed, towels stacked in the linen closet. When they'd arrived, Mae had seemed enchanted by the condo, which he knew was a much nicer place to stay than the cheap motel on the highway. With all their cell numbers exchanged, Mae had yawned and was clearly exhausted. She'd said she'd be asleep in about ten minutes. He'd texted Aimee that Mae was settled and that he'd back in a couple hours but if Summer got worse, or if she needed him, he'd come straight away.

If she needed him.

Talk about an understatement. To make her dream come true, she needed to be *married* to him.

Even the word *married*, echoing in his head, had his stomach twisting, that acidic blast making its way up his throat.

He hadn't elaborated on what he'd be doing for the next few hours, because he had no idea. He figured he'd drive aimlessly and try to think, to process all that Mae had said, but what was there to think about? He and Aimee weren't married—and they weren't going to be.

He drove around town, passing through Main Street and stopping at the park, which barely had any snow on the grass. The sidewalk plowers and the normal fall temps had gotten rid of most of the white stuff, but as he stared at the lingering flakes here and there, all he could think about was Aimee. Snowbound at her cabin.

Naked in her bed.

Beside him every step of the way these past few days.

And now her dream was grabbing distance away, and because he was who he was, she wouldn't be able to adopt Summer.

A new ache spread in his chest.

He left the park and drove around some more, wishing he could go to the Dawson Family Guest Ranch and walk over to the river and his favorite big boulder to sit on. He'd done a lot of processing there a year ago. Including the very first steps to healing, which had taken its unsweet time. But it was forty degrees and too cold for that.

An hour later, driving aimlessly, he wanted to call or text Mae to check in, make sure she was all right, but he didn't want to wake her. She was so young but she'd been on her own for almost a year and had been incredibly strong and resourceful. She'd be okay for tonight.

He drove to the police station and parked in the lot but kept the engine on, staring out at the one-story limestone building that had helped change his life, given him a fresh start and a new purpose. Given him Summer. He saw himself walking in and noticing the big pink thing on his desk and thinking it looked like an infant car seat but couldn't possibly be because why on earth would *that* be on his desk?

Surprise.

The lights were on inside the station; someone was always on duty overnight, but Reed was in no state to see anyone. He noticed the door open and someone coming out. He squinted and saw it was his cousin Rex, on the late shift tonight. He turned and called something back to whoever else was still on duty inside, then stepped out into the night.

Reed saw him notice his SUV idling in the parking lot for no good reason, and he came over. Reed lowered the driver's-side window.

"On the trail of Summer's mother?" Rex asked.

"Actually, the case is solved." He told Rex the whole story, his cousin's eyes widening with every new development. Particularly the last.

That Mae wanted her baby to go to a married couple.

"The jewelry shop in town opens at 9:30 a.m." Rex said.

"Not following," Reed said.

Rex rolled his eyes and jogged around the side of the SUV and got in the passenger seat.

"Propose to Aimee," Rex said. "Get married. Raise that baby."

Reed gaped at his cousin. "For a second, I thought you were serious. You know my history."

"Yeah, I do. I also know you love Aimee. And you

love that tiny baby too. I could see it a mile away at the birthday party, Reed. Everyone could."

Reed shook his head, his head feeling hollow, his gut twisting. "I can't go there. I'm never going there again." How could he? How could he ever put himself in the position to possibly lose everything again?

He wouldn't survive it.

"Aimee isn't your ex-wife. Summer isn't Kayla. This is a second chance at the most beautiful, the most fundamental things about life. Grab it, Reed."

Rex just didn't understand.

But as soon as he had the thought, Reed knew that that wasn't exactly true. Or true at all. Rex understood plenty about second chances.

But Reed had just come around to being able to hold a baby without his heart aching, his knees shaking. *That* was his second chance.

Marriage—no.

"Marriage isn't an option," Reed said. "I can't."

"I'm here to tell you that you can. And that you should. It's not often I tell people besides criminals and my children what to do. But I'm telling you. Marry that woman. There's no waiting period in Wyoming. You can get married at the town hall tomorrow, start adoption proceedings the same day. I'm sure Aimee knows many good private-adoption attorneys."

You can get married at the town hall tomorrow...

Wait. Hold on.

An idea started forming. A very unexpected idea.

It was a way to make this work. For everyone to have what they wanted and needed.

And he could do it.

"It'll be an arranged marriage," Reed said with a nod, the idea seeming more and more perfect. "For a purpose. To adopt Summer."

They'd probably want it to be platonic in order to keep things even-keeled. That would be hard, given how attracted he was to Aimee, but he'd be spurred on by the purpose itself, the importance: that this was about Summer. About giving Aimee her heart's desire. About Mae finally getting what she needed and wanted.

If Reed was anything, it was *controlled*. He could do this. He could marry Aimee Gallagher on paper, make it legally binding, without putting his heart on the line, as long as they'd have an agreement over the basic vows.

This wasn't about love and happily-ever-after and forever and new beginnings. It was about making a *family*.

Yes, this was the answer. The only answer.

The more the idea bounced around his head, the more he realized he'd hit on the solution.

Aimee could have her dream.

Mae could have her wish.

And he'd share his life with a great woman who he respected and admired. He would help raise the baby he'd come to care deeply about. He couldn't see any downside. It wasn't like he ever wanted to marry for *real*.

It was win-win for everyone.

"Um, Reed, I'm not talking about an arranged marriage." He glanced at Rex to find his cousin staring at him as if he had grown a few extra heads.

"It's the perfect solution, though," Reed said, excitement building where there was despair just five minutes ago.

"Is it?" Rex asked. "You sure about that?"

"Yes, for several very good reasons."

Rex sighed. "This should be interesting. Just know—I'm available day or night if you need to talk." He hopped out of the vehicle, then came around to the driver's-side window. "Good luck."

As he watched Rex head toward his own SUV, Reed couldn't wait to get to the cabin. To propose an arranged marriage.

Aimee was going to be so happy.

For the past two hours, Aimee had been afraid to even look at Summer. Afraid she'd wake up and cry and Aimee would have to go into the nursery and pick her up. Because if she did, her heart would shatter.

She loved that baby girl, with everything she was. And her mother was giving Summer up for adoption.

To a happily married couple in a loving home.

Her chest ached and she had to sit down. She dropped onto the sofa and buried her face in her hands.

To be so close and then, wham, the rug was yanked out from under her.

But from what I've seen, just sneaking around and peering in the living room windows, the two of you are deeply in love and care so much about Summer.

That was all *Aimee's* love and yearning that Mae had seen. Yes, Reed did care about Summer. But he didn't love Aimee. He didn't *want* to love her.

She dropped her hands and sucked in a deep breath, letting her head fall back against the sofa cushion. What she would give to marry Reed Dawson, the man of her every dream, and for the two of them to adopt Summer—the infant she loved with all her heart.

They'd be a family.

But that wasn't going to happen.

Aimee had to accept, accept, accept, because what was there to fight here? She and Reed weren't married. They weren't even dating.

She was relieved Reed had stayed away from the cabin the past two hours because she'd needed that time to cry and grieve for what was never even hers. She was more herself now but could feel how fragile she was on the inside, ready to shatter.

She heard a car pull up, and a moment later, Reed came bursting through the door. She stood up. He looked a lot different than he had when he'd left. Then, his expression had been strained, uncertainty radiating from him. Now he seemed…excited, his blue eyes gleaming.

"Aimee," he said, hanging up his coat and then hurrying over to the sofa. He sat down beside her and took her hands in his.

"What happened?" she asked. "What's going on?"

"Everything," he said. "I've been thinking. We make a really great team. We've seen that the past few days. And we both love that baby girl. I think we should enter into an arranged marriage and adopt Summer together. I want to do this for you, Aimee. I want to make your dream come true."

Aimee stared at him, her mouth dropping open. She could hardly believe what she was hearing. An arranged marriage?

She was so confused that she couldn't find her voice for a moment.

"What are you talking about?" she asked. "An arranged marriage?"

"For a purpose—to adopt Summer."

Aimee pulled her hands away from his and moved over a little. "But not a real marriage?"

"Well, it'll be legal, of course."

"I mean in other senses. How would this arranged marriage work?"

"I thought about that," he said. "I think we need to be platonic, Aimee. Otherwise, we'd be a real couple—married."

"Yes, that's what most married people are. Couples."

"But that's not what I want—it's not what I can offer. An arranged marriage is the one way I can do this," he said, his voice a bit ragged.

Oh, Reed. Her heart went out to him even if she wanted to bop him on the head.

"We could marry at the town hall in mere hours," he said, hope lighting his voice again. "There's no waiting period in Wyoming. And then we can meet with an adoption attorney and get the legalities and paperwork started."

Aimee felt her eyes well with tears. She couldn't speak, couldn't form words. She just sat there, shaking her head.

"Aimee? Are you okay? I thought this was what you wanted. Isn't it the perfect solution?"

He'd proposed. She could marry him tomorrow. They could start the adoption paperwork immediately afterward. Summer would be their baby.

They'd be a family.

Except, except, except.

He thought he was being kind. He thought he was being her *friend*. He didn't understand just how much this hurt.

"Aimee?"

Finally, she looked at him. "I did everything wrong. Five years' experience and I acted like a rookie. I wasn't supposed to get attached to Summer. And I wasn't supposed to fall in love with you, Reed."

Now it was his turn for his mouth to drop open. He stared at her in absolute surprise. Then concern filled his eyes.

Because he was doing what he'd said he wouldn't. He was hurting her. Breaking her heart.

"If you *wanted* to get married, Reed, if you *loved* me, I'd marry you in a heartbeat. *Then* all my dreams would come true. But how can I marry you—in this arranged marriage you're talking about?"

"But I can marry you under those terms, Aimee. I can marry for Summer's sake. For yours. I don't want to get married, but I can do it this way. When it's arranged for a very important, beautiful purpose—adopting Summer."

She shook her head again, the tears falling. She wiped them away. "Reed, there's no way I'd say yes to *this*. I want a husband who loves me. Who *wants* to be married to me. Summer deserves parents who love each other, who are committed to building a life together with her, as a family. And Mae made her feelings clear—that's what she wants for her baby. Not just a piece of paper, but a real marriage. A real family. I won't do something underhanded to get what I want. She's been through too much. We owe her more than that. We owe Summer more than that."

He ran a hand over his eyes. "I didn't think of any of that. Of being underhanded. Dammit. That's not what I want. That's not who I am."

"I know. You were thinking of me, Reed. Because—" She paused, about to take a very big risk here. "Because maybe you *do* love me. Propose to me for that reason and my answer will be yes."

Please say you love me. If you say so, I'll believe you. You're the most honest person I know.

He dropped his face in his hands for a moment. "Aimee, I—"

She waited. *Please, please, please. Let the past go. Love me enough to crack open your heart fully. Let me in all the way.*

Please.

"We're backed into a corner here, Aimee. I want to do the right thing. For you, for Summer, for Mae. I feel like marrying is the *right* thing to do. Not the wrong thing. Not the underhanded thing. We will have a loving, caring home. Let's do this, Aimee."

She let out a breath. "And so we'd marry, but have separate bedrooms? Continue taking turns in caring for Summer? We'd essentially be housemates?"

He was silent for a moment.

"Well, yes," he finally said.

She took both his hands and looked at him. "Tell me you don't love me, Reed."

Her heart wedged into her throat. She could barely breathe.

"Aimee, this is about Summer."

"It needs to be about all of us," she said.

"You know my history. You know I can't do—"

He stopped talking and her heart broke. She wasn't getting through to him. Or maybe she was fooling herself to think there was anything to reach. If he did love her, surely that would take precedence over his guarded heart, which was under lock and key. Love would take the reins here, not his past.

He didn't love her.

And once again, she had to accept it.

She squeezed her eyes shut, willing herself not to burst into tears.

A cry came from the nursery.

"I'd like the rest of the night with her," she said, her voice shaky. "I'd like to say a real goodbye to Summer." *And to how close I came to having what I want most.*

Reed looked like *he* might cry. He didn't, but she'd never seen him with such pain in his eyes.

Oh, Reed, you're doing this to yourself. Why can't you see that? Last time, it was done to you.

"You're breaking your own heart this time around," she dared to say.

He closed his eyes for a second and then stood up. "I think it's best that I don't stay here. I'll crash at Rex's."

Aimee couldn't even nod. She didn't watch as he walked away. She heard the door opening, then closing. Then his vehicle started.

Summer cried again.

This time, Aimee did too.

Chapter Sixteen

Aimee cried through the diaper change at 5:00 in the morning. Cried through putting fresh pj's on Summer. Cried through her bottle—and particularly hard at the big burp that had come out of that little sturdy body in her fairy wings pj's.

Several hours after Reed left, Aimee finally pulled herself together. Summer needed a caregiver, not a sobbing mess. She had to do her best for the baby, even if this was it, their last night together.

Talk about breaking your own heart. Aimee would barely make it through to morning.

With Summer in her infant bouncer, eyes now thankfully curious and alert, Aimee sent a group text to her sisters.

I need you guys was all she managed to type. Plus a sad-faced emoji.

Marin texted back in two seconds. Are you okay? What's wrong?

Aimee burst into tears again.

We'll be there in 15, Ella texted. Hang on.

Aimee put the phone down and let the tears come. "Sorry, Summer," she said, trying to catch her breath. "I think it's going to be a very tearful day."

The beautiful baby was looking at her with those slate blue eyes.

Aimee leaned back against the cushions. She couldn't help but wonder what Reed was doing. Spilling his guts to his cousin? Driving around? He had to be as miserable right now as she was.

The doorbell rang, her sisters there in record time. Aimee dragged herself to the door to open it. Ella and Marin took one look at her, then they looked at each other with concern and led Aimee over to the sofa.

"Where's Reed? Where's Summer?" Marin asked.

"Reed's at his cousin's. Summer's right there," Aimee said, pointing to the other side of the coffee table.

They both craned their necks, then looked back at Aimee.

She told them the whole story, starting with Summer burning up with fever, the knock on the door from Mae and Reed leaving last night—with her heart.

Well, half her heart was still here, in that bouncer. But all of it felt broken.

"An arranged marriage?" Ella asked, her blue eyes truly confused. "What does that even mean?"

"The way he sees it, we'd be getting married officially, but we'd be more like roommates, partners—working together to adopt and raise Summer, but not having any kind of romantic relationship. It wouldn't be about love. Or at least, not love for each other."

Marin slowly shook her head. "But that man does love you. It's the first thing Ella and I said to each other when you two left our dinner party." She seemed about to say something, probably about how awkward that dinner had been, but she clamped her mouth shut.

Ella nodded. "It was so evident to us. The way he looked at you, talked to you, talked *about* you."

Marin was quiet for a second. "Unlike how John looks and talks to me. And he probably agrees with his mother that I don't have good taste and can't be trusted to choose my own wedding gown." She grimaced and quickly shook her head. "Ugh, I'm sorry for being so self-absorbed. This isn't about me. Aimee, Reed will come around. He has to."

Aimee knew that wouldn't be happening. "I don't think he will. He's gone through too much, lost too much, was too broken by his marriage. This is the best he can do."

"So maybe you could just say yes?" Marin said quietly. "Everyone gets what they want, right?"

Ella tilted her head.

"Like I told Reed, I want to marry a man who loves me. I need to."

"But Mae only said she wanted Summer to go to a married couple in a caring, loving home," Marin said. "You and Reed could provide that in an arranged marriage."

Aimee slowly shook her head, her eyes welling. "My vows need to mean something. And how can I possibly be happy in an arranged marriage when the husband

I'm madly in love with will be in his own separate bedroom? A platonic marriage? With Reed? I'd go out of my mind. I'd be absolutely miserable. And then what kind of mother could I be if I'm constantly struggling with how I wished things could be different?"

Marin bit her lip.

Ella nodded. "I understand."

"But Summer will go to someone else. Are you really okay with that—especially when there's a way you could keep her? All couples have problems and work through them, right? That's marriage." Her shoulders slumped. "Wait, I'm focusing on the marriage part and not the platonic part. That's not going to work."

"No, it won't. And even if Reed can't bear to keep his hands off me, he'll go back to his bedroom in the middle of the night, trying to keep his head and heart at a distance. I'll have a broken heart every day. I can't live like that."

Ella sighed. "I'm so damned sorry, Aimee. You deserve all the happiness in the world. You deserve everything you want. This isn't it."

"No, it's not," Aimee said, leaning her head back against the cushions.

"I wish he were here," Ella said. "Reed, I mean. I'd try to talk some sense into that man." She held on to Aimee's hand, then rested her head on Aimee's shoulder.

Aimee managed something of a smile. But it faded as she thought of him running after his ex-wife to the front door of the house they'd shared, their two-year-old in her arms, her red suitcase at her feet. The very painful things she'd said about their marriage, about his lack of rights to the daughter he thought of as his own, about how the little girl would forget him.

How could Aimee's heart not go out to Reed? How could she not understand that he wanted to protect himself after such an experience? She got it—she really did.

She just wished things could be different.

"So this is your last day with Summer?" Marin asked, glancing at the baby who was now looking at the little, dangling pastel mobile on the bouncer.

She nodded. "I guess Reed and I will meet with Mae at some point this morning and tell her we can't get married. That we're sorry to let her down."

Marin stood up and walked over to the sliding glass doors, taking glances at Summer, biting her lip, staring at the ground. And then she burst into tears.

"Marin?" Ella said.

"I'm breaking up with John," Marin said.

Aimee gasped. "What? I thought—"

"Now it's my turn to have an epiphany, Aimee. You're giving up adopting Summer because it would be wrong to marry a man who doesn't love you. Am I really going to marry a man I don't love just so I can have a ring on my finger?" She shook her head. "To be honest, I don't think John loves me either. I just tick off enough boxes, so he asked. And I said yes."

"Oh, Marin," Aimee said, the tears back.

Ella grabbed the box of tissues from the coffee table and gave a bunch to Aimee, then popped up and gave some to Marin.

"We have each other," Aimee said. "Always and forever. When things are really hard, like now, we've got each other."

Ella started crying and sat back down on the sofa. Marin hurried over and they fell into a group sisters' hug.

"Yeah, I called that one," Rex said, dropping a supportive hand on Reed's shoulder in the kitchen of his house. He had a luxe cabin on the guest ranch, a good two miles from where all the action was. When Reed had arrived last night, his cousin had taken one look at him, set him up in a guest room, and let Reed know he'd give him space but if he wanted to talk, just knock on his door.

Now, Reed tried to form words, but he just stood there, his legs like lead, his heart so heavy he was surprised he hadn't tipped over face first.

"I'll make coffee," Rex said.

Reed dropped down on a chair at the table. "I'm blowing it. Blowing up my life, blowing up Aimee's life. I'm even going to disappoint Mae in the process. What the hell?"

"Yeah, you are," Rex said, sitting at the end of the sofa to give Reed some space. "So what are you going to do about it?"

"What *can* I do? The thought of marrying for real, repeating vows promising love and commitment, starting all that over—it feels impossible."

"*Do* you love Aimee?" Rex asked.

Reed took a slug of his beer. "Everything's just jumbled up." The flashes were coming back. His ex telling him Kayla would forget him. His ex telling him everything he did wrong in his marriage, that it was all his fault. Which it was.

He cared very deeply for Aimee Gallagher. But he'd

been a bad husband once. And he'd paid the price. He couldn't do it again. Not the way Aimee wanted.

"If only she'd accept the proposal as is," Reed said. "Everyone gets what they want."

Rex stared at him. "Oh yeah? What is it you're getting that you want from an arranged marriage?"

"I'm getting a life with Aimee and Summer. I really care about them, Rex."

"So you do want to marry Aimee and adopt Summer."

Reed took another slug of his beer. "With boundaries set up, yeah."

"You didn't answer my question. Do you love Aimee?"

Reed got up and walked to the wall of windows that faced Clover Mountain in the distance. He'd stared at the mountain for hours, for days, last year when he'd felt his absolute worst, when he never thought he'd come through whole. "I don't want to love Aimee. I don't want to love anyone."

"But you do, Reed."

That part of his life was over. He had so many walls up around his busted heart that he couldn't get to it if he wanted to.

So you're going to break all these hearts instead. Including your own.

This wasn't what he wanted. How the hell was he going to fix this?

Reed had an invitation to stay in Rex's guest room as long as he wanted, but he found himself needing to get out, needing air, needing the mountain and the sound of the river and everything about this ranch that had restored him last year. He walked a good couple of miles, grateful it wasn't biting cold. But all the refreshing air and the walk did was make him feel alone.

He got in his SUV and drove around some more, ending up parking in his condo development, glancing up at his living room windows. How in the hell was he going to tell Mae that he and Aimee weren't getting married? That she had to pick a different couple to adopt Summer, to raise the baby girl they all loved so much?

He closed his eyes for a second and let out a hard breath.

Just as he was about to pull out of the spot, he noticed a familiar guy getting out of his own car and walking toward the middle building where Aimee's sisters lived. He squinted—was that John? Marin's fiancé?

The guy stopped and dropped his face in his hands. For a minute, he started pacing in front of the building. Then he sat down on the black wrought-iron bench across from the door, his head in his hands.

Okay, what was this? Something was definitely wrong. Reed got out of his SUV and jogged over. "John?"

The guy's head darted up. It *was* John, but his eyes were glassy and he looked at Reed without recognition.

"Reed. Aimee's…friend," Reed explained, hoping to jog his memory. "From the dinner party."

John stood up and paced a bit and then sat back down. "Marin dumped me this morning. She said we don't love each other. That our relationship isn't solid. That we aren't close and had no business being engaged, let alone getting married."

And quite clearly, the guy was not taking it well. Which was a surprise. Based on what Reed had heard and seen with his own eyes, Reed would have figured that John wouldn't be devastated. But he sure seemed to be.

"Sorry," Reed said.

"But I do love her. I thought she loved me."

"You love her?" Reed asked.

"I do. A lot. I'm just…bad at this. My last girlfriend told me I was a know-it-all right before she ended things. That I talked too much and always said the wrong thing. I've always been…kind of awkward that way. But I thought Marin and I really had something."

"Like what?" Reed asked. He had the feeling he was going to have to lead the guy to some answers, when he himself, of all people right now, was the last person who should be giving advice about relationships.

"Like…when we're alone together and don't even have to speak. I'm so comfortable with her. I feel like she just gets me. I thought it was like that for her too."

Huh. "If you really love her, my advice to you is to knock on her door and tell her so. State your case. Lay it out. But do it with feeling, John. If you want something bad enough, it'll come naturally."

John's face brightened. "I was even thinking that maybe Marin and I could see a couples' counselor. I'd be willing to do that—and really work on myself, if that's what she needs."

"Tell her that. The most important things you said here was that you love her and that you want to go to couples' counseling. And that you feel she gets you and that you get her."

John stood. "I'm gonna go right now."

He hadn't known that Marin had broken the engagement. He had a feeling that Aimee had told her sisters about their situation and that it had woken Marin up to some hard truths. But who knew what would happen between Marin and John now?

He was about to head back to his SUV when John called his name.

Reed turned. The guy jogged up to him. "I forgot to say thank you. If I hadn't run into you, I probably would have just gone home and sulked all day, telling myself that it was over and I had to accept it. At this rate, you and Aimee will be married before Marin and I will, but that's okay, right?"

"Why do you think Aimee and I are getting married so fast?" he asked, wondering where that had come from. Aimee had very likely told her sisters they were not getting married.

"When you and Aimee were over here, I kept thinking that things are supposed to be like you two are. The way you look at each other and the things you say to each other and about each other. The way you seem to understand each other so well, even when you're not saying anything at all. I want that with Marin. I just don't know how to do it. I mean, it's crystal clear you love Aimee. But I know it's not crystal clear to Marin I love her. I'm gonna change that, starting tonight."

Reed was speechless for a moment. So much of what this guy said had slammed into his head and was now echoing around, making too much sense.

"One last piece of advice?" Reed said.

"Let me have it."

"Get your mother out of the relationship. Trust me on

that. Put your foot down. It's you and Marin. Not you, Marin and your mom's opinions."

Understanding lit John's eyes. "Yeah. You're absolutely right. My sister's a real pill too."

Reed laughed. "Go get your woman."

As John ran at full speed toward the condo's double doors, Reed felt something inside him shift, give way. He wasn't sure what, he just knew that he felt…lighter.

He was going back to the ranch, back to his big rock by the river. He had some thinking to do.

No, he amended. He had some *feeling* to do.

Chapter Seventeen

Summer's cry from the nursery roused Aimee from her thoughts on the living room sofa. Her sisters had stayed for a while, and they'd moved into the kitchen for coffee and toast, but both had had to leave.

As she'd said goodbye at the door, she'd asked Marin if she was okay and Marin said no, that it was entirely possible that she actually *did* love John and just didn't love how things were between them. Aimee had said that she could end the engagement without ending the relationship, and that maybe they could work on things. Marin had brightened.

After a long hug and promises to call with any updates, the twins had left.

She got up and went to the nursery, where she scooped up the precious baby. She cuddled her against her chest for a bit, then went into the kitchen, where the stroller was, settling her down while she made up a bottle.

She'd likely do this only a couple more times before Reed came to take Summer away.

The stupid tears threatened again and she blinked them back. She'd gotten through her divorce and losing her parents, and disappointing relationships and a hard time with Marin. Surely in about fifty years, she'd get through this.

She tucked the bottle in the pocket of her hoodie sweatshirt and wheeled Summer over to the sofa and fed her, the baby drinking happily, no sign of her earlier fever.

"So, Summer, I just wanted to say thanks. For everything you taught me these past few days. How to really care for a newborn, which you absolutely can't learn in a parenting class. And you've made it clear to me that I really want a child of my own. I was hoping it would be you—"

Her phone pinging with a text interrupted her.

She eyed her screen. Reed.

I'm outside on the porch. Can we talk?

No, she wanted to text back. *No, we cannot. No, you can't break my heart some more.* She didn't need to hear more of his reasons and sorrys and I can'ts.

"Should I go see what he has to say?" she whispered to Summer.

Summer was drinking and staring at absolutely nothing and didn't respond. Aimee took that as a yes.

She stood up and walked with Summer, still having her bottle, in her arms. With a deep breath, she opened the door.

Reed stood there, filling the doorway like he had the

first day he'd been in her kitchen. Looking so gorgeous, so familiar, so everything to her.

"I've spent the last half hour sitting on the big rock by the river at my cousin's dude ranch, the one I sat on for hours last year when I felt completely dead."

She bit her lip and stepped back, and he came in. She shut the door behind him but stayed put in the entryway. She didn't want to invite him in. Didn't want to sit on the sofa with him or have a hundredth cup of coffee in the kitchen.

She couldn't listen to him tell her he didn't love her without saying it.

She'd done enough of that already.

"I think I loved you from the first day I met you, Aimee. When you opened up to me in this cabin and told me who you were. You enabled me to open up when I'd planned on keeping my past under layers of cement."

She'd gasped inwardly at the first line about loving her, too shocked to reply. Seeming to take her silence as a request to continue, Reed kept talking.

"You've cracked me open, Aimee Gallagher. You and Summer. I *do* love you. More than anything in the world. Certainly more than holding on to the past. I can't let it control me anymore. I can't lose you, I can't lose Summer. I love you. So much."

Tears welled in Aimee's eyes. She didn't have a free hand to blot them, but Reed did, and he used the back of his fingertips to wipe them away.

"I never want to make you cry again," he said. "Unless they're happy tears."

"These are." She was so happy she really did think she'd explode with it.

"Can I hold her?" he asked, his gaze soft on the baby.

"Sure," she said. Summer was finished with her bottle. Aimee held on to that while Reed carefully took her and walked over to the sliding glass doors. He leaned his head down and kissed Summer's forehead.

"This is our baby," he said. "Yours and mine."

"Mine and yours." The tears came again. She put down the bottle and ran over to the man and baby she loved with all her heart.

"I love you and I want to marry you because you're the best thing that ever happened to me," he said. "You're everything to me, Aimee. I was scared to face it. Scared to admit it. But the truth is the truth. And sometimes, you just have to accept it."

Aimee laughed. "Right?"

She wrapped her arms around them both, wanting to pinch herself to make sure this wasn't a dream, that she wasn't still in bed in la-la land. She did give herself a little pinch...but she was still here.

"Oh, and by the way, I love you too, Reed. I know I said so already, but I want to scream it from the rooftops. I love you so much."

"We're a family now," he said. "But we were from the first minute. We just didn't know it."

Something told her that Summer, in all her week-old wisdom, had known it.

While Aimee was in the shower and Summer was napping in her bouncer, Reed texted Mae that she was invited to a wedding tomorrow.

I'm so happy, Mae texted back. Will you and Aimee set up the meeting with the adoption attorney?

Will do. Happily, he typed.

An hour later, the meeting set up for tomorrow morning, Reed texted Mae about it. She sent back a heart emoji and said she'd like to have the day to herself to explore Bear Ridge and soak up where Summer would be raised. Reed asked if he could call her, if they could talk, and she said yes.

"You're welcome to stay at my place, use anything you need. If we can take you to lunch or dinner, just let me know, okay?"

"I appreciate that. I know I'm doing the right thing by giving Summer up for adoption. It's hard, though, you know? So I don't want to spend time with you guys or Summer. I just need to say my goodbye to her in my own way. You'll pick me up for the meeting tomorrow morning?"

"Nine o'clock," he said.

"Okay. I'll be ready. As ready as I'll ever be. You have no idea how good I feel about you and Aimee adopting her. Thank you, Reed. I'll thank Aimee tomorrow. After the meeting, I think I'm gonna take the bus down to Blue Smoke—there's a rodeo there and I can get a job pretty easily, I figure. In a month, I should have enough to get to California."

Her dad's dream. Her dream.

"Actually," he said. "I spoke to my mother this morning and I mentioned your dream of moving to California and swimming in the Pacific. Having a complete fresh start. Turns out she's in Santa Barbara right now—my parents are spending their retirement traveling the South and West in an RV. They're visiting with an old college friend of my mom's. She owns a beachfront restaurant in Santa Barbara—and she could use another waitress. You have a job and place to stay waiting. Her daughter's a college student, waitressing there, and needs a roommate. The apartment isn't fancy or right on the beach, but it's walking distance."

Mae gasped. "Are you serious?"

"Yup. Plane fare is on me. My parents and my mom's friend will pick you up at the airport."

"Oh my gosh, Reed. I don't know what to say, except thank you."

"My pleasure."

"I'm going to be okay," she whispered.

"Yeah, you are."

When Reed disconnected the call, Aimee was standing in the hallway, her blond hair damp around her shoulders, tears in her eyes.

"Her dreams are coming true too," she said.

"Just like ours."

She threw her arms around him, her robe coming undone. Last night, they'd spent hours in bed, looking at each other, snuggling, making love, talking. He'd never get enough of Aimee.

"How about we go back to bed until our daughter wakes up," he said. "And then we have a quickie wedding to plan."

They dashed to Aimee's bedroom. *Their* bedroom. The robe came off along with Reed's clothes, and they got under the covers, facing each other on their sides.

"I called the town mayor—he happens to be a buddy of the family's. He can marry us at 5:00 p.m. tomorrow."

"Perfect," she said, pressing a soft kiss on his lips. "I

can't believe that at five-ten-ish or so, I'll be married to the man of my every dream."

"Same for me. But woman."

She smiled. "I'm going to be a Dawson. One of thousands in Bear Ridge. I kind of like that."

"No one likes that you're going to be a Dawson more than I do," he said and kissed her nose. "So we'll have a big party tomorrow night, but keep the ceremony small? Your sisters and Rex and Ford? Double the required witnesses."

Plus the baby girl who'd changed both their lives.

Epilogue

"I can't believe you're getting married before me," Ella said to Aimee in the back room of the Bear Ridge Town Hall the next afternoon.

"And me," Marin added. "But that's a good thing." She smiled and squeezed Aimee's hand. Surprise of all surprises, Marin had indeed ended the engagement— but not her relationship with John. Marin and John had talked all day and night and had committed to couples' counseling and starting fresh. Aimee had a very good feeling about their future now.

Aimee pulled both her sisters into a group hug. "I love you two so much," she said. Her sisters had decided to wear "bridesmaid" dresses, which really just meant they were both wearing pretty blue dresses they had in their closets and both had twisted up their long hair into fancy chignons.

"Don't make me cry—either of you—or I'll look

like a raccoon for the wedding photos," Ella said. "And they're forever!"

All their eyes misted, anyway.

In fifteen minutes, at 5:00 p.m. on this supposedly ordinary weekday afternoon, Aimee would be marrying Reed Dawson. The town's mayor had cancelled his early-bird dinner plans at the diner for the occasion and would be officiating the ceremony. Aimee's sisters would be in attendance, as would Reed's cousins Rex and Ford, and then tonight, the Dawson clan was throwing a reception for the happy couple tonight in the ballroom of the Dawson Family Guest Ranch. Apparently, Rex's and Ford's wives were busily planning the party now. Reed had texted Aimee a few minutes ago that he'd heard Pimoni's Italian Café was providing the hors d'oeuvres *gratis*. When Danica had stopped in to place a big order, the owner had said Reed was one of their best customers and there would definitely be minibites of chicken Milanese among the offerings.

Aimee's heart had been bursting all day with all the kindnesses, all the well wishes and congratulations. She couldn't wait to become part of the Dawson family.

She stood back a bit and stared at her reflection in the antique standing mirror in the corner. She'd managed to look very bridal and was afraid she *was* going to cry and ruin her makeup. *Keep it together*, she told herself, or *you'll* look like a raccoon before you even step outside and see your groom. Oh, who was she kidding? She was way too emotional right now to try to bother not crying. That was what waterproof mascara was for.

"Kinda makes you wonder why it's taking almost a year to plan my wedding but it took an *hour* to plan yours," Ella said. "Same result at the end of the day." She grinned and shook her head.

"So true," Aimee said. "I can plan your wedding in an hour if you want."

Ella's eyes widened. "I'll stick with the fancy ballroom of the Dawson Family Guest Ranch, but thanks." She grinned. "I can't believe you're beating me there too, by having your reception there."

Aimee could barely believe it herself. It still felt like a dream.

"For an hour of planning, you look amazingly bridal," Marin said, looking at Aimee's reflection in the mirror.

For the very special occasion of her marriage to Reed Hughes Dawson, Aimee chose a pretty off-white suit that she'd bought for Easter a few years ago but had never actually worn. The skirt was lace and the lapel of the jacket kind of curved. She'd never noticed that the suit looked bridal. Or maybe she had and that was why could never bring herself to wear it. She'd added a pair of blush-colored pumps, and each sister had given her something from that famous old wedding rhyme: *Something old, something new, something borrowed, something blue.*

Something old was their mother's pearl drop earrings. Ella had dashed to a gift shop the minute she'd heard about the wedding this morning and bought a sexy black lace garter, which she'd presented to Aimee as something new—and something supersexy. Marin had taken Aimee's wrist and put on her seed pearl bracelet for something borrowed, and the something blue, they'd all decided, was the groom himself: Bear Ridge PD.

At this very moment, Mae was on a plane to Santa Barbara, California, where she would be met in baggage claim by Reed's parents to start a whole new life. Mae had decided that attending the wedding would be too much for her, too much a part of things. And so Aimee and Reed had said their goodbyes to Mae at the airport in Brewer a few hours ago. Mae hadn't wanted Summer to be there; she wanted a clean break, and so they'd dropped off the baby with Rex's wife, Maisey, who'd be bringing her to the ceremony.

"I knew you two were madly in love and should get married," Mae had said. "I guess I just made it happen sooner than it might have."

That turned out to be A-OK with both Aimee and Reed.

The three of them had met with an adoption attorney that morning who Aimee knew through her work with Family Services. It was to be a private, closed adoption, which was Mae's choice, but Aimee and Reed had assured her that she was welcome to visit; that they would tell Summer about her origins from the get-go and she would grow up knowing that her birth mother loved her. Mae had tearfully hugged them goodbye and thanked them for making her and her father's dream of California and the Pacific come true.

Aimee had a feeling they wouldn't see Mae again, but she knew they'd keep that door open if Mae ever changed her mind. Aimee had mentioned that to Reed on the way back from the airport, and he'd agreed. They'd both teared up and sent up a wishful prayer that Mae would find her way and achieve all she wanted in her life, and they both knew that would be the case. She'd have support in California and would be just fine.

A tap came at door. "Showtime!" Aimee heard Rex call out.

Her heart was beating a mile a minute. When the door opened, she'd step out with her sisters on either side, both holding an arm, and she'd walk down the three-foot long "aisle," which was really just a long black mat, and see her husband-to-be standing near the podium with the mayor and Rex and Ford.

She was afraid she'd get so emotional that she'd dissolve into tears and ruin even her waterproof mascara.

But the door opened, and Aimee heard the wedding march playing—from Rex's phone—and she and her sisters were too busy smiling at that for her to cry.

She stepped out and saw Reed standing there, facing her, flanked by his cousins. He wore a tuxedo and was so handsome she could barely breathe for a moment.

In his arms was an infant, their daughter. Aimee sucked in a breath, her heart feeling like it might burst out of her chest. Summer wore a frilly pink headband and pink pj's with little red hearts all over them, which Ella had found in the gift shop when she'd bought the garter.

Their baby was at their wedding, treasured guest of honor.

Aimee's sisters walked her to where Reed stood, and then he stepped forward and took her hand and they turned to face the officiant.

A bright and shining new beginning for three.

* * * * *

Don't miss these other great Christmas romances!

The Rancher's Christmas Star
By Stella Bagwell

Holiday at Mistletoe Cottage
By Nancy Robards Thompson

Their Convenient Christmas Engagement
By Catherine Mann

*Available now wherever
Harlequin Special Edition books
and ebooks are sold!*

Chapter One

Ian Steele leaned back in his full grain leather chair, the one he'd just dropped three grand on, and looked out at the sparkling waters of San Francisco Bay. The light in his office this time of day was soft, golden. The sun filtered in through the blinds in warm rays, making the dust particles in the air look like stars. He'd always liked San Francisco this time of year. It was almost Christmas, but it didn't necessarily feel *Christmassy,* which suited him just fine. He could almost look out the window at the sailboats bouncing over the swells and mistake it for summertime.

There was a soft knock on his door, but he didn't take his eyes off the view below. "Come in," he said evenly.

"Ian, there's a call for you on line one."

At the sound of Jill's voice, he swiveled around to see her standing with her hands clasped in front of her stomach. She always looked apologetic these days, like she didn't want to upset him. He could be an ass, but she was the consummate professional, which was why he'd hired her in the first place.

He smiled, trying his best to put her at ease. But truth be told, he'd probably have a better shot at swimming across the bay without being eaten by a shark. She had the distinct look of someone standing on broken glass.

"Who is it?" he asked.

"Stella Clarke. Says she's from Christmas Bay." She frowned. "Where's that?"

Ian stiffened. It had been years since he'd thought of his hometown. Maybe even longer since he'd heard anyone mention Christmas Bay. He'd cut that part of his life out as neatly as a surgeon. He was too busy now, too successful to spend much time dwelling on things like his childhood, which quite frankly didn't deserve a single minute of reflection.

"Tiny little town on the Oregon Coast." He rubbed his jaw. "What the hell does she want, anyway?"

His assistant's eyebrows rose at this. Clearly, she was taken aback. Ian was usually smooth as scotch. Unruffled by much of anything.

Clearing his throat, he leaned back in his brand-new chair. He had the ridiculous urge to loosen his tie, but resisted out of sheer willpower. "Did she say? What she wants?"

"She has a favor to ask. She said she knows you're busy but that it won't take much time."

Typical Stella. Exactly how he remembered her. He could see her standing in the living room on the day he'd arrived at the foster home, when his heart had been the heaviest, and his anger the sharpest. Wild, dark hair. Deep blue eyes. Even at fourteen years old, she'd been a force to be reckoned with. Even with all she'd probably endured. Just like him. Just like all of them. She'd been whip-smart, direct, always trying to negotiate something for her benefit.

But he couldn't exactly talk. Now he made a living out of negotiating things for his own benefit. A very nice living, as a matter of fact. As one of the Bay Area's top real estate developers, he'd been snatching up prime property for years, building on it and then selling it for loads of cash. He had people standing in line to do his bidding. The question was, what was this favor she was talking about? And how much time would it actually take?

He looked at his Apple Watch, the cool metal band glinting in the sunlight. Almost noon. He had a meeting across town at two thirty, and he hadn't eaten yet. He could have Jill take her number, and he could call her back. Or not. But for some damn reason, he was curious about what she wanted. And whether he'd admit it or not, he was itching to hear her voice again. A voice that would now be seasoned by age, but would no doubt still be as soft as velvet. He hadn't talked to her since he'd graduated from Portland State. They'd run into each other at a swanky restaurant in the city where she'd been a server. They'd awkwardly met for coffee after the place closed, and it hadn't gone well. At all.

"Thanks, Jill," he said. "I'll take it. Have a good lunch."

She smoothed her hands down the front of her cream-colored pencil skirt. "Do you want me to bring you something back?"

He smiled again. "No. Thank you, though. Why don't

you take an extra half hour? Get some time outside if you can. You've been working hard this morning, and the weather's nice. Enjoy it."

"Are you sure?"

"Positive. Go."

She reached for the door and pulled it closed behind her.

He looked down at the blinking button on the sleek black phone and felt his heart beat in time with it.

Picking it up, he stabbed the button with his index finger.

"Ian Steele," he said in a clipped tone.

"Ian? It's Stella Clarke. From Christmas Bay…"

He let out an even breath he hadn't realized he'd been holding. He'd been right. Her voice was still soft as velvet.

"Stella."

He waited, imagining what she might look like on the other end of the line. Wondering if that voice matched the rest of her. If she was that different than she'd been ten years ago. Because back then, the last time he'd seen her, she'd been very beautiful, and very pissed.

At least, she'd been pissed with him.

There was a long pause, and she cleared her throat. "How have you been?" she asked.

She was obviously trying to be polite, but he didn't give a crap about that right about now. He had things to do, and opening a window into the past was definitely not one of them.

"What do you want, Stella?"

"Well, it's nice to talk to you, too."

"I know you didn't call for a trip down memory lane."

"I took a chance that you might care about what's happening here," she said evenly. "Even if it's just a little."

"Why would I care about Christmas Bay?" He had no idea if that sounded convincing or not. Because he thought there might be an edge to his voice that said he did care, just the tiniest bit. Even if it was just being curious as to why she was calling after all this time. Curiosity he could live with. Caring, he couldn't. At least not about that Podunk little town.

"Because you have memories here, Ian."

He shook his head. *Unbelievable.* Of course she'd assume his memories at Frances's house were good ones. Worth keeping, if only in the corner of his mind.

The thing was, though, she was actually right. Not that he'd ever admit it. There were some good memories. Of course there were. Of Stella, whom he'd always gravitated toward, despite her sometimes-prickly ways. She was a survivor, and he'd admired that. She was a leader and a nurturer, and he'd admired that, too. He'd seen in her things he wished he'd seen in himself growing up. Things he'd had to teach himself as he'd gotten older, or at least fake.

And there were other memories that weren't so terrible. Memories of Frances. Of his aunt. And snippets of things, soft things, that he'd practically let slip away over the years, because they'd been intermingled with the bad stuff, and tarnished by time.

He gripped the phone tighter, until he felt it grow slick with perspiration. Those decent memories were the only reason he hadn't hung up on her by now. Those, and his ever-present curiosity.

"What do you want, Stella?" he repeated.

And this time, the question was sincere.

"I can't believe I just did that," Stella muttered under her breath.

Sinking down in her favorite chair in the sunroom, she looked over at Frances, who was wearing another one of her bedazzled Christmas sweaters. Her fat black-and-white cat was curled up on her lap, purring like someone with a snoring problem.

"Uh-oh," Frances said, stroking Beauregard's head. "What?"

Stella worried her bottom lip with her teeth, and gazed out the window to the Pacific Ocean. It was misty today. Cold. But still stunningly beautiful—the ocean a deep, churning blue gray below the dramatic cliffs where the house hovered. One of the loveliest houses in Christmas Bay. But of course, she was biased.

She'd moved in when she was a preteen and brand new to the foster system. At the time, she'd thought Frances's two-hundred-year-old Victorian was the only good thing about her unbelievably crappy situation. After all, it was rumored to be haunted, and how cool was that? But she'd also been a girl at the time, and incredibly naive. She had no way of knowing that Frances herself would end up being the best thing about her situation. Frances and the girls who became not only her foster sisters, but her sisters of the heart. Getting to live in the house had been a bonus.

Now, as the thought of selling it crept back in, along with the thought of Frances's Alzheimer's diagnosis, which had changed things dramatically over the last few years, Stella felt a lump rise in her throat.

Swallowing it back down again, she forced a smile. This was going to be hard enough on her foster mother without her falling apart. Selling was the right thing to do. They just had to find the right buyer, that was all. Frances's only caveat was that a family needed to live here. A family who would love it as much as her own family had. As much as all of her foster kids had over the years.

"I asked someone for a favor," she said. "And now I'm wishing I hadn't."

"Why?"

She took a deep breath. "Since *Coastal Monthly* is doing that Christmas article on the house, I thought it would be a great time to kill two birds with one stone. Drum up some interest from potential buyers, and get the locals to stop telling that old ghost story."

Frances leaned forward, eliciting a grunt from Beauregard. "What do you mean? How in the world would you do that?"

It had been a long time. Almost fifteen years. Frances might have Alzheimer's, but her long-term memory was just fine. Stella wasn't sure how she'd react to this next piece of information. Maybe she'd be okay with it. But maybe not.

She braced herself, hoping for the former. "I called Ian Steele…"

Her foster mother's blue eyes widened. She sat there for minute, and Stella could hear the grandfather clock in the living room ticking off the seconds.

"Wow," Frances finally muttered. "Just…wow."

"I know."

"How did you find him?"

"I googled him and he came right up. He's this big shot real estate developer in San Francisco."

Frances sucked in a breath. "You don't think he'd want to buy the house, do you?"

"No way. He hates Christmas Bay, remember?" Still, Stella couldn't shake the fact that he'd seemed to perk up when she said the property was for sale. He'd asked several specific questions, the real estate kind, until her guard had shot up, leaving her uneasy.

"It's been a long time, honey. People change."

She shook her head. "Not Ian."

"Then why call him?"

"Because I thought if he gave the magazine a quick interview over the phone, it could help when the house goes on the market. You want a legitimate buyer, not some ghost hunters who will turn it into a tourist trap. You know people around here still talk about that silly story, and he's the only one who can put it to rest."

Frances looked skeptical. "But would he want to?"

"I'd hope so after what he put you through while he was here. Including making up that story in the first place and spreading it around. It's been years. I'd assumed he'd matured enough to at least feel a little bad about it."

Frances was quiet at that. She'd always defended Ian when he'd been defiant. He'd had this innate charm that seemed to sway most of the adults around him, but Stella had been able to see right through him. Maybe because she'd come from a similar background. Abuse, neglect.

Nobody was going to pull the wool over her eyes, not even a boy as cute as Ian.

Suddenly looking wistful, maybe even a little regretful, Frances gazed out the window. The mist was beginning to burn off, and the sun was trying its best to poke through the steely clouds overhead. Even in the winter, Frances's yard was beautiful. Emerald green, and surrounded by golden Scotch broom that stretched all the way to the edge of the cliffs of Cape Longing. As a girl, Stella thought it looked like something out of *Wuthering Heights*. As a woman, she understood how special the property really was. And how valuable.

She truly hadn't believed Ian would be interested in the house, or she wouldn't have called him. It wasn't the kind of real estate he seemed to be making so much money on in the city, at least according to the internet. He and his business partner bought properties and built apartment buildings and housing developments on them, and the Cape Longing land was smaller than what they were probably used to. But after talking to him, even for just those few painful minutes, Stella knew he was more calculating than she'd given him credit for. If he smelled a good deal, even if it was in Christmas Bay, he might just follow his nose. Which was the *last* thing Frances needed.

"So, what did he say?" her foster mother asked. "Will he do the interview?"

"He wouldn't say. I never should've called him. I could just kick myself."

"At least you got to talk to him again."

Stella bit her tongue. *Yeah, at least.*

"Did he say how he was?" Frances asked hopefully.

She was so sweet. And it made Stella indignant for her all over again. She'd loved and cared for Ian like he was her own, seeing something special in him, even under all the surliness and anger. She'd told him that often, but it didn't matter. He'd made his time with her miserable, and had ended up running away. He'd disappeared for days, worrying Frances sick, and ultimately breaking her heart when he was sent to live with a great-aunt instead.

Stella had a hunch it was *because* of the love Frances had shown him, not in spite of it. If Ian sensed anyone getting close, he ran. He was a runner. She'd be willing to bet he'd run all these years, and had ended up in San Francisco, still the same old Ian. Just older. And maybe a little more jaded, if that was possible.

Stella liked to think that despite their similar background, one that had helped her understand him better than most people might, she'd turned out softer, more approachable. And she credited Frances for that. Maybe if Ian had stayed put, he might've had his rough edges smoothed out some, too.

She smiled at her foster mother, determined not to say what she was thinking. Determined to show some grace, at least for the time being. "We didn't get that far," she said. "I guess he had a meeting or something."

Frances nodded. "So, he's done well for himself?"

If his website was any indication, he was doing more than well.

"He seems to be."

"I wish things had turned out differently," Frances said. "I wish I could've reached him."

"It wasn't because you didn't try, Frances. We all did."

"But maybe if we'd tried harder..."

Frowning, Stella leaned forward and put a hand over Frances's. Her foster mother smelled good this morning. Like perfume and sugar cookies. She was in her early sixties, and was a beautiful, vital woman. Nobody would ever guess that she struggled with her memory as much as she did. So much so that her three foster daughters had moved back home to help her navigate this next chapter of her life.

In the corner of the sunroom, one of the house's two Christmas trees glittered. The decorations were ocean themed, of course. The blue lights glowed through the room like a lighthouse beacon. Christmas cards from previous foster children, now long grown, were strung around one of the double-paned windows. The old Victorian came alive over the holidays, and its warmth and coziness was one of the reasons Stella loved it so much. She knew it would be heartbreaking to sell it. Frances was right to want a family living here. Somehow, it softened the blow.

"You were the best thing to happen to us," Stella said quietly. "I'm just sorry he couldn't see that."

Frances smiled, but it looked like she was far away. Lost in her memories.

Stella scratched Beauregard behind his ears, before leaning back again with a sigh. Lost in some of hers.

Ian shifted the Porsche into second. This was the first time he'd driven it in the mountains, and not surprisingly, it hugged the hairpin turns like a dream. If he was in the mood, he'd be driving faster. After all, why own a German-engineered sports car if you weren't going to break the speed limit every now and then? But he wasn't in the mood. And getting to Christmas Bay any faster wasn't exactly tempting.

Gritting his teeth, he glanced out the window to the ocean on his left. Then at the GPS to his right. He'd be there in less than half an hour. Plenty of time to wonder about this decision. Yeah, the Cape Longing property might be the deal of a lifetime (*if* he could convince Frances to sell to him), but was it worth stepping foot back inside the little town he'd left so long ago? He wasn't so sure.

Which brought him back to Frances again. And to Stella. Ian could smooth talk anyone. Anyone having second thoughts, or experiencing cold feet, was putty in his hands after about five minutes. Less, over drinks. But true to form, Stella had been immune to everything he'd thrown at her over the phone. The conversation had turned stilted in *less* than five minutes, which he wasn't used to.

Thinking about it now, he bristled. She'd always been different than the rest of the kids he'd known in the system. Foster kids were usually wise, but she was wiser. They were tough, but she was tougher. They had walls, but Stella had barricades. He'd never been able to scale them, and then he'd just stopped trying. He didn't need anyone, anyway. Not Frances O'Hara, not Kyla or Marley, and sure as hell not Stella. So, he'd done anything and everything in his power to test them. He'd stolen, lied, smoked, drank. You name it, he'd done it. And for the cherry on the crapcake, he'd come up with that dumbass story about the ghost, knowing what a headache it would be for Frances. Knowing how it would get around and eventually stick in a town that was known for every kind of story sticking. Especially the bad kind.

But now, he had a chance to rectify it. That's what Stella had said. *Rectify.* Like he owed them something by talking to *Coastal Monthly* for their fluffy Christmas piece. *It's not like it matters*, he'd said evenly. *These days, a story like that only helps sell houses.*

And that's when she'd told him that Frances wanted a family living there. Someone who would love it as much as she did.

When he'd hung up, he'd gotten an idea. Why *not* do the interview?

He'd tracked down the lady writing the article, and she'd practically begged him to come up to Christmas Bay so she could take pictures. And if he got a good look at the property in person, through the eyes of a real estate developer, well, then… What could it hurt? Other than shocking the hell out of Stella, who'd asked him to talk to the magazine but definitely would *not* expect him to do it in person. No way would she have wanted to open up that can of worms. She'd suspect a deeper motivation, and she'd be right.

In the beginning, money had been the driving force. Of course it had. But as he made his way up Highway 101, his Porsche winding along the cliffs overlooking the ocean, he had to admit there was another reason he was doing this. For once, it had nothing to do with money and everything to do with wanting to see Stella again. Just so she could see what he'd become. Just so he could flaunt it in her pretty face.

He downshifted again and glanced over at the water. It sparkled nearly as far as the eye could see. It was deep blue today, turquoise where the waves met the beach. The evergreens only added to the incredible palate of colors, standing tall and noble against the bluebird sky.

It had been so long since Ian had been up this way that he'd almost forgotten how beautiful it was. Easy, because the Bay Area was beautiful, too. But in a different way. There were so many people down there that sometimes it was hard to look past all the buildings and cars to see the nature beyond. On the Oregon Coast, the people were sparse. So sparse that it wasn't unusual to go to the beach and not see anyone at all. The weather had something to do with that—it was usually cold. But the scenery? The scenery was some of the most spectacular in the world, and Ian had been a lot of places.

Swallowing hard, he passed a sign on his right. Christmas Bay, Ten Miles. Ten miles, and he'd be back in the town where he'd been the most miserable, the loneliest and most confused of his entire life. But also, where he'd caught a glimpse of what love could look like if he'd only let it in. But he hadn't let it in. In the end, he hadn't known how. And he'd been too pissed at the world to try, anyway.

There was absolutely no other reason, other than maybe a little spite, that he wanted to come back here again. No reason at all.

That's what he kept telling himself as the trees opened up, and Christmas Bay finally came into view.

Stella opened up the front door to see a woman in trendy glasses standing on the stoop. She looked the part of a journalist. Her hair was in a messy bun, and she had a camera bag slung over one shoulder. It was a beautiful day, perfect for pictures, but it was cold, and she was dressed appropriately for a December day on the Oregon Coast—rain boots and a thick cardigan.

When she saw Stella, she smiled wide. But her gaze immediately settled on the entryway behind her. It was obvious she couldn't wait to get a look inside.

"Hi, there," she said, holding out a hand. "Gwen Todd. And you must be Stella?"

Stella shook it. "I'm so glad the weather cooperated."

"Oh, I know. I thought it was going to pour. We got lucky."

"Please come in," Stella said. "Frances has some coffee brewing."

Gwen stepped past her and into the foyer. Before Stella could turn around, she heard the other woman gasp. She couldn't blame her. The house was incredible. Three stories of stunning Victorian charm. Gleaming hardwood floors, antique lamps that cast a warm, yellow glow throughout. A winding staircase that you immediately wanted to climb, just to see what treasures waited at the top. A widow's walk on the third floor that looked out over the cliffs, where Ian said he'd seen a ghost all those years ago. A coastal cliché that the entire town had latched onto, but that her family would finally shake free of today. At least, Stella hoped they would. It was just an article—it wasn't going to go viral or anything. But for the locals, for someone most likely to buy this house and live happily in it, it would be a start.

Gwen Todd ran her hand along the staircase's glossy banister. "Oh, it's just lovely. I've always wanted to see inside."

Stella had heard that more times than she could count.

From certain places in town, you could see the house, perched high above Cape Longing, its distinctive yellow paint peeking like the sun through the gaps in the trees. It had been built when Christmas Bay was just a tiny logging settlement, and Frances's grandparents had had to get their supplies by boat, because the mountain roads were impassible by wagon in the winter and spring. As the town had grown, the house had become a fixture, near and far. It even had its own display in the local maritime museum—the fuzzy, black-and-white pictures taking people back to a time when the West was still fairly wild.

And Gwen Todd was clearly a fan. Shaking her head, she looked around, enthralled.

Stella smiled. She understood how Gwen felt, because that was exactly how she'd felt as a girl, walking through the doors of this place for the first time. In absolute wonder and awe. For a kid who'd gone from surviving on ramen noodles in a broken-down trailer on the outskirts of town, to this? It had been almost too good to be true. For the first six months of her new life with Frances, Stella had expected someone to come and take her away at any moment. Or worse, for her mother to get her back. She'd had nightmares about being deposited back into that cruelty and filth. Into that never-ending cycle of neglect and abuse. It wasn't until after the first full year that she'd begun to trust her good fortune. That she'd been able to start opening her heart again. Cautiously, and just a little at a time.

Now, standing here, those days seemed so far away, they were just as fuzzy as the pictures in the museum down the road. But other times, they were clear as a bell, and those were the days that tended to hit her the hardest. When the pain and memories were too sharp to take a full breath. Thank God for Frances. Otherwise, there was no telling where she would've ended up. Or *how* she would've ended up. She hadn't spoken to her biological parents in years. She simply had nothing to say to them.

Gwen looked at her watch, just as Frances walked in holding out a reindeer mug full of steaming coffee. This time of year, Frances served all her drinks in Christmas mugs. She was proud of her collection.

"Oh, thanks so much," Gwen said. "This will help wake me up before Mr. Steele gets here."

Stella froze. Frances froze, too.

"I'm sorry," Stella managed. "What?"

"Mr. Steele. He's supposed to be here at eleven, but I think he might be running late…"

Stella stared at Frances, who sank down in a chair by the staircase. She looked pale.

"Oh…" Gwen set her coffee cup down. "Oh, no. I thought I mentioned that he'd be coming?"

"I don't think so," Stella said. There was no way she'd mentioned that. Stella would've remembered.

"There were so many calls back and forth, I must've totally spaced it. I'm so sorry. Will it be a problem?"

Gwen looked genuinely concerned, but if she'd known exactly how Ian had left things all those years ago, Stella knew she'd be downright horrified. He hadn't stepped foot inside this house since he'd left with his social worker at sixteen. Frances had been crying. She'd stood at the window watching them pull out of the driveway with tears streaming down her face. She'd felt like she'd failed him. Which was ridiculous, but that's how she'd felt, which made Stella furious with him all over again.

She forced a smile to ease Gwen's mind. And maybe her own, too. There was always the chance he'd show up and apologize to Frances for how he'd treated her back then. Or that he'd acknowledge that what he'd said at that coffee date years ago had been horribly untrue— suggesting their sweet and loving foster mother had only taken them in for the money. A disgusting comment that had brought up every single insecurity that Stella had ever had about finding a genuine home. But she doubted he'd do either of those things. She also doubted that he was coming back to Christmas Bay simply to do this interview and help Frances sell her house. No way. He had other motives in mind. Probably like getting a good look at her property, since, like an idiot, Stella had practically waved it in his face.

"It's okay," she said. "We just haven't seen him in a long time. He was one of Frances's foster kids, and he left…suddenly."

Gwen frowned, glancing at Frances, and then back at Stella again. "Are you sure? I feel terrible about this. I wouldn't want it to be awkward for you."

Too late.

Frances shook her head. "No, honey. Don't worry. He's come all this way to do the interview, so that says a lot. Maybe this is a blessing in disguise."

As if on cue, there was the roar of a car coming up the drive. All three of them moved over to the bay window and looked out, like they were waiting for Santa

Claus or something. Stella crossed her arms over her chest, annoyed by her own curiosity. She didn't care that she'd be seeing Ian again. She couldn't stand him and his giant ego. And she managed to believe that. Mostly.

Outside, a beautiful silver sports car pulled into view, mud from the long dirt driveway spattered on its glossy paint job. Stella's heart beat heavily inside her chest as she saw the silhouette of a man through the tinted windows. Short black hair, straight nose and strong jaw. Sunglasses that concealed eyes that she remembered all too well. Blue, like Caribbean water. But not nearly as warm.

Letting out a low breath, she watched as the door opened, and he stepped out. Tall, broad shouldered and dressed impeccably in crisp, white-collared shirt and khaki slacks. Like the car, the clothes looked expensive. Tailored to his lean body in a way that she'd really only seen in magazines. So, this was how Ian had turned out. Probably with an even bigger ego than she'd remembered.

Frances looked over at her. "I can't believe how handsome he is. He looks so different."

There were differences. But there were also similarities, and those were what made Stella's chest tighten as she watched him swipe his dark sunglasses off and walk toward the front door with that same old confidence. That same old arrogance that had driven her bananas as a kid. That had driven them *all* bananas.

But there was no doubt he'd grown into that confidence. As a woman, she could imagine feeling safe and secure in his presence. And at that, she recoiled. Nothing about Ian Steele should make her feel safe. He was a piranha, only here for a meal. She'd bet her life on it.

Beside them, Gwen cleared her throat and touched her hair. Probably taken with his looks—something that made Stella want to snap her fingers in front of her face. *Snap out of it, Gwen!*

Instead, she walked over to the front door and opened it with her features perfectly schooled.

He stood with his hands in his pockets, gazing down at her like she was some acquaintance he was meeting for lunch. Instead of a girl he'd shared a home with, a family with, for two tumultuous years.

He smiled, and his straight white teeth flashed against his tanned skin. Two long dimples cut into each cheek. *Good God, he's grown into a good-looking man.* The kind of man who stopped traffic. Or at least a heart or two.

Stella stood there, stoic. Reminding herself that it didn't matter how he looked. It only mattered that he gave this interview and went on his merry way again. Got back in his sports car and got the heck out of Christmas Bay.

"Stella," he said, that Caribbean gaze sweeping her entire body. He didn't bother trying to hide it. "It's been a long time."

She stiffened. If he was trying to unnerve her, it wasn't going to work. He might be trying to brush those two years underneath the rug, but she sure wasn't going to. He'd made their lives miserable, and had left a lasting scar on Frances's heart. Something she refused to minimize or forgive. And that slippery smile said he wasn't the least bit sorry about what he'd said over that fateful coffee date. Whether he'd meant it or not, he'd definitely wanted to wound her, probably since she'd stayed and found happiness in Christmas Bay, and he hadn't. No, he wasn't sorry. Not by a longshot.

"Ian," she said. "Exactly the same, I see."

His smile only widened at that. "Now, how can you say that? It's been years."

"Oh, I can tell." She glanced over her shoulder into the living room. Frances and Gwen were talking in low tones, obviously waiting for her to bring him inside. She looked back at him and narrowed her eyes. "I know exactly why you're here."

"I don't know what you're talking about."

"Cut the crap, Ian. Frances wouldn't sell to you if you were the last man on earth."

Rubbing the back of his neck, he seemed to contemplate that. "Oh, you mean because the house is coming up on the market, and I'm a real estate developer, you just assumed I'm here to schmooze…"

"I *know* you're here to schmooze," she whisper-yelled. "But it's not going to work. You're not going to just waltz in here after all this time and get what you want. Life doesn't work that way."

"Oh, I beg to differ. It does, in fact, work that way." He leaned back in his expensive Italian loafers and looked down his nose at her. "Are you going to invite me in, or are we going to stand here and argue all day? I mean, don't get me wrong, the sexual tension is nice, but there's a time and place for it."

She felt the blood rush to her cheeks. "Give me a break."

He smiled again, his eyes twinkling. She wanted

to murder him. But that wouldn't be good for the sale of the house, either, so she stepped stiffly aside as he walked past, trying not to breathe in his subtle, musky cologne that smelled like money.

When Frances saw him, she took a noticeable breath. Then she stepped forward and pulled him into a hug. He was so tall, she had to stand on her tiptoes to do it. But he bent down obligingly, even though Stella could tell his body was unyielding. Ian had always had trouble with giving and receiving affection.

Stella couldn't bring herself to feel sorry for him. He'd had plenty of opportunities to be loved. Frances had tried, but he'd only pushed her away. It was what it was.

Still, she couldn't help but notice how his jaw was clenched, the muscles bunching and relaxing methodically. How his gaze was fixed on the wall behind Frances, stony and cold. Like he just wanted to retreat. And before she could help it, there was a flutter of compassion for him after all. Because she could remember feeling the same way a long time ago.

After a second, he pulled away and looked down at her with a careful smile on his face. Not the almost playful one he'd given Stella a minute before. This one was more structured. Like he'd been practicing it a while. Like fifteen years, maybe.

"Hi, Frances," he said. "It's good to see you."

Stella could see that she was having a hard time with a reply. Her eyes were definitely misty. Poor Frances. She'd just wanted the kids who'd passed through her doors to leave happy. She'd wanted to give them a home, whether it was for a few months, or the rest of their childhoods. The fact that she hadn't been able to give Ian any of those things still bothered her. Probably because, despite that carefully crafted smile, his pain was clearly visible. It had been brought right to the surface by this visit. Stella had to wonder if he'd been prepared for that when he'd hatched this asinine plan.

"Ian," Frances said. "You grew up."

"Probably all those vitamins you made me take."

"Well, they worked. Just look at you."

Gwen stepped forward and fluttered her lashes. She actually fluttered her lashes. Stella wanted to groan.

"Oh, I'm sorry," Frances said. "Gwen, this is Ian Steele. Ian, this is Gwen Todd, from *Coastal Monthly*."

Ian took her hand, appearing just short of kissing it. Gwen didn't seem to mind. In fact, her cheeks flushed pink.

"Gwen, it's a pleasure."

"Thank you so much for making the drive up," she said. "I know it's a long one, but I'm so glad you did."

Stella eyed him, waiting for him to admit to wanting to take a look at the house, even in passing. Otherwise, why not do the interview over the phone? But he didn't. He just smiled down at Gwen innocently. *Who me? I just want to help with the article, that's all...*

Frances took all this in with interest. If she was worried about Ian's true intentions, she didn't let on. She just seemed happy to see him again. Which, in Stella's opinion, he didn't deserve. But that was Frances for you. Kind to the core.

Clapping her hands together, Gwen smiled. "Are we ready? I thought maybe we could start with some pictures of the upstairs, Frances. Maybe the widow's walk?"

"Sounds good to me."

"Me, too," Ian said.

Stella stepped forward, narrowly missing Ian's toe. All of a sudden, Frances's spacious living room seemed as big as a postage stamp. She stepped back again, putting some distance between them, but not before catching his smirk. Of course he was enjoying this. Of course he was.

"The widow's walk is where Ian said he saw the ghost," Stella said tightly. "Are you sure you want to put that in the article, Frances? Maybe we shouldn't focus on that part?"

Frances frowned. "That's true…"

"Well, that's no problem," Gwen said, fishing her camera out of the bag. "We'll just start with a few by the Christmas tree, and then we can go outside to the garden. The sun is coming out. The light should be perfect."

Stella smiled, relieved. As long as things went smoothly, this article might actually end up painting the house in the light it deserved, which was what she'd hoped for in the beginning. And maybe she was just being paranoid as far as Ian was concerned. Maybe after he got a look at the place, he'd dismiss it like he probably dismissed so many other things in his life. After all, this was Christmas Bay, and what she'd told Frances was true. He hated Christmas Bay.

He stepped up to the bay window and looked out toward the ocean. The muscles in his jaw were bunching again, his blue eyes narrowing in the sunlight.

"My God, I'd almost forgotten that view," he said under his breath. Almost too softly for anyone else to hear.

But Stella heard. And even though it had been years

since she'd seen Ian Steele, or that look in his eyes, she recognized it immediately.

This was something he wanted. And he intended to get it.

Chapter Two

Ian walked behind Stella, having trouble keeping his eyes off her amazing rear end. She'd been slightly overweight as a kid, always refusing to get into a swimsuit at the city pool. She'd worn a T-shirt and shorts instead, which he'd thought was dumb. She'd looked just fine, but the girls he knew had a way of obsessing over things like that. If it wasn't their weight, it was their skin. Or their hair. Or a myriad of other things. Even the prettiest ones, who had absolutely nothing to worry about, worried, anyway. Stella had been that way.

But he could see those days were long gone. She was no longer the girl in the oversize clothes. She was a confident, stunningly beautiful woman, who was looking over her shoulder at him like she wanted to stick a knife between his ribs.

"Be careful," she said. "The railing is wobbly."

They were climbing the stairs to the widow's walk

after all. Frances had changed her mind, and thought it would be a fitting end to the article to have a picture of Ian standing there, looking out over the ocean. A grown man, coming back to the place where he'd spent so much time as a boy. A place that, as a confused, overwhelmed kid, he'd once said was haunted, but that he now realized was only a sweet old house that didn't deserve a dark reputation. The whole thing was a little too cute for his taste, but that's what people around here liked. Stella was absolutely right, thinking this article would help sell the house. That is, if he didn't get his hands on it first.

He smiled up at her, running his hand along the railing. "I remember."

She didn't smile back. Just turned around and kept climbing, her lovely backside only inches from his face. Good Lord, he really was a jackass. But he couldn't help it. She had a gorgeous body, and his gaze was drawn to it like it was magnetized. It wasn't like he wasn't used to gorgeous bodies, either. The women he usually dated were high maintenance, and keeping themselves up was part of their lifestyle. But Stella's body was soft, curvaceous. Something he could imagine running his hands over, exploring, undressing. Her skin would probably be just as velvety as her voice, and at the thought, his throat felt uncomfortably tight.

Taking the last few steps up the narrow, winding staircase, he stepped out behind her on the widow's walk. Frances and Gwen were already standing near the iron railing, looking out over the ocean. He stared at it, too, and for a few seconds, all thoughts of Stella's body were forgotten in favor of the house's property value.

He fished his sunglasses out of his front pocket and

put them on. The yard below was spacious and pretty. A peeling white picket fence that was covered in climbing vines and rose bushes enveloped it like a hug. In the summer, the whole space was alive with colorful, fragrant blooms that made the garden look like something out of a fairy tale. In the winter, it was more subdued, but still a beautiful, luscious green.

Beyond the yard was the ever-present Scotch broom that butted right up to the edge of the cliffs that dropped into the sea. Cape Longing was one of the most dramatic stretches along the Oregon Coast, and finding land here that was prime for development was rare. Ian's wheels were turning so fast, he could barely think straight. *Condos.* He could picture a small row of expensive condos or townhouses. Simple, midcentury modern style, with lots of glass and metal. Balconies that overlooked the sea. Perfect for reading, or having a glass of wine, or entertaining in the evenings. Bachelor pads, or a couple's paradise… They could go in any direction, appeal to anyone. And with a setting like this, he could sell them for more than he'd even dreamed.

He looked up to see Frances smiling over at him.

"I hope you have some good memories of being up here," she said. "I know this used to be your favorite part of the house."

He smiled back, determined not to let that get to him. Determined not to tumble back into the past, to those lonely nights when he'd sat up here, looking out at the ocean reflecting the full moon above. Feeling scared and alone, and then ashamed for feeling so scared and alone. He guessed that's where that stupid ghost story of his had come from. Underneath everything, it had been a cry for help, a bid for attention. And now he was going to debunk it very publicly, in this article. If he owed Frances anything, that was it. And then they'd be even as far as he was concerned. She wasn't going to look at him with those doe eyes, and make him feel guilty for seeing a good business opportunity here. She just wasn't.

"I wasn't always easy to live with," he said, "but I do have some good memories of this place."

He was in the beginning stages of buttering her up, but maybe that was a bridge too far. It's not that it wasn't true—he did have good memories. Not that he'd ever admitted that…until now. But he could feel Stella watching him from a few feet away, her gaze like a laser beam boring into his head.

"Oh, really?" she muttered.

He turned to her. She knew exactly what he was thinking. He didn't know how, but she did. Not that it mattered. Frances was the only one who mattered here. It wasn't Stella who would be choosing a buyer, it was Frances.

"Really," he said.

"I'm glad to hear that," Frances said. "So glad."

Gwen was fiddling with her camera, looking like she was trying to get the lighting right. "So, this was where you said you saw the ghost?" she asked, holding the camera up and peering through the lens.

"This was the spot," he said. "Only, you know by now I didn't really see anything."

Gwen lowered the camera again. "So, why did you do it? Why did you make up that story?"

"Because I had a problem with the truth back then. Troubled kid, going off the rails—you know the drill."

Gwen nodded. Behind her, Frances frowned, her expression sad.

Back then, Ian hadn't believed her when she'd said she cared about him. He hadn't believed anyone when they'd told him anything. His mother had lied over and over and over again. About her relationships, about Ian's future with her. About everything. So, he'd learned to lie, too. And he'd learned to use lies to get exactly what he wanted.

Stella kept watching him. Maybe waiting for him to apologize. What the hell—he needed to stay on Frances's good side, anyway.

He let his gaze settle on the older woman with the kind eyes. He'd resented her so much back then. She'd been just another adult forcing him into a mold that he'd never wanted or asked for. *Troubled kid, going off the rails*... But he could never quite lump her into the same category as his parents and everyone else who'd let him down over the years. She was different then. She was different now.

"I'm sorry, Frances," he said. He had been bitter about his time in foster care, and she'd been a convenient target. She'd remained one for a long time, even after he'd left Christmas Bay. But she hadn't deserved his behavior. Today, he found he could say the words, but he still couldn't forgive her in his heart. Even though that was ridiculous, of course—none of it had been her fault. But he still couldn't get past her role in all of it. He'd been taken away from the only home he'd ever known and placed with a complete stranger, and the anger had nearly eaten him alive.

But he could at least say the words. And the words were all he needed right now.

She smiled, clearly moved. *Goal achieved.*

"Honey, you have nothing to be sorry for. It's all behind us now."

It wasn't behind them. Not by a long shot, since he was acutely aware that he was still lying for his own benefit. In this case, that benefit was her house. But he'd said he was sorry, and she seemed to accept it, and in that way, they could move forward. He could pile on the charm, convince her to sell, make a ton of money and leave Christmas Bay in his rearview mirror. This time for good.

"Frances," Gwen said, "why don't you move over to the railing next to Ian, and I can get a picture of you both."

"Oh, that's a good idea. Stella, why don't you get in here with us?"

Stella shook her head. "No, that's okay. This one can be just you two."

"Are you sure?"

"Positive."

Ian watched her as Frances walked over, leaning into his side for the picture. She watched him back, her blue eyes chilly. Her long dark hair moved in the ocean breeze. It was wild around her face, wavy, but not quite curly. Her skin was pale, delicate. Almost translucent, and there was a spattering of freckles across her nose. She was so pretty that he could almost forget how he'd never been able to stand her.

But even as he thought it, even as Gwen told them to smile and say cheese, he couldn't believe that same old line he'd always repeated to himself. He hated Frances.

He hated Stella. He hated Marley and Kyla, and all the other foster kids who'd come in and out of the house during his time there. But the truth, which Ian still had trouble with, was more complicated than that. More layered. He hadn't really hated them. The truth was, he'd *wanted* to hate them, and there was a difference.

"Perfect," Gwen said, lowering the camera again. "I think that's about it. I've got everything I need. I'll call you if the gaps need filling in, but I think this is going to be a great Christmas article."

Frances touched Gwen's elbow. "Let me walk you out."

And just like that, Ian found himself alone with Stella. Just the two of them, facing each other on the widow's walk, the salty breeze blowing through their hair. He caught her scent, something clean, flowery. Something that made his groin tighten.

"We might as well not beat around the bush," he said evenly. "I'm going to be honest with you."

"Well, that's a first."

"I'm interested in this property, you're right. I think it's a great development opportunity."

Her lovely eyes flashed. "I knew it. I knew that's why you came."

"I came because I owed it to Frances. And I was curious about the house, too."

"You're so full of it, Ian. You were *only* curious about the house."

She was going to think what she was going to think. There was nothing he could do about it, and he didn't care, anyway.

He leaned casually against the railing and smiled

down at her. Something he remembered had always driven her crazy. "Now that I've seen it," he said, "I'm going to talk to Frances about making an offer."

"Forget it. She'll never sell to you."

"Says who?"

"Says me."

"Last I checked, you don't own it."

She glared up at him. "No, but she'll listen to me. She'll listen to Marley and Kyla. And all we'll have to do is remind her that she wants a family here."

"She may have some romantic notion of selling to a family, but in reality, money talks. And I think she'll sell for the right price."

"You're insufferable," she bit out. She was furious now. Her cheeks were pink, her full lips pursed. Before he could help it, he wondered what she'd be like in bed. All that passion and energy directed right at him. But that wasn't a fantasy that had a chance of coming true anytime soon. By the looks of it, she'd rather run him over with her car first.

"Don't assume Frances would just sell to the highest bidder," she continued. "She doesn't need the money. Despite what you've always thought."

She was obviously talking about that idiotic comment he'd made about Frances's motives that night at the coffee shop in Portland. Something he'd said out of bitterness. It had been a rotten thing to say, not to mention categorically untrue. Stella hadn't given him a chance to take it back, though. She'd gotten up and slammed out before he could utter another word. Fast-forward almost ten years, and now here they were.

"I didn't mean that," he said huskily. "What I said back then."

She crossed her arms over her chest.

"And I know she doesn't need the money *now*," he continued. "But what about later? On the phone, you said she's got Alzheimer's. That's why she can't handle the house anymore. Retirement homes are expensive. Care facilities are even more expensive. This would give her a nest egg for her future. She's smart—she's got to know she'll need one."

Stella gaped at him. "Oh, you are disgusting. You're even lower than I thought you'd be when you showed up here, and believe me, that's pretty low."

"How is it low? The way I see it, I'd be helping her out."

"You *would* see it that way." She shook her head, her dark hair blowing in front of her face. She tucked it behind her ears again and took a deep breath. "She wants a family here, and that's the only thing that's going to sway her. Believe me, you don't stand a chance."

He put his hands in his pockets. "Hmm."

"What?"

"I'm just saying, if she wants a family living here, I might fit the bill there, too."

She laughed. "What? Come on."

"I don't have a family. Yet. But eventually I might, and it'd be great to have the house checked off the list." She was right. He *was* low.

Stella watched him suspiciously. "You just said this place is a great development opportunity. You expect me to believe you'd actually live here?"

"I might. For a while."

"Baloney. You're just saying that to get what you want."

"Believe me, don't believe me. Doesn't matter to me, Stella. What matters to me is what Frances believes. And by the way, this whole archrival thing we've got going on? It's only making me want the house more."

"Oh, really."

"Really."

"You'd buy a house out of spite?"

"No, I'd buy a house to make money. I'd sell it out of spite."

She glared up at him. She was fuming. But if she thought she was going to stand in his way, she was wrong. Nobody stood in his way. At least not people who didn't want to get bulldozed.

After a second, she looked away. She stared out at the ocean that was sparkling underneath the midday sun. He couldn't be sure, but he thought her chin might be trembling a little. And if it was, that would be a surprise. A crack in her otherwise impenetrable armor.

"Hey," he said.

She didn't look at him. Just continued staring at the water.

He took a breath, not sure what to say. Taken off guard by her sudden show of emotion. Ian could take a lot of things, and did on a daily basis. But the sight of a woman crying had always unnerved him. Talk about an Achilles' heel. He remembered walking in on Stella crying once when they were kids. She'd been trying to be quiet, so as not to call attention to herself. She'd looked up at him, her cheeks wet with tears, and the expression on her face had nearly broken his heart. He remembered very clearly wanting to cross the room to hug her, to comfort her. To take some of her pain away, just a little.

"You can tell me to go to hell," he said now. "But I'll give you some advice, Stella. Sometimes there's such a thing as caring too much."

At that she looked back at him. And he'd been right. There were tears in her eyes. He had to stop himself before he reached for her, because really, she was a stranger to him. He didn't know her anymore, and he didn't care to know her. He was only here for a business deal.

"She's eventually going to forget all the memories she has of this place," she said. "The only thing that comforts her is the thought of someone making new memories here. For me, as far as Frances is concerned, there is no such thing as caring too much."

He grit his teeth. *There's no such thing...* He wondered how it was that they'd ended up so differently. Her caring too much, and him not caring at all. They were two stars at the opposite ends of the universe. And she still shone just as brightly as she had when she was fourteen. Maybe he was jealous of that. Deep down. Maybe he wanted to love just as fiercely as Stella Clarke did.

She lifted her chin. "So, yes, Ian. You can take your money, and your offer, and you can go to hell."

And she walked out.

"Here's your room key, sir." The woman smiled up at him, wrinkles exploding from the corners of her brown eyes. Her Christmas tree earrings sparkled, coming in a close second to her sweater. She looked like Mrs. Claus.

"Thank you," he said.

"There's a vending machine right down the breeze-way, and if you want to rent a movie, we have a pretty good selection of DVDs, but the front desk closes at nine."

He took the key card and tucked it in his back pocket, preoccupied with the events of that afternoon. Frances owned a candy shop on Main Street, and she and Stella had gone back to work right after their meeting with Gwen. That had left him zero time to approach her about the house, so he'd made the incredibly annoying decision to stay in Christmas Bay overnight.

He'd called and asked if he could meet Frances for coffee before heading home tomorrow, and she'd seemed genuinely happy about that. He'd make his move then. Her defenses were already down because of this cheesy article. If he could frame the sale in a way that would tug on her heartstrings, it would be easier than he'd thought.

Pushing down the slightest feeling of guilt, he grabbed a razor, comb and toothbrush from a rack beside the counter and paid quickly, not wanting to encourage any more small talk with the Jingle Bell Inn front desk lady. He'd already had to endure enough nosy questions— what brought him to town, where had he bought a car that fancy, etcetera, etcetera. All topped off with a story about someone who'd stayed here not long ago who drove a Ferrari. The kind Tom Selleck had in *Magnum P.I.* He'd smiled and nodded politely. But inside, he was dying. This was exactly the kind of interaction he never had to deal with in the city. In the city, people couldn't care less why you were staying overnight. They just took your credit card and told you where the best seafood places were.

Gathering his things, he told the lady to have a good evening and walked out the door. The sun was just beginning its fiery descent toward the ocean. The sky was a brilliant swirl of pinks and purples, and the salty breeze felt good on his skin. He breathed in the smell of the water, of the beach, letting the air saturate his lungs. Letting it bring him back, just a little, to the last time he was here.

He'd left his aunt Betty's and Christmas Bay the second he'd graduated from high school—right after he'd turned eighteen and was done with the foster system for good. His mother had made some weak overtures about him coming to live with her again, and letting her "help" him with college. He hadn't been able to tell her off fast enough. This, after an entire childhood of not caring whether he was coming or going, or that he'd basically served as a punching bag for her ever-revolving door of boyfriends.

He slid the key card into the lock, watching the light blink green, then opened the door and walked into the small room with his stomach in a knot. He really couldn't believe he was back here after all this time. He'd never planned on it. His mother had passed away a few years ago, and the only relative still living here was a great-aunt who was in a retirement home across town. He'd gone to live with her after he'd left Frances's house for good. She'd tried to make a connection with him, and had been the only one in his family who ever acted like they cared at all. But he'd kept her at an arm's length, anyway, protecting himself the best way he knew how. The thought of coming back to visit her had never crossed his mind. He'd left. And that meant leaving her, and everything else, behind, too.

Opening the sliding glass door, he stepped onto the balcony with the beginnings of a headache throbbing at his temples. The guilt he'd felt earlier had settled in his gut like a small stone. If he had any chance of convincing Frances to sell to him, he needed to bury that guilt, along with any strange pull he was feeling toward Stella. These people were simply part of his past. They had no place in his future. And if they registered in his present at all, it was only because they were a means to an end.

It wasn't in Ian's nature to let fruit like this slip through his fingers once he realized how ripe it was for the picking. And no matter what kind of bleeding-heart reasons Frances had for wanting to sell her house to a family, he knew he'd been absolutely right about her needing the most money she could get out of it. What kind of local family would be able to come up with the cash to outbid him? What he was doing would only end up helping her, not hurting her.

Sinking down in one of the plastic deck chairs, he watched the waves pound the beach. In the distance, a woman was being dragged along by her golden retriever, the dog barking joyously at the water. Up ahead, two boys in hoodies were playing football in the sand. Other than that, the beach was empty. So unlike San Francisco, where the amount of people on a sunny winter day could make you feel like you couldn't catch your breath. Which, normally, he didn't mind. The hustle was what he liked about California. The opportunities, the possibilities. But the deep breathing you could do up here was undeniable.

He leaned back in the chair and pulled out his phone to do some quick calculations. How much the house might be worth on the market, how much the land alone might be worth and what kind of builders might be interested. Ian had instantly seen a few luxury condos perched on that cliff in his mind's eye. But honestly, it would be a great place for a high end spa, too. Maybe even a small, quaint hotel... He'd been worried the house would be on the National Register of Historic Places, but miraculously, it wasn't. Probably because it had always been a private residence and nobody famous had stayed there. Or maybe Frances's family had never gotten around to listing it. He knew there was an in-depth nomination process. Either way, his initial worry that he'd run into red tape was null and void.

Looking out over the water, he rubbed his chin. The golden retriever was in the surf now, its owner standing with her hands on her hips, looking resigned. She'd lost the battle. Despite his headache, Ian smiled. It was a Norman Rockwell kind of moment. But then again, Christmas Bay was a Norman Rockwell kind of town. Scratch that. It was for some people. For people like him, he remembered how dead-end and limiting it really was. Yeah, Frances would definitely be thanking him after this. Even if he did have to stretch the truth initially, she'd thank him in the end.

He'd bet on it.

"Frances, I'm not sure you realize who you're dealing with here, that's all."

Stella leaned against the counter next to the cash register, watching her foster mother go from window to window with a bottle of Windex and a wad of paper towels. She was just about done, and the glass was crystal clear. It wouldn't last, though. When you worked in a candy shop, you got used to fingerprints everywhere. Even some nose prints thrown in for good measure.

Frances didn't turn around. Just kept spraying and wiping, spraying and wiping. "I know you're worried, honey. But we're only going to have coffee. I'll just see what he has to say."

"I *know* what he's going to say."

"I keep telling you, people change."

"Yeah, sometimes they get worse."

"You still think he's selfish."

"Does the Pope wear a funny hat?"

Frances laughed. "Well. That would be a yes."

"I'm just saying, we spent an hour with the guy, and that was plenty. He's only here to make money. He doesn't care about the house."

Frances did turn around at that. "What kind of person would I be, what kind of foster mother, if I didn't at least hear him out? If I didn't give him a chance to prove himself?"

Stella sighed.

"You're just going to have to trust me on this one, Stella. I know my memory is going, but it's not gone yet, and I need to give him a chance."

Frowning, Stella chewed the inside of her cheek. Damn him. Frances was already being swayed by that big-city charm. By those blue eyes, and that calculating smile. He probably knew exactly how Frances felt about him, and was going to use that to his fullest advantage. But at the end of the day, this was Frances's house, Frances's decision. All Stella could do was try to advise and be there for support.

"I do want you to come, though," Frances said, walking over and setting the Windex on the counter. "Would you do that for me?"

Stella's chest tightened. She hadn't been prepared to see him again so soon. Or maybe ever. The thought of looking up into that smug face made her want to chug a glass of wine.

She licked her lips, which suddenly felt dry. "What about the shop?"

"We'll close it. It's just for a little while."

Well, there goes that excuse.

She forced a smile. "Then of course I'll come."

"But you have to promise not to kill him."

"I can't promise that."

Frances reached out and took her hand, suddenly looking serious. Almost desperate in a way, and Stella knew she was asking for reassurance. And comfort.

"I can't explain it," Frances said, "but I just want him to leave on good terms this time. Things with Ian have bothered me for years. This is a way to fix it, even if it's just to smooth it over. I need that. Can you understand?"

She could. She knew the sale of the house was the beginning of smoothing a lot of things over for Frances. She was settling her affairs, mending broken fences, looking back on mistakes she felt she'd made. And no matter how much Stella mistrusted Ian, she had to respect how Frances felt about him. Her foster children were her children. No matter how long they ended up staying with her. And having one of her children out there in the world, alone, unanchored, was too much for her to take, without at least having coffee with him and hearing him out, apparently.

Stella squeezed her hand. Frances had beautiful hands. Soft, and perfectly manicured, her nails usually painted some kind of fuchsia or cotton candy pink. Today, they were Christmas themed, green with little red polka dots.

"I can understand that, Frances," she said. "And I won't kill him. I promise."

Chapter Three

Ian sat in the sunroom of the old Victorian, with Stella sitting directly across from him. Frances had gone into the kitchen to get the coffee and pastries, insisting that "you kids sit and chat" for a minute.

So far there hadn't been any chatting. Just the chilly gaze of a woman who looked even more beautiful today than she had yesterday, if that was possible. She wore a gray Portland Trail Blazers hoodie and had her dark hair pulled into a high ponytail. Her face was freshly scrubbed, her cheeks pink and dewy. She still looked like she wanted to push him in front of a bus, though. Which was fine. Whatever.

He smiled at her and leaned back in the wicker chair. Everything in this room was wicker. Even the coffee table. It felt like he'd been teleported back to 1985.

"I wasn't expecting you to show up today," he said.

"You seem like you'd rather be doing something else. Like getting a root canal, maybe."

Her lips twitched at that. But if he thought the teasing would get her to relax, he was sadly mistaken.

"That would be preferable, yes."

"Then why are you here?"

"Frances asked me to come, and I couldn't say no."

"Even though you wanted to."

"Exactly. But I promised I'd behave, so this is me behaving."

"Good to know. I'd hate to see you misbehaving."

A tubby black-and-white cat sauntered in with a hoarse meow, and blinked up at him through yellow eyes. Then it proceeded to wind itself around his ankles.

Ian stared down at it. He hated cats. He was allergic. In fact, he thought he could feel the beginnings of a tickle in his nose.

"Beauregard," Stella said. "No."

The cat looked over at her, unconcerned. Then he turned around and rammed his little head into Ian's shin.

"Beauregard." She leaned down and snapped her fingers at him, but he ignored her completely. Ian had to work not to laugh. He didn't like cats, but he did appreciate them. They did what the hell they wanted, when the hell they wanted to do it. If they came to you, it was because you had something to offer. If they left, it was because something else was more appealing at that moment. As a human, he could relate.

He reached up and rubbed his nose. Definitely a tickle.

"Oh, I see you've met Beauregard," Frances said, appearing in the doorway with a tray. "Just nudge him with your foot if he's being a pest."

Ian nudged him, but the cat only seemed encouraged by the contact. He immediately came back for more.

"Oh, dear," Frances said, setting the tray down on the coffee table. "I think you've made a friend."

Ian looked down at him dubiously.

Sitting beside Stella, Frances handed over his coffee. "Black, like you said."

"Thank you."

"Honey," she said, handing Stella a cup. "Here you go."

"Thanks, Frances."

"That's homemade blackberry jam for the scones. Kyla and Marley made it last summer." She smiled over at Ian. "They came back to Christmas Bay, too. They're busy with their own families, but we see each other nearly every day, don't we Stella?"

Stella took a sip of her coffee, eyeing him over the rim of the mug. A Christmas tree, draped in blue lights, twinkled next to her. The ocean outside the windows was gray and misty today. The perfect backdrop to the house on the cliff. It all felt like a movie set, and he was about to deliver his lines. The ones he'd rehearsed last night. The ones Frances wouldn't be able to resist.

He took a sip of his coffee, too, and burned his tongue. Wincing, he set it on the coffee table.

"Frances," he said evenly. "I want to talk to you about your house."

Clasping her hands in her lap, she waited. She'd obviously known this was coming. Stella sat beside her with a tight expression on her face. But whatever warning she'd given Frances, it obviously hadn't been enough to dissuade her from meeting with him today.

Sensing an opening, he leaned forward and put his elbows on his knees. "I'd like you to consider selling it to me."

She nodded slowly. "Is that the reason you came up here? To make an offer on the house?"

"I could've made an offer from San Francisco," he said, pushing down that annoying sliver of guilt that kept pricking at his subconscious. It was absolutely true. He could've made an offer from California, but he'd come up to do the interview, and he'd done it. He'd also come up for the house, but again, she didn't have to know that. Right now he needed to work the seller. He'd done it a thousand times before. Frances was no different.

"I wanted to do the interview for you. But when I saw this place again..." He clasped his hands and looked around. "Well, I really couldn't resist."

"It's a beautiful house," Frances said. "And you have to know what it means to me."

"I do."

"I was raised here. And my parents and grandparents, too. And then all of you kids..."

He clenched his jaw. *You kids...* He still couldn't believe she thought of him as more than just a shithead teenager who'd slept here for a couple of years.

Pushing that down, he smiled. "I know. The emotional value far exceeds the monetary value. But I have to be honest, Frances. That's a lot, too."

"I don't care about the money."

He didn't believe that. Everyone cared about the money.

He licked his lips. Stella watched him steadily, saying *I told you so* with that cool gaze of hers.

Taking a page from the cat's playbook—who right that minute had his sizeable girth spread out on Ian's foot—he ignored Stella and doubled down on Frances. If he wasn't careful, he'd lose control of the room, and he never lost control of the room.

"I know you don't," he said softly. Shaking his head. Milking the moment. "I know you want someone living here who will love it just like you do."

Her kind eyes, which had been slightly guarded a minute ago, warmed at that. He could hardly believe it was going to be this simple. But he went on, not wanting to lose any ground, and not trusting Stella to interrupt when he was just getting to the good stuff.

"I'm not married yet," he said. "But of course, I'd like to be someday." For such a whopping lie, it rolled off his tongue fairly easily. He just had to keep reminding himself that it could be true. Technically. Anything was possible.

"And I'd love this house just as much as you do, Frances," he finished. That part was downright true. He'd love the massive payday it would bring, and that was practically the same thing.

Stella sat there stiff as a board. It was obvious she was trying to keep her mouth shut, but was having a hard time of it. He was sure he could handle her and whatever she threw at him, but it would be nice if he could get in a few more minutes with Frances before she started winding up.

"I'd love to believe that," Frances said.

Stella cleared her throat.

He ignored that, too.

"So, you're saying if you bought the house," Frances said, "you'd want to live here."

"That's what I'm saying."

"But you haven't been back to Christmas Bay since you left after high school, right?"

"You hate Christmas Bay," Stella said flatly. "Why would you live in a town that you hate?"

He held up a hand. "Now, I never said I hate it." That was also true. He hadn't said it. He'd been thinking it.

"Oh, come on, Ian."

"I have complicated memories of Christmas Bay," he said. "But now that I see it as an adult, it's obviously a great place to raise a family."

Stella made a huffing sound. But Frances's interest seemed piqued.

"Honestly," she said. "I love the idea of someone I know buying the house, over complete strangers…"

He smiled.

"And you really think you'd want to settle down here? It's awfully fast. Or have you been thinking of settling down for a while?"

Stella had been taking a sip of her coffee, but she coughed at that.

"Sorry," she croaked. "Went down the wrong pipe."

Ian narrowed his eyes at her before looking back at Frances. "Oh, you know. For a while now." If he was keeping track, that would go in the whopper column. But it couldn't be helped. She'd painted him into a corner.

"How convenient," Stella muttered under her breath.

"Now, Ian," Frances said. "I'm going to tell you the truth. If you made an offer, I think I'd consider it before I'd consider anything else. But I just can't get past what a change this would be for you, coming from the city. What about your job?"

"Oh, I could work remotely for a while. And I'm used to traveling. That wouldn't be a problem."

"But would you be able to acclimate back into small-town life?"

Ian resisted the urge to shift in his seat. He needed to appear convincing, and squirming around like a fibbing third grader wasn't going to get him anywhere.

"It would be an adjustment," he said. "But I've been wanting to make a change for a while, so…"

Frances nodded thoughtfully. He almost had her, he could feel it. But then again, he'd been expecting it. Ian did this for a living, and he was good at it. Really good. By this afternoon, he'd be on the phone with his office, getting the ball rolling. This should be an easy sale, barring anything popping up with the inspection. But that really didn't matter, either. It was the property he was after, not the house, and he'd pay whatever he had to for it.

He leaned back in his chair, the wicker squeaking obnoxiously under his weight. He felt confident, in control. The guilt that had been plaguing him earlier was tucked away in the farthest corners of his mind, ignored. It was all going to work out exactly how he'd hoped. He'd get a kick-ass piece of land, and Frances, whether she realized it or not, would be better off. Taken care of financially. Sure, she'd hate him in the end, but that was inevitable. He could live with it. He'd lived with a lot worse.

Stella continued to stare at him, her eyes cold. Under different circumstances, he probably would've asked her out by now. Taken her to the nicest restaurant he could find, and impressed her by ordering the most expensive bottle of wine. If she'd been a stranger, he would've done his damnedest to get her into bed afterward, too. He'd push that dark mane of hair off to the side, and move his lips along her jaw, down her throat. He'd work to get her to look at him the way so many other women did. He might even turn himself inside out for that.

But it was only a fantasy. Because she wasn't a stranger. She'd never liked him before, and she sure as hell didn't like him now. Again, he reminded himself that he didn't care.

Still, as he stared back at her, he knew that deep down, where that sliver of guilt lay, he did care. Just a little. Just enough to swallow hard now, his tongue suddenly feeling thick and dry in his mouth.

Frances took a sip of her coffee. Then another, as the clock ticked from the other room. The cat continued purring on his foot, and he thought his eyes felt itchy now. Or maybe that was just his imagination.

"I know you want the house, Ian," she finally said, setting the coffee cup down again. "And I want you to have the house."

His heart beat evenly inside his chest.

"On one condition…"

He raised his brows. Stella raised hers, too, and looked over at her foster mother. Even the cat, probably sensing the sudden stiffness in Ian's body, shifted and yawned.

"If you're serious about this," she continued, "if you're

serious about living in Christmas Bay again, I want you to stay for a few weeks. Until Christmas Eve."

He stared at her. Stella stared at her, too.

"If you can work remotely," she said, "that shouldn't be a problem. You can get reacquainted with the town, with the people. Stella can show you around and introduce you. Then, you can truly decide if you want to put down some roots here. And if that's how you feel in your heart, I'll be able to tell. I'll be able to see it written all over your face."

Ian felt his mouth go slack. The house—his great investment opportunity, a deal so sure, he'd been writing up the papers in his head—was so quiet you could hear a pin drop. Outside the windows, there was the muted sound of the ocean, the waves slamming against the cliffs of Cape Longing. He felt his pulse tapping steadily in his neck as he let her words, her surprisingly genius condition, settle like a weight in his stomach.

Well, son of a bitch.

He hadn't been expecting *that*.

Stella couldn't stop gaping at Frances. She knew she was doing it. She must've looked like a sea bass, but she couldn't help it. The shock was all-consuming.

Across the room, Ian was apparently just as shocked. He didn't look like a sea bass—unfortunately he was too handsome for that. But he did look like Frances had dropped a sizeable bomb right in his lap.

He seemed at a loss for words. Stella couldn't blame him. She was in the same boat.

"I'm sorry," she managed after a minute. "What?"

Frances folded her hands in her lap, her Christmas sweater sparkling in the morning light. This one had a sequined snowman emblazoned on the front.

"You heard me," she said evenly.

Ian glanced over at Stella, and for the first time since he'd arrived, he looked taken aback. She had to hand it to Frances. She'd surprised them both. And she'd done it on her own terms. If she was going to sell the house, she was going to sell it to whomever she chose. She was not a forgetful old lady who couldn't handle her affairs. She could still manage just fine, and she was going to prove it.

Stella felt a distinctive warmth creep into her cheeks. She loved Frances so much, but she realized she'd been coddling her for the last few weeks. Treating her like a child. She stared at her shoes, ashamed.

Still, Ian *staying* here? And having to show him around? It was worse than him just making an outright offer. Much worse.

Taking a deep breath, she settled her gaze on Frances again, this time trying to center herself. "Frances, can we at least talk about this?"

"There's nothing to talk about. I was up half the night thinking about it, and it makes perfect sense."

Ian frowned, clearly wondering how he'd been so close to a deal, only to let this wriggle right out of his grasp. Normally, Stella would be gloating, but she couldn't even bring herself to do that. What a cluster.

"I trust your instincts, Stella," Frances said. "You might think I'm dismissing all your concerns, but it's actually because I've been listening that I'm doing this.

By spending time with Ian, you'll be able to gauge his true feelings."

She turned to Ian then. "And I love you to pieces, Ian. I know you probably have a hard time believing that, but I do. However, I need to know you're not just here for the real estate. And this way, I'll know."

Ian swallowed visibly. "Frances…"

"There's really nothing you can say to make me change my mind. It's made up. If you're serious about the house you'll stay, or you won't and I'll find another buyer. It's as simple as that."

Stella watched her foster mother, impressed with her badassery, and at the same time horrified that she appeared to mean everything she'd just said. Ian was going to stay. *Until Christmas Eve.*

That is…unless he didn't. She looked over at him, wondering if Frances had called his bluff. There was always that possibility, and she felt the stirrings of hope in her belly. Maybe she wouldn't have to spend any more time with him after all.

He seemed deep in thought. His dark brows were furrowed, his jaw working methodically. He looked far away, weighing how much he actually wanted the property, no doubt. Was it really worth two weeks of his life? She guessed he already had more money than God. Why did he need more?

But right as she was thinking it, his gaze shifted to Frances, and there was something in his eyes that told Stella her foster mother might've just met her match.

"It's a deal, Frances," he said evenly. "On Christmas Eve, you'll see that I'm the right buyer for this house."

* * *

"I'm still not sure what you mean," Carter said, sounding confused on the other end of the line. "You're *staying* there?"

Ian sighed and leaned back against the motel bed's headrest. There was a light rain falling outside, and the ocean churned, grumpy and gray beyond the beach. He really didn't care to repeat himself—he wasn't in the mood. But the fact was, he was going to have to be doing a lot of that in the days to come. Telling people over and over again why he was here. His associates, his employees, Christmas Bay locals. He swallowed a groan. *God.* The Christmas Bay locals. If the front desk lady was any indication of the amount of nosiness around here, he'd have to tell everyone his business. And would any of them swallow his reasons for wanting to come back here? They'd have to if he had any hope of convincing Frances.

He felt his shoulders tighten. And it wasn't just Frances anymore. It was Stella, too. And having to convince her was what had him worried. Plenty.

"Yes," he said, gripping his phone tighter than he needed to. "It's a long story. But in order to secure this sale, I need to put the time in."

"Yeah, but two *weeks*?"

He could almost see his partner leaning back in her corner office chair, the bay sparkling behind her. She'd think this was ridiculous, of course. She'd think Ian was losing his edge if it was taking him two days to make a sale, much less two weeks. But if he didn't secure it, as far as he was concerned, that *would* be losing his edge, and he wasn't about to let that happen. Two weeks was a long time, but it would be worth it in the end. Another notch in his belt, another win for his company. And his bank account. All he needed was for Carter to take over while he was gone and deal with their clients in person. He could Zoom until the cows came home, but some of them were finicky and needed to be handled like high-strung racehorses. Zoom meetings didn't always cut it.

"Two weeks," Ian said. "Just trust me on this."

"Okaaay. Two weeks. I can't wait to hear all about it."

That was a lie. Carter didn't actually care if Ian camped out on the moon, just as long as he made them money. She was just as cutthroat as he was. Maybe even more so, and that was saying something in this business.

"Listen," Ian said. "I'm going to drive down tomorrow and pick up some clothes. So if you need me for anything, I can swing by the office before heading back. I'll call on the way down, okay?"

"Sounds good. Talk then."

Ian hung up and rubbed his temple. The headache from yesterday had turned into a full-blown pain in the ass. What he really needed to do was get in the car and head to the little market in town. Pick up a few groceries for his room. He had a microwave, minifridge and a coffee pot, thank God. He'd be living on macaroni and cheese and granola bars for a while. *Great*. This really couldn't get much worse.

But it could get worse, he knew that. He could put in the time and effort for this property, and by Christmas Eve, he might not be able to convince Stella that he was being genuine. He might not be able to convince Frances to sell to him, and then what?

He scraped a hand through his hair. He'd just have to cross that bridge when he came to it. Right now, he was going to have to gird his loins and head into town.

Lord help him.

Stella watched seven-year-old Gracie, wearing a pink slicker with the hood flopping on her shoulders, run up the beach.

"Don't go too far!" Kyla yelled through her cupped hands.

At that, Gracie turned and waved. She was so cute. Dark hair, dark eyes. Maybe one of the cutest kids Stella had ever seen. And she was about to get a brand-new stepmom. Kyla was going to marry Ben Martinez, Christmas Bay's police chief and the love of her life, next spring. She was positively glowing.

But as she walked alongside Stella now, the wind blowing her shoulder-length hair in front of her face, she looked more worried than anything.

"I'm not sure I like this," Kyla said. "It has trouble written all over it."

Stella pulled her cardigan tighter around her, watching as Gracie bent down to inspect something in the sand, then shoved it in her slicker pocket. Stella hoped it wasn't alive. "Tell me about it. I haven't liked it from the beginning."

"And this was Frances's idea? Actually, don't answer that. It sounds exactly like something Frances would do."

Stella nodded. "I know. She definitely wants to know Ian's serious, but there's also a part of her that wants to show us she's still in control. I'm proud of her. I mean,

I'm super annoyed, but you have to hand it to her. It's kind of brilliant."

"So, what are you going to do?"

"What can I do? The only way to know for sure if Ian's serious is to spend some time with him, like she said. And even then, I'm not sure he'll ever be honest with us. What if he keeps up this charade about wanting to live in the house?"

"Then she'll have to trust you when you tell her it's just a charade."

Stella looked out over the water. It was gorgeous today. A little windy—the ocean was choppy and un-settled—but the sun was out, warming everything up.

"That's true," she said. "But two weeks... It seems like a lifetime."

Kyla hooked her arm in Stella's. "I'm sorry you got stuck with this."

"Me, too. But Frances is worth it. The house is worth it. I'll just have to keep reminding myself of that every time I have to be within five feet of him."

Kyla laughed. "He's still that bad?"

"Worse."

"But good-looking."

Stella turned to her. "Who told you that?"

"Frances. On the phone this morning."

"What do his looks have to do with anything?"

"Nothing...but just how good-looking are we talking?"

"Kyla."

Her foster sister shrugged. "I'm just saying, you're single..."

"Gross. He's an ass."

"But a good-looking ass."

Stella raised a hand to shield her eyes from the sun, watching as Gracie drew in the sand with a stick. "I guess."

"Listen, you don't have to do this all by yourself. Ben and I can help. Bring him over for dinner or something. Take him to see Marley and the baby. Really lay it on thick. Maybe he'll decide he's in over his head and will give up. I mean, how much Christmas Bay can a person take, if they hate everything about Christmas Bay?"

Stella contemplated this, her wheels turning. "That's true…"

"I bet after a few days, he'll start wondering what the hell he's doing here and will leave early."

"Kyla," Stella said slowly. "You just gave me the best idea."

"Uh-oh."

"He'd *definitely* have second thoughts if he has a miserable time. Remember when Frances took us crabbing in middle school, and we were all hungry and cold, and Marley ended up falling in the water?"

"The infamous crabbing day. How could I forget?" Stella smiled. *"Exactly."*

"Are you going to take him to the bay and push him in?"

"Don't tempt me. But why should we have to sugar-coat anything? Living in a small town isn't like a Hall-mark movie. There are all kinds of things about it that drive you crazy. I'm just saying, I'll show him around. I'll introduce him to people. With the sole purpose of reminding him why he hated it here to begin with."

"Oh, you are *bad*."

"Not half as bad as he is." Stella lifted her chin as a

flock of seagulls squabbled overhead, dipping and bobbing on the chilly breeze. "He dealt the cards," she said. "Now I'll show him I can play."

Don't miss
Their Christmas Resolution *by Kaylie Newell,*
available September 2023 wherever
Harlequin® Special Edition books
and ebooks are sold.

www.Harlequin.com

#3013 THE MAVERICK'S HOLIDAY DELIVERY
Montana Mavericks: Lassoing Love • by Christy Jeffries

Dante Sanchez is an expert on no-strings romances. But his feelings for single mom-to-be Eloise Taylor are anything but casual. She knows there's a scandal surrounding her pregnancy. But catching the attention of the town's most notorious bachelor may be her biggest scandal yet!

#3014 TRIPLETS UNDER THE TREE
Dawson Family Ranch • by Melissa Senate

Divorced rancher Hutch Dawson has one heck of a Christmas wish: find a nanny for his baby triplets. And Savannah Walsh is his only applicant! Who knew that his high school nemesis would be the *perfect* solution to his very busy—and lonely—holiday season...

#3015 THE RANCHER'S CHRISTMAS STAR
Men of the West • by Stella Bagwell

Would Quint Hollister hire a woman to be Stone Creek Ranch's new sheepherder? Only if the woman is capable Clementine Starr. She wants no part of romance—at least until Quint's first knee-weakening kiss. But getting two stubborn singletons to admit love might take a Christmas miracle!

#3016 THEIR CONVENIENT CHRISTMAS ENGAGEMENT
Top Dog Dude Ranch • by Catherine Mann

Ian Greer is used to finding his mother, who has Alzheimer's, anywhere but at home! More often than not, he finds her at Gwen Bishop's vintage toy store. He admires the kind, plucky single mom, so a fake engagement to placate his mother—and her family—seems like the perfect plan. Until a romantic sleigh ride changes their holiday ruse into something much more real...

#3017 THE VET'S SHELTER SURPRISE
by Michelle M. Douglas

Sparks fly when beautiful PR expert Georgia O'Neill brings an armful of stray kittens to veterinarian Mel Carter's small-town animal shelter. Mel has loved and lost before, and Georgia is only in town short-term, so it makes sense to ignore their mutual attraction. But as they open up about their pasts, will they also open up to the possibility of new love?

#3018 HOLIDAY AT MISTLETOE COTTAGE
The McFaddens of Tinsley Cove • by Nancy Robards Thompson

Free-spirited photojournalist Avery Anderson just inherited her aunt's beach house. And, it seems, her aunt's sexy, outgoing neighbor. Hometown hero Forest McFadden may be Avery's polar opposite. But fortunately, he's also the adventure she's been searching for.

**YOU CAN FIND MORE INFORMATION ON UPCOMING HARLEQUIN TITLES,
FREE EXCERPTS AND MORE AT HARLEQUIN.COM.**

HSECNM0923

Get 3 FREE REWARDS!

We'll send you 2 FREE Books plus a FREE Mystery Gift.

FREE Value Over **$20**

Both the **Harlequin® Special Edition** and **Harlequin® Heartwarming™** series feature compelling novels filled with stories of love and strength where the bonds of friendship, family and community unite.

YES! Please send me 2 FREE novels from the Harlequin Special Edition or Harlequin Heartwarming series and my FREE gift (gift is worth about $10 retail). After receiving them, if I don't wish to receive any more books, I can return the shipping statement marked "cancel." If I don't cancel, I will receive 6 brand-new Harlequin Special Edition books every month and be billed just $5.49 each in the U.S. or $6.24 each in Canada, a savings of at least 12% off the cover price, or 4 brand-new Harlequin Heartwarming Larger-Print books every month and be billed just $6.24 each in the U.S. or $6.74 each in Canada, a savings of at least 19% off the cover price. It's quite a bargain! Shipping and handling is just 50¢ per book in the U.S. and $1.25 per book in Canada.* I understand that accepting the 2 free books and gift places me under no obligation to buy anything. I can always return a shipment and cancel at any time by calling the number below. The free books and gift are mine to keep no matter what I decide.

Choose one: ☐ **Harlequin Special Edition**
(235/335 BPA GRMK)

☐ **Harlequin Heartwarming Larger-Print**
(161/361 BPA GRMK)

☐ **Or Try Both!**
(235/335 & 161/361 BPA GRPZ)

Name (please print)

Address _____ Apt. #

City _____ State/Province _____ Zip/Postal Code

Email: Please check this box ☐ if you would like to receive newsletters and promotional emails from Harlequin Enterprises ULC and its affiliates. You can unsubscribe anytime.

Mail to the Harlequin Reader Service:
IN U.S.A.: P.O. Box 1341, Buffalo, NY 14240-8531
IN CANADA: P.O. Box 603, Fort Erie, Ontario L2A 5X3

Want to try 2 free books from another series! Call 1-800-873-8635 or visit www.ReaderService.com.

*Terms and prices subject to change without notice. Prices do not include sales taxes, which will be charged (if applicable) based on your state or country of residence. Canadian residents will be charged applicable taxes. Offer not valid in Quebec. This offer is limited to one order per household. Books received may not be as shown. Not valid for current subscribers to the Harlequin Special Edition or Harlequin Heartwarming series. All orders subject to approval. Credit or debit balances in a customer's account(s) may be offset by any other outstanding balance owed by or to the customer. Please allow 4 to 6 weeks for delivery. Offer available while quantities last.

Your Privacy—Your information is being collected by Harlequin Enterprises ULC, operating as Harlequin Reader Service. For a complete summary of the information we collect, how we use this information and to whom it is disclosed, please visit our privacy notice located at corporate.harlequin.com/privacy-notice. From time to time we may also exchange your personal information with reputable third parties. If you wish to opt out of this sharing of your personal information, please visit readerservice.com/consumerschoice or call 1-800-873-8635. **Notice to California Residents**—Under California law, you have specific rights to control and access your data. For more information on these rights and how to exercise them, visit corporate.harlequin.com/california-privacy.

HSEHW23

HARLEQUIN
PLUS

Try the best multimedia subscription service for romance readers like you!

Read, Watch and Play.

Experience the easiest way to get the romance content you crave.

Start your **FREE TRIAL** at
<u>www.harlequinplus.com/freetrial</u>.